BIGFOOT AND THE BABY

BIGFOOT AND THE BABY
Ann Gelder

Bona Fide Books
Tahoe Paradise, CA

ISBN 978-1-936511-44-0

Library of Congress Control Number: 2013956391
Cover Design: Vicky Shea, www.ponderosapinedesign.com
Copy Editor: Mary Cook
Photo Imaging: photosync/javarman/Shutterstock
Orders, inquiries, and correspondence should be addressed to:
    Bona Fide Books
    PO Box 550278, South Lake Tahoe, CA 96155
    (530) 573-1513
    www.bonafidebooks.com

This thing of darkness I
Acknowledge mine.
~William Shakespeare, *The Tempest*

For Trevor

PART ONE: VALENTINES

CHAPTER ONE

Jackie Majesky's unborn daughter knew the world was ending. To Jackie, that much was clear. In her restless thrashing, Mollie feared for the world. She grieved for it. Yet the sorrow radiating from her tiny heart occasionally—rarely—felt like joy.

"Hush, sweetheart," Jackie whispered, pushing her plate aside and laying both hands on her belly. "It's almost time for Daddy's show."

The Lions Club of Morton, California, was holding a fundraiser for blind children. As the fried-chicken dinner wound down, men in yellow vests moved among the rows of tables, pouring coffee and offering slices of cherry pie. Jackie's husband, Kyle, swallowed his piece in three nervous gulps. Crumbs tumbled onto his uniform pants, which Jackie pointed out to him.

"Thanks," he whispered, brushing them off. It would have been awful, though not entirely uncharacteristic, if he'd done his gun-safety demonstration covered in crumbs.

The club president, Merritt Stokes, stepped up to the podium and thumped the microphone with his finger.

"Good evening," he said, his bushy eyebrows twitching happily. "Thank you all for coming out tonight, and for your generosity in supporting this important cause. Blind children throughout the greater Bakersfield area have new hope tonight because of you."

1

Jackie could not fathom how people like Merritt functioned. How did they not think about the Apocalypse all the time? If Jackie's pastor's calculations were correct, those blind children would never even grow up. It was now 1986, and the portents were unmistakable. There was war and famine and disease. A guy with a red mark on his head, lending him a powerful resemblance to the Antichrist, controlled Russia. Two weeks ago, the Challenger space shuttle had exploded, literally writing the End of Days on the sky. Yet the Lions persisted in raising funds, even as God was about to wipe out everything.

At least when the blind children got to heaven, Jackie told herself, they would all see.

"Now for the entertainment portion of the program," Merritt said. Kyle rose to stand beside him, a bit stiffly (his back wasn't what it used to be). "Of course, Kyle Majesky needs no introduction. He's been a cop here in Morton for fifteen years. He's my friend and your friend, too. He may not be the speediest thing on two legs"—here Merritt elbowed Kyle, who grinned down at his potbelly—"but he's just about the funniest. So let's give him a big old round of applause."

Jackie clapped with her hands above her head. She whispered, "It's Daddy, sweetheart," to Mollie, who was not soothed. Katie, their other daughter, pushed her potato salad around on her plate. Katie was nearly fifteen, and a punk. Punks did not applaud on general principle.

Kyle wiped his hands on his uniform pants. He removed his gun from its holster and set it on his outstretched palm, like a turtle he'd found. He looked up at the audience and winked.

"Well," he said. "Tomorrow's Valentine's Day. So I went out and bought Nancy a little present."

Subtly, Jackie began massaging her temples. She had hoped Kyle would not do his Ronald Reagan impression this evening. Why couldn't he just use his own voice when he did these demos? No amount of head ducks or lopsided smiles could turn her plump husband with his little-boy lips into the craggy president. He probably thought Reagan was more interesting than he was, and better. Which, Jackie conceded, was true. But that was no reason to pretend to be someone he was not. Kyle's imitation only reminded her of the differences between him and Reagan, who would be the first one taken to heaven in the Rapture. About him, there could be no doubt.

Katie mashed her potato salad into batter, leaning so far forward that Jackie could see the red roots of her hair. That mop—black and random, modeled on some scrawny singer—did not quite conceal her own reaction to her father's performance.

"Now, I know what you're thinking," Kyle said, as Jackie shifted to rubbing the hinges of her jaw. "It's like Nancy says to me. This gun-safety stuff is so complicated. I'll never remember all those steps. But it boils down to one simple rule. Guns are always loaded. That's right. Even an unloaded gun is loaded." Head duck, grin. "I know that might not make any sense at first, but my first priority for Nancy is her safety. So I tell her: Don't trust. Verify.

"Now, I'll unload it," Kyle said. He slid the clip from the Glock and held it up to the crowd.

Goose bumps scampered down Jackie's back. It still happened whenever her husband demonstrated brisk competence with his weapon. Look at that sweet smile, she thought, those expectant blue eyes. He'd actually lost some of that spare tire he'd been carrying—possibly because the past months had been a little rocky for everybody. Last November Jackie had found the Lord, and since then a digital clock had been glowing in her mind like a gathering headache. As she had been reminding them on a daily basis, Kyle and Katie still had not accepted Jesus as their Savior. If the Rapture came this minute, the Lord would be obliged to take Jackie and Mollie with him to heaven and leave the other two behind to suffer.

Help me at least get through to him, Lord, Jackie prayed silently. She knew that once Kyle was saved, Katie would follow. She loved her father too much to do otherwise.

Kyle paused, gun in one hand, clip in the other. He must have felt Jackie's dark eyes pulling at him—the La Brea Tar Pits, he'd once called them, trying to say they were irresistible. He turned to her. If his face mirrored hers, then she looked terrified.

Kyle nearly dropped the clip, but he snatched it away from gravity and laid it on the table. The crowd murmured. He shifted the gun from his left hand to his right in order to wipe the palm of his empty hand on his thigh. Then came the shot and Kyle's great yelp of pain.

The audience gasped. With supreme delicacy, Kyle set the gun on the table, gritting his teeth. He turned on his left heel, once, twice. His right foot flailed weirdly.

"Everyone OK?" he said, and sat down on the floor.

Benches overturned. Kyle was surrounded by Lions. They proffered napkins, wadded-up vests, water, aspirin.

"Call an ambulance!" someone shouted.

Katie elbowed her way through the crowd as Jackie stood frozen at the picnic table with her hands over her ears. She knelt beside her dad, who now lay in a fetal position. The look on Katie's face, Jackie thought, was so beautiful. She couldn't hear what she and Kyle were saying to each other. Katie smiled. Katie had a great smile, even though her front teeth were slightly buck. Maybe there was no need to get her braces after all, Jackie thought, with a disproportionate sense of relief. Katie's smile was a surprise, like a little firework.

By the time Jackie could move again, the ambulance had arrived and Kyle was sitting up. He hopped over to the gurney and scrambled onto it. The crowd clapped sporadically as he was wheeled out, and Kyle lifted his head, straining against the straps that held him down.

"Just like I told Nancy," he called out, a pale, giddy echo of Reagan. "The gun is always loaded. There was still a bullet in the chamber. That's a lesson I bet you'll never forget."

Katie climbed into the ambulance after him, shooting a glare at Jackie that took her breath away. Fumbling for the car keys, Jackie tried to stroke her belly. "He's fine, sweetheart," she whispered to Mollie as she raced to the parking lot. The ambulance dissolved into the Central Valley fog. Jackie tried to catch up with it, flooring the Reliant's accelerator to little effect. Mollie thrashed up a storm.

જ

Tonight on *The Weird Frontier*, we meet Dottie Mayflower of Yakima, Washington. It is Dottie's contention that her dog has been reincarnated as Bigfoot.

"Two years ago Chester was hit by a car. My husband had died just a month before, and he always used to walk the dog. Chester was big, a German shepherd mix, and I'm a small woman with arthritis.

"It was raining that night. We were walking along our street when he saw something on the other side. He bolted and my feet slipped right out from under me. I couldn't hold onto the leash. Chester ran right into the street. The car drove right over him, never even tried to stop. They had to have seen him. They had to. I will never understand the human race.

"I had the wind knocked out of me. But I saw Chester's tail was moving. I thought he was still alive. I called to him, but no sound came out. Finally I was able to stand and go to him. He was dead, nothing but a mass of blood and fur, and this expression on his face, I will never forget it. He died thinking he had been betrayed. I had let him run into the car. His tail was only wagging from the breeze.

"After that I just wanted to die. I stopped making meals for myself. The neighbors came by and brought me food. They said I should get another dog, but I couldn't think of it.

"Then early one morning, after about six weeks, something told me I should go outside. It wasn't a voice, just a sort of a pull, like a dog on a leash. Only the leash was looped around my heart. I put on my robe and went out onto the front lawn.

"The sun had just come up. There was frost on the grass, glowing like, and in the middle of the frost was a man. Or I should say, it was the shape of a man, only a little larger and covered with fur. I could see no features. The figure was darker than a shadow. But the smell was unmistakable. Wet dog. It was Chester, back to visit me."

"How did you know?"

"It was the love I felt from him."

"Forgive me, but . . . did you ever think it could be your husband?"

"It was Chester. And he said to me, 'All is well. And all will be well forever.' He forgave me, you see. He wanted me to know."

"I'm sorry to press, but if it was indeed your dog, why didn't he just come back in that form, so you could resume your life together as before?"

"Chester has other things to do now. He visits people the world over, and he talks to them in their own language, whatever that happens to be. They always understand immediately what he is saying. He is saying, 'Peace.'

"He still visits me whenever I'm feeling especially lonely. He stands there on the lawn, and I look at him through the window. And he tells me, 'All is well.'"

"What shit," said Katie, out of habit.

Actually, she liked *The Weird Frontier*, a show that chronicled paranormal occurrences all across America. She usually watched it with her dad. The host, Topper Moss, was a pith-helmeted Brit with a face like a hatchet, though not in an unflattering way. His deadpan delivery made it hard to figure out if he believed the stories he was telling, or not. Katie and her dad had a running bet of ten dollars. Kyle thought Topper did believe. Katie disagreed, because, how could he?

On this occasion, her father being otherwise occupied, Katie was watching the WF with her best friend, Stick. It was Valentine's Day night. Despite recent events, her parents had gone out to dinner at their favorite restaurant, her dad pegging along on his crutches and grinning like he'd won the lottery. They were probably back by now, but Katie had no wish to go home and witness the fallout. Given how rattled her mother had been since the accident, their "date" could not possibly have gone well.

Besides, Katie owed Stick a little company. This morning she'd found his valentine stuck in the vent of her locker door. It was the only one she'd received, not that she'd expected any at all. The card was in the shape of a ladybug, and between its spots Stick had carefully written, "Let's jam." He played the guitar in a band called The Coma Cluster with his two older brothers. Prog rock, billions of pointless notes, the opposite of punk. They needed a vocalist.

Stick did another shot of Jim Beam and lowered himself back onto his elbow. Slowly, inexorably as a dune, he undulated toward Katie's semifetal position on the floor. She felt the shadows of his fingers on her backbone.

She sat up. Stick yanked back his hand and pretended to study it in the light of the television. His fingers were amazingly long and padded at the tips, like a gecko's. He poured himself yet another shot, threw it back, and offered the bottle to Katie. She shook her head and lay back down.

It was nearly midnight, Stick's last chance to celebrate Valentine's Day in the manner Katie now realized he had been planning for some time. She heard his knuckles crack as his fingers reached for her once again, pausing to consider various landing sites on her back.

She decided to stay put. Stick was a good guy. She would give him something, today of all days. Besides, she was almost fifteen. It was past time she had some experience.

Fingertips, light as the legs of an insect, touched her shoulder.

"Do you want a backrub?" Stick said.

Katie said, "All right."

She flattened herself on the floor, face planted in the orange carpet, arms out in front of her. Stick gulped audibly. He threw one leg over her ass, but was too terrified to sit down, so he balanced on his knees as he began to knead Katie's shoulders. They were embarrassingly tense, thanks to her parents. It felt like peach pits were buried under her skin.

"Mmmph," she said, trying to sound encouraging.

Stick kept going. He moved down from the shoulders, digging under her shoulder blades. Katie winced but said nothing. She wasn't wearing a bra. She hadn't thought she needed one, although it now occurred to her that she'd been mistaken. Stick's fingers fanned out along her ribs. He inched them around to the front, where he began to probe like a doctor looking for lumps, a process Katie's mother had recently described to her in some detail.

As Katie had read in magazines, technique could be learned. The problem with Stick went much deeper. A year ago he had lost both his parents. They'd died in a car accident while racing to his allegedly dying grandfather's bedside. Now he and his brothers, ironically, lived with Grandpa. Katie could hear the old man snoring away in his bedroom. Meanwhile, in the kitchen, Stick's twin brothers catalogued their Star Trek cards and jabbered in their special code.

All Stick had was music and Katie, and Katie was not much. Yet he refused to see how awful his life was—or worse, if he did see it, he gave in. Life kicked him in the teeth and what did he do? He shrugged. With his guitar he spun out walls of fuzz, when what was called for was rage.

"Get off me." Katie rolled over, quick as a cat. Stick crouched, also like a cat, staring back at her. "I like you as a friend, but that's it," she said, tucking her T-shirt into her jeans.

"Yeah, well, same here. Me too," he said. "I was a little drunk, that's all." He slumped onto the floor, his legs splayed out in front of him.

Now Katie really owed him something. She sat up and beckoned for the Jim Beam. Stick passed it over with a sigh.

"I was thinking," she said, wiping her mouth with the back of her hand, "that we should, you know, jam. Like you keep saying. I want to be in the band with you and your brothers."

"Really?" Stick pushed the cloud of hair off his face.

He thought she was joking. But she wasn't. She was going to help him tonight, after all. She would teach him, through song, to fight the power.

"Three things," Katie said. "One: we get a new name. It can't be The Coma Cluster anymore."

"Obviously."

"Two. Your brothers do not wear their Star Trek uniforms on stage."

"I can arrange that."

"Three. We do not sell out, ever. We play for free, and we never forget who our real fans are. We make our own tapes and give them away. We denounce hypocrisy, greed, cruelty, and all bullshit. We are one big fuck you to the system."

"That's our new name?" said Stick, confused.

"No, stupid." An image flew into Katie's mind: her dad climbing onto the gurney, waving and joking. "We are The Patients."

CHAPTER TWO

It might be useful to note here that Morton, California, was just over one hundred miles northeast of Los Angeles. That distance maintained a cultural gulf between the two cities as vast as the ocean. Yet, borne on the westward breeze, along with various agricultural effluvia, the promise of Hollywood still infected the dreams of Morton's citizens. Their symptoms invariably flared up in the presence of a camera. At first, they pretended to ignore it. But eventually, shyly but with unmistakable expectation, they turned toward the lens. This happened even with security cameras in convenience stores. Who ever watches all that black-and-white footage of little smiles, little head tosses, little shifts to a more macho posture while standing in line with a package of toilet paper? No one, to my knowledge. Yet the people could not help hoping, as the camera clicked or rolled, that their recorded image would summon a black limousine, one soft spring morning, to their house.

The chauffeur emerges and, with practiced deference, opens the back door. A robust man in a black suit steps out. He pauses on the driveway to light his cigar and contemplate the humble home that has nurtured the tremendous talent within. The house's front door swings open, and there, in a blazing pool of sunshine, stands the dreamer. The robust man looks up and nods knowingly. The dreamer is then swept into the luxurious backseat and out of Morton forever.

∾

On Valentine's Day night, The Rustic, Morton's best restaurant, was packed to the gills with couples in love. Many of the same people who had witnessed Kyle's gun-safety demo last evening were here. They all made a point of coming over to shake his hand and offer their congratulations. For, although the aforementioned limo had not yet arrived for him, Kyle had every reason to believe it was on its way. A Los Angeles TV station had gotten wind of his accident and had included a brief item on the eleven o'clock news last night—one of those *Guess what some hick from the outlands has done now?* kind of pieces. But Kyle didn't mind. The story, as it were, had legs, if not wheels. And they were going to carry Kyle and his family to places they'd never even dared to imagine.

His bandaged foot rested on a chair. His crutches leaned against the table. In front of him, like proud soldiers, stood a row of drinks. People had been bringing them over all evening. The joke, which Kyle appreciated, was to make each drink more ridiculous than the last. The one Merritt Stokes had just presented was blue with skewered cherries alternating with chunks of pineapple and an umbrella.

"Heard you on the radio this morning," said Merritt. "You did good."

A representative of *Batso's Morning Mayhem* had phoned at 6:00 a.m., and within minutes Kyle had made his national media debut. Batso, broadcasting out of LA, was a phenomenon across the country, and everybody at The Rustic, at least all the men, had heard the show.

The Batso interview had gone like this:

"So, Kyle, that was one colossal f—— up!"
"Yeah."
"You shot yourself in the foot, man!"
"Yeah."
"Doing a gun safety demonstration! I mean you just can't have a more perfect f—— up than that!"
"I know."
"I think Kyle deserves the Batso salute, don't you? Batsos, all together now: YOU F——ED UP, MAN!"

So it had been a little short, Kyle thought. The point was, he was on the radar. And his blip was growing bigger by the minute.

"Enjoy your dinner," Merritt said, delivering a parting back wallop. Jackie aimed an insincere smile at Merritt's wife.

Jackie twisted a ringlet of brown hair around her finger. The gesture meant she was mulling something over, which, these days, she did often. She stared, unseeing, at her plate, the candlelight sharpening the angles of her nose and chin. Jackie's looks suited her serious nature, Kyle thought. He admired the way she worried about the universe.

Jackie's prime rib sat in a pink puddle. Kyle took a swallow of the blue drink and smacked his lips. "A fine bouquet," he said, "with hints of marshmallow and horse manure."

Jackie sighed and patted her stomach. Mollie was acting up again, apparently. Kyle could sympathize. He too had something inside him struggling to get out.

In fact, now was as good a time as any for Valentine's Day Surprise Number One.

"I've decided to quit my job and become a comedian," Kyle said to his wife.

Jackie winced and shifted in her chair. Evidently Mollie had delivered a flurry of kicks.

"I was never cut out to be a cop," Kyle explained. "Who's the guy who gets hung up on the chain-link fence while his partner's busting the meth heads? I'm fat, I've got a bad back, I haven't been promoted in fourteen years. The foot thing was a sign."

"A sign from who?" said Jackie, slowly.

"From God, all right? I do believe in him, just not the same way you do. I think God wants me to be a comedian."

This was Jackie's territory, and she rose up to claim it. "God does not want you to be a comedian," she said, jabbing the tablecloth with her index finger.

"How do you know?"

"Wars? Diseases? The space shuttle exploding? It was all predicted in the book of Daniel, Kyle: *Then the iron, the clay, the brass, the silver, and the gold were broken to pieces together . . . and the wind carried them away.* The foot thing, as you call it, was a sign from God that you have to get right with him immediately. Otherwise you're shooting yourself in the foot. He's speaking to you, Kyle, in your language. Don't you get it?"

"You don't think I'm good enough." Kyle was referring to his impressions.

It was ever thus. The people he loved the most had always doubted him the most.

In 1970, Kyle was still living in the city of his birth, Las Vegas. He had recently obtained a full-time position as a busboy at the Tahitian, the casino where his father dealt blackjack. Burt frequently reminded his son that he had pulled quite a few strings to get him that job, at the Tahitian's fanciest restaurant no less, and that he expected Kyle to work his way up to waiter and then maître d'. Kyle did not want to end up like his father, worn down to a nub of pure anger by years of serving the public at its worst. Still, the money had allowed him to move into a studio apartment, achieving some respite from the anger and his mother's compensatory fawning. Working at Smuggler's Cove also allowed him to sidle up to certain celebrities' tables—not that he had yet mustered the courage to do so—and introduce himself. And it got him free tickets to all the shows.

One autumn evening, Rich Little headlined at the Tahitian. To cap off the evening, Little had done his renowned impression of Nixon. As Kyle raptly observed the master from his corner table, it dawned on him that Little's Nixon lacked something crucial. He had the jowls, the hunch, and the peace signs, or make that victory signs. But Little didn't have the eyes right. There was something of the trapped animal in Nixon's eyes, and for some reason Little could not convey this. Possibly he couldn't imagine being trapped himself.

After the show Kyle went to an out-of-the-way men's room and worked up his own Nixon in front of the mirror. He hunched and sank his neck into his shoulders. He shrank his eyes down to suspicious sparks in the grim expanse of his face. He made V signs and said some nasty things about hippies.

That's when it happened. Though his physical features were actually quite different from his target's, he saw and felt himself merging with Nixon. The transformation was thrilling and also a little frightening. His limbs tingled. A bizarre being loomed in the mirror—Kyle and Dick Nixon, fused.

He ran over to his father's table, because he knew if he hesitated, that amazing thing he had become would vanish and probably never return. Barely catching his breath, he did Nixon right there in front of all the gamblers.

But Burt just glared at him, like Kyle had stuck a knife through his heart. He growled, "So this is what you've chosen to be? A mocker of men who try to do something on behalf of their country? You choose not to serve your nation in combat, and yet you mock its president at this time? You are a mocker, Kyle. That's all you are. A mocker, not a doer."

By coincidence, later that very night, Kyle had met Jackie, who was visiting the casino with her mother. And fifteen-odd years later, here she was telling him, just like his dad, that his impressions were not appreciated.

"This is the most serious time in all of history," Jackie was saying, cradling Mollie with one hand and jabbing at the tablecloth—which evidently represented this time in history—with the other. "It's mankind's last chance."

"Then I have to take the leap now," Kyle said. "Go out with no regrets. It's not as though money would be a problem, right? We could live on credit and never have to pay."

Jackie still had not touched her prime rib. Kyle felt sorry for it. As his wife seemed unable to respond to his last point, he refreshed himself with the blue drink and went on.

"I love doing impressions, Jacks. It's like I let someone else take me over. Suddenly I have their voice, their gestures, their *spirit*." His hands became claws, grasping the delight that was fleeing from him even now. "Like at the demo last night. I was me and Ronald Reagan, both at once. It was amazing."

"Until you shot yourself."

Kyle reached again for the blue drink but reconsidered and tucked his hands under the table. "You know, Jacks, you're a little hard on people sometimes."

"Oh?" Jackie stared at Kyle. He could not help detecting a little pride in that expression, along with the shock.

"It's because you want life to be predictable," he explained. "That's what all this religious stuff is about, in my opinion. You want to predict what's going to happen so you can control it. But the fact is we're all going to die someday. You and I and Katie and Mollie are all going to die. And there's nothing we can do about it."

"There *is* something we can do." On the word *is*, Jackie pounded both fists on the table. The silverware and Kyle jumped together. "You can do it right now," she said. Bang. "Ask Jesus into your heart." Bang. "Just ask him." Bang. "Right now."

At nearby tables, heads turned, and conversations quieted. For the second time in two days, Kyle was the center of a significant public drama. Suspense built. Would he give his wife what she most wanted, on Valentine's Day of all days? Would he ask Jesus into his heart, so Jackie would stop banging and everyone could go back to eating in peace?

"No," Kyle said.

Jackie's face sank into anguish. Her fists remained clenched as the chatter around them slowly resumed.

"I won't do it," Kyle said, "because I don't believe things work that way. It would make me a liar. God doesn't want liars in his heaven."

He reached for the blue drink and once again pulled his hand back. It was surprisingly easy, he realized. Just say no, like Nancy Reagan herself said.

"I'll tell you what I will do, Jacks. I'll give up booze. Alcohol's a sin, right? So I will sin no more. Not in this area, anyway."

Kyle signaled for the waiter and told him to take all the drinks away. His eyes lingered on the tray as it disappeared, a plate of jewels. He raised his glass of water and intoned: "I swear off liquor forever. I will not set foot in a bar again, not even The Missing Link. When we get home, I will dump all the beer I own into the gutter."

Jackie picked up her glass of sparkling cider but set it down again without drinking. Her faith in her husband, Kyle saw, had not yet been fully restored.

He cleared his throat to deliver Valentine's Day Surprise Number Two. "Seriously, money isn't going to be a problem for us," he said. "David Letterman's associate producer called me this afternoon. He heard me on Batso. I did Reagan for the guy and also Rambo, and he said he'd call back next week. I'm going to be on Letterman, Jacks."

"Holy . . . *the* David Letterman?"

"The man himself."

That did it. Instantly, Jackie was laughing, leaning back in her seat and patting her stomach to make sure Mollie had heard the good news. Jackie didn't watch *Late Night*, or any TV anymore, other than *The 700 Club*. But even she understood Letterman's power. That one name washed away the past half hour, the past twenty-four hours. Kyle's wounded foot was gone. Even the Apocalypse was history, at least for the moment. Jackie laughed like she used to, when Kyle used to tickle her. From the corner of his eye, Kyle saw Merritt Stokes give him a thumbs-up.

In time Jackie, stroking her belly, stopped laughing and began to dream.

When Jackie was Katie's age, her mother had bought her magazines. Tessa had come to Morton from a distant planet, which is to say, Santa Fe. The daughter of artists, she had wanted her own children to be sophisticated, despite being stuck in the California version of Appalachia.

"Do not say 'tarnation,'" Tessa told the girls. "Do not say 'them's.' We are not, I repeat, not Okies. Here, read this."

She gave Pam and Jackie *Vogue* magazine to inspire the teenagers with visions of their future selves—long, brightly colored, European. They did not ask how they were supposed to get there from where they were now. Tessa herself had never achieved anything but the bright colors, which she foisted on Jackie and Pam through instructions in beadwork, textile painting, and weaving. Nevertheless, per Tessa's instructions, the girls plucked their eyebrows down to threads and buried their eyelids in shadow. They wore their skirts short, their jeans tight. They wore their handwoven berets at rakish angles, but Jackie shoved hers in her book bag as soon as she escaped her mother's sight. Unlike Pam's, Jackie's hips did not sway; the fringed ends of her belt did not suggestively brush her thighs. She folded her arms over her low-buttoned shirt and smiled icily at the football players.

Pam soon gained a reputation as a slut, charges which Jackie did not look into very thoroughly. But Jackie secretly sided with the majority, those girls who cast wary glances at both her and Pam while trading recipes in the lunchroom. Jackie wanted those recipes. At times she was prepared to approach the table and beg for them. But she did not, and the girls chattered on, happy in their knowledge that they were utterly and permanently normal. Those girls thought Jackie too open, too free. If only they knew she was a column of stone on the inside. Yet, in a tiny pock in that stone, hope trembled like a dewdrop. Someday, she believed, her inside would catch up with her outside. She'd grow into the relaxed and even sexual person she was now disguised as, at least after she was married.

We must say a word now about Jackie's father. That word is "gorgeous." Leo was a tool pusher on drilling rigs, black-haired and dark-eyed from a suspicion of Incan blood in his veins. He strode the platforms shirtless, his tanned torso streaked with oil, which might as well have been honey to the potter's daughter who'd beckoned him to the roadside to ask for directions. Even after they were married, the astonishing sight of his body every morning had driven Tessa to briefly take up photography. She used lighting to emphasize the three comet-shaped shrapnel scars just above his left hip. As an artist, Tessa understood that such flaws were the source of true beauty.

"What do you think?" Pam asked Jackie, approximately twelve years later, as they lingered over the photos of their father in his thin pajama bottoms.

"Huh," was all Jackie could manage. Who was this man gazing up at her? Not her father, not yet.

More years passed. Jackie and Pam moved on to other idols, though Jackie cast the occasional wistful glance at the softness spreading over her father's muscles. His scars elongated, his skin turned pebbled and striated like the desert. Still, he swaggered, he strode. Nothing could hurt him—not the German bullets he'd marched through like rain on the beach at Normandy, not the monstrous drill that could pulverize a human being on its way into the earth's breast. His eyes burned, saturated with sunshine.

He left when Jackie and Pam were in high school. The girls weren't surprised, after years of screaming fights between him and Tessa and week-long disappearances only tangentially related to the extraction of oil from rock. The girls made a point of blaming their mother.

"Wouldn't you leave?" they whispered to each other. "She's just too weird."

For her part, Tessa seemed to confirm that assessment. She invited her ex-husband for every festive occasion, official or trumped-up. And if Leo wanted to bring a guest along, Tessa seemed to think that was fine; her kids invited their friends over all the time, so why couldn't he? "Your hair is so beautiful," she'd say to the new girlfriend, a different one every time. "You're so cute together." Meanwhile, Jackie and Pam mimed shooting themselves in the head. The last time Jackie would ever see her father was at Tessa's Halloween party in 1970. He came as a pirate, with a wench in tow who was Pam's age.

The next day, Tessa snapped. She collected Jackie and Pam from their jobs at the IGA and the truck stop, respectively, and drove them to Las Vegas for a "Celebration of Freedom." What this turned out to mean was watching their mother get drunk and throw herself at every man in the casino. The only lesson they could have learned, had they not been too old and too appalled to take any instruction from their mother, was that life without a man was not worth living. Any man would do—sweaty men with pinky rings; drunk men; married men accompanied by their wives; a man wearing a sequined jacket and knickers, late for his show, in which he rode a white horse and twirled a baton. She draped herself over them all and giggled and fawned until they sloughed her off. The spectacle sent Pam over the edge. After that trip she started wearing caftans and eating only nuts and seeds. Six months later she fled to the Oregon border. She eventually became a teacher in a school that met in a trailer.

For Jackie, the only saving grace of that night, and at the time it felt like salvation, was meeting Kyle.

He sat at the end of the bar, watching Tessa slobber on the bartender. From time to time he took a swallow of a bright-colored drink. He had on a brand-new short-sleeved shirt and polyester pants. That and the look on his face, which Jackie interpreted as elemental grief, told her he'd just come back from the war. She was the only one who saw this wrecked man.

"Hi," said Jackie, sliding onto the bar stool beside him. The beads on her belt clattered against the stool's chrome edge. Kyle flinched.

"Sorry," she said. "I was wondering what you were drinking. It looks good."

"Tequila sunrise," said Kyle. "I never had one before. I liked the name."

"It's pretty," Jackie said.

"Can I get you one?"

"Sure."

Kyle raised a finger at the bartender, who gratefully uncoiled Tessa's arms from his neck. Tessa fell on the bar and whined, "Come back, honey. I need you."

"That's my mother," Jackie said. She couldn't believe she had just revealed this to a stranger. But she felt this stranger would understand. He nodded and stirred his drink with his finger.

"My mom's like that, too," he said. "Part of the territory when you grow up in Vegas."

"My mom's never like this. We've never even been here before."

"Where are you from?"

"Morton, California," Jackie said, in the apologetic yet defiant tone all Mortonians used when telling others where they lived. A man from Vegas would no doubt wonder how anyone could live in the city known—if it was known at all—as the armpit of Bakersfield. She sipped her tequila sunrise, which tasted like orange juice on fire, and answered the question Kyle was too polite to ask.

"I like Morton because people are respectful," she said. "They would never spit on soldiers or anything, not like other places."

"That's cool," said Kyle, shifting on his seat.

They never wanted to talk about the war, Jackie thought. But she had to say something. "I wish I knew how to say thank you," she said. "To the soldiers, I mean. The sacrifice. I just can't imagine . . ."

"I know," Kyle said.

His face, already mournful, aged twenty years in an instant. Jackie took this as confirmation that he'd experienced dreadful things in those jungles and rice paddies. Later, she would learn that this was Kyle's look of shame for having achieved nothing in his life. In fact his father had just finished publicly berating him on this very matter on the casino floor. When he'd finished, all that was left of Kyle was a tuft of red hair on the carpet. The tuft had crawled over to a bar stool, where it was now reconstituting itself with liquor.

Jackie started to cry. "I'm sorry," she said to Kyle. "It's everything. The war. My parents. My dad left us, and my mom—oh, God, where did she go?" Jackie looked around for Tessa. She wasn't at the bar anymore. She didn't see her sister, either.

"Come on. Let's look for her," said Kyle.

They found Tessa dozing in a chair in front of a slot machine. Her red halter dress had come loose at the neck, and one breast, barely restrained by a strapless bra, was foraying out into the noise and light. A small crowd had gathered to laugh. Kyle picked Tessa up and carried her up to the hotel room, where Pam lay stoned and mesmerized by the TV test pattern. Jackie and Kyle returned to the casino.

Kyle introduced her to his dad, a squat, bespectacled man who warmed considerably when Kyle brought up the subject of World War II. Burt made it known that he would have served heroically in that conflict, if not for his terrible eyesight. He taught Jackie blackjack and related it to the Allied strategy in the Battle of the Bulge. The pit boss, a man whose body was an almost-perfect sphere, gave them a full cup of nickels for the slot machines. Kyle told her how the dealers slipped mickeys to unruly customers, how the drug made them shit and barf uncontrollably, and how the dealers would then drag them out by the dumpsters and pull their pants off. Kyle's next-door neighbor growing up had been a real hit man. Kyle used to walk his dog, a white poodle named Ruth.

These horrible stories made Jackie laugh until she couldn't speak. Kyle's sadness and Jackie's dissolved together like fog in sunshine. There were no clocks in the casino, no windows, but Kyle seemed to know exactly when dawn was approaching. He led her outside to show her the greatest wonder yet: the serpentine pool. They walked along its flanks until it slipped through a waterfall and vanished under the building. On the other side, Kyle told her, was a swim-up bar.

As the sun rose Jackie and Kyle lay by the pool in a chaise lounge. Kyle wrapped his arms around her and kissed her hair. The waterfall blushed. Two middle-aged women waded out through it, covering their daiquiris with their hands.

"You, um, want to get married?" Kyle said.

"Yes!" Jackie shrieked.

To seal the deal, they jumped fully clothed into the pool and passed through the waterfall. They toasted their decision with Champagne at the bar and sat on the pool steps, dripping with chlorinated water and plans. Jackie was already taking the wedding photos in her mind: Kyle in a navy-blue dress uniform, herself in strapless satin, the two of them promenading under a canopy of crossed swords. Jackie couldn't believe her luck—a war hero wanted to marry her, to live with her in full view of her mother, who would learn, at last, what a good man really was. They would in fact have to live with Tessa until they got on their feet; fortunately her house had plenty of room. Kyle told Jackie he wanted to become a cop. It had been his dream since childhood, he assured her, though in reality he'd made the idea up on the spot. Jackie had just told him, bashfully, of her fondness for uniforms.

A month later, when Kyle was visiting her in Morton for the second time, she found out the truth. On the vinyl beanbag chair in her bedroom,

Kyle had just finished revealing to her the mysteries of the universe. Jackie suspected the universe possessed even greater mysteries than these; at the moment, however, she was preoccupied. In their daily phone conversations, Kyle had told her nothing about the war. She hadn't pushed, opting to wait for him to bring it up. Now Jackie was seeing large swaths of his body for the first time, all dusted with pinkish freckles. His skin was too tender, too free of scars. It reddened as it peeled away from the beanbag.

"We should talk about the war," Jackie said. "I know it's hard. But we're going to be married. Whatever happened to you in 'Nam, I need to know."

"Oh," said Kyle, laughing hard, "you must have misunderstood."

He was not a soldier, he explained. He was a twenty-five-year-old busboy. "My number never came up," Kyle said. "I got lucky."

He did not look like he felt lucky. An expression descended over his face—the same one that had first drawn her to him at the Tahitian. Even now, she wanted to wrap him in a blanket and sing to him.

"It's no big deal," she said. "I misunderstood, like you said. There are other ways to be a hero."

Back then Jackie could easily dispose of her dreams and replace them with new ones. As a matter of fact, she'd just seen an ad in the paper that the Morton Police Department was recruiting. She liked cops nearly as much as soldiers. Kyle could become a cop in Morton, she told him. He could still serve and protect. He'd have a weapon and a sharp blue uniform.

Nevertheless, from then on, Jackie could not see Kyle as clearly. She couldn't capture him—he was smoke in a glass. *Better or worse?* an eye doctor might have asked, dropping in one lens after another. But Jackie could not tell. How could she know what she was supposed to see in the first place? Jackie had fallen for a soldier on a bar stool, had given that man her virginity. And he had never existed.

Under these circumstances, marital relations proved somewhat complicated. But Jackie loved, and wanted, Kyle all the more because he took her rejections so well. His patience with her made her ache for him the moment he rose, unfulfilled again, from their bed and got himself a beer. Back then she had actually admired the way Kyle used beer. It never made him sloppy or loud or mean. It simply kept him from overreacting to life's little disappointments, which drove other men crazy, or at least out of the house for good. She sometimes wished her dad had taken up drinking.

She followed Kyle out to the living room in her bathrobe, sat on his lap, and touched her forehead to his.

"Want to try again?" she said.

"Not just now. Game's on."

"I want to be with you."

"I know."

It was her fault, Jackie knew. She allowed her mother's experience with her dad to make her distrust Kyle. It could not be his fault that the moment she tried to relax and let him inside her, her mother barged into her mind. In reality, Tessa was a mile away, babysitting Katie, teaching her candle making or another of her thousand useless crafts. But in Jackie's imagination, she stood right next to the bed, watching Kyle's struggling rump with an expression of triumph. *You don't know this guy. You've never known him. How do you know he won't up and leave you tomorrow?* Jackie reminded herself that Kyle wasn't like her father. Kyle had moved to Morton from Las Vegas, away from his family and all the glamour, to live with her. He had become a policeman, just like they'd planned. He was funny and patient and decent. A true friend. Yet in spite of her luck in finding such a man, Jackie could never fully give herself to him. How did people do it, she'd wondered—let themselves go and tear at each other like animals?

"Come on, Kyle."

"Not now."

She went back to bed and stared at the yellowed ceiling the way better-situated people gazed at the ocean. She knew its every lump and wave. She noted the spider she'd smashed with a broom years ago, its body in the shape of an 8 (or an infinity, depending Jackie's position) still stuck above the dresser.

Then, last summer, Jackie had started running. It had suddenly struck her, the desire to lope across the earth and feel it spinning away under her feet. Maybe it was something she'd seen on TV, or that spider, with its multiple legs accusingly and permanently knotted. Summer was the worst possible time to take up running in Morton. Temperatures reached a hundred by ten in the morning. Citizens were warned to stay indoors and keep breathing to a minimum, lest the toxic brew of car exhaust, refinery emissions, pollen, and fertilizer fell them like so many cattle on the killing floor. Nevertheless, Jackie rose at five every morning and put on her running shoes. She eased the screen door shut behind her so as not to wake her family. The sky was the color of a policeman's uniform. Faint silver stars poked through the haze like buttons. The air settled softly on her skin. She pushed off.

One morning she came back, taut and exhilarated, and found Kyle sitting on the edge of the bed. He wore that expression that still came over him from time to time, when Jackie least expected it. Like he'd lost everything. This time, the look inflamed her. She shoved him onto the bed, tearing off her shorts and jogging bra and kicking her running shoes across the room.

"Whoa, there," Kyle said, as Jackie gnawed and sucked at his neck, his chest, his belly. "What the hell? Let's not get crazy."

She pulled him on top of her, licking, clawing. Kyle slid his boxers off, his face a muddle of wonder and confusion. Jackie howled at his every touch, and shuddered, for real, when he came inside her.

"I love you," she whispered.

He rolled off, and still she wanted more, took his hands, tried to place them everywhere on her at once.

"I have to go," Kyle said. "Early shift."

Jackie fell back, frustrated and happy. She had turned a corner. That morning, she later calculated, Mollie came into being.

As the weeks went by, Kyle left for work earlier and came home later. He was pulling (or requesting) an unprecedented amount of overtime, or else he lingered for hours at The Missing Link. He submitted to Jackie's attacks, but warily, never abandoning himself the way she did. He sat on the edge of the bed, flinching from the fresh bites and watching her lace up her silver Nikes—making sure, Jackie thought with a smile, she was not going to come after him again that morning. Her husband's fear intrigued her. The thought of it powered her up and down Morton's streets.

She bought a Walkman and borrowed some of Katie's tapes, to Katie's horror. Punk rock pounded through her like power. It loosened her limbs and her hair, letting her run farther and faster than logic told her was possible. She became an airplane rushing down the straightaway, nose lifting as her wheels relinquished the ground. She buzzed over Morton's geometries, the box houses and squares of lawn and wadded balls of trees along the dry river bed. Banking left, she soared over Front Street, lined by mostly empty stores as a strip mall encroached from the south. She passed the oil fields, pricked by pumps and filigreed with silver pipe. Then she broke free. The plane swooped over dizzying rows of almond trees, orange trees, carrots, cotton, and asparagus. There were roses even—she always forgot about the roses—and great brown patches of cattle in feedlots.

It was all here, Jackie thought. Everything people needed—food, clothing, flowers, energy. Morton was the country's very engine, its heart, and yet it was mocked. People despised what they needed most. The insight struck Jackie so suddenly that she laughed and ran faster, guzzling Morton's questionable air by the mouthful.

In Morton, as the rains come and the nights lengthen, the overheated land sighs with relief—and a cold, dense cloud stretches over the valley and lies there, like a drugged cat, until spring. Occasionally wind or rain will nudge it aside, but just when you think it has departed for good, it plops back down, heavier and more sluggish than ever. In the past, as the fog descended, Jackie had taken to her bed with even more of a vengeance than the rest of the year. This was the season of abandonment. Everyone else refused to admit it. Into the fog they dragged mountains of food; toys with grasping, tangled arms; greenery. Tinny music seeped from every nook and cranny as motorized Santas rocked on rooftops. For Jackie it was hell on earth. But not this year—the Year (actually five months, all told) of Running. She bought a bright yellow rain suit with reflective stripes so she would not get hit by a car when she ran.

"You look like the Gorton's Fisherman," Kyle joked one morning, two weeks before Thanksgiving. She laughed with him. She tied up her new pair of silver Nikes, having worn the old ones out already, and ran off, a ray of sun splitting the cloud.

She came home more energized than ever before. Katie was in school. Kyle was working. Jackie was three months pregnant, although she still did not quite believe it. She had experienced none of the sickness or fatigue that Katie had brought on, unintentionally of course. Mollie did not feed off her mother; if anything, the opposite was true. The child was a ball of light.

Jackie paced the house. Her mind landed on a thousand things and lifted off, finding no object for its powerful sense of purpose. Today she had run seven miles and could have gone much longer. She showered, drank a smoothie. She cleaned the whole house. She attacked the long-neglected oven as the radio reminded women to reserve their Thanksgiving turkeys now, lest they disappoint their families and die broken and alone. These days, Jackie laughed at such fears. Her limbs thrummed. She scrubbed and scrubbed.

Peering into the oven's dark recess, she pictured a person whom she had actually never seen—a gentle monster whose eyes glowed from terrible sorrow. Hunter was the proprietor of The Missing Link, Kyle's favorite bar, and a real Vietnam vet. Kyle had said he was covered in tattoos, names of fallen comrades and places where unspeakable slaughters had taken place. He also said Hunter was an agoraphobe who never went outside. He lived in a small apartment over the bar, and the regulars, like Kyle, did errands for him and brought him food.

On certain nights when Kyle stayed late at The Link, Jackie used to rouse Katie from her slumber, buckle her into the backseat, and drive to the bar. She would park in the lot and take Katie by the hand. The plan was to lead the cute five-year-old inside to shame her father into coming home. Jackie had even coached Katie to say, "Please come home, Daddy," in a voice cobwebbed with sleep. But each time, she faltered at the edge of the parking lot. As Jackie heard the music inside, the cheer as someone raised a toast, she felt she had no right—nor any desire—to tell Kyle to leave. She wanted, rather, to come in. To become a member of Hunter's kindly crew. Yet one could not simply barge into someone else's world and ask to join it. That sort of thing had to arise naturally, and for Jackie, it never did.

So, to Katie's relief, she'd eventually halted these midnight forays. Instead, on those late nights, she lay alone in bed, telling herself she was helping Hunter by letting Kyle stay at The Link with him.

Jackie now knew what she must do, which was to stop making everything so complicated. She should simply do something nice for Hunter, regardless of what he thought of her. She decided to make him macaroni and cheese, from Kyle's mother's recipe, not a box, as had shamefully become her habit.

Jackie put on her rain suit and Nikes and ran to Vons and then ran back with the bag of ingredients banging a bruise into her thigh. She grated mounds of cheese with her right bicep bulging, and drizzled in two sticks of butter. Inspired, she stirred in chunks of last night's HoneyBaked Ham.

With unbearable anticipation she watched through the oven window as the offering bubbled and browned.

Saving out two servings for Katie and Kyle and a smaller one for herself, she scooped the gurgling mass into a Tupperware bowl. Steam engulfed her creation as she sealed it in, and wrapped the bowl in a towel from the bathroom to keep it warm. In the garage she found her old steel-frame backpack, which she'd used approximately three times in the past ten years on family camping trips. She brushed off the cobwebs and shoved the bowl inside, zipped up her rain suit, retied her Nikes, and shouldered the pack. She set off, her warm, heavy burden nudging her back.

The Link's white exterior made it blend in with the fog, although the second story, where Hunter's apartment was, remained an oily dark brown. From a distance, the building seemed to float in midair.

Inside, the bar was dark. The neon beer signs were turned off and a cardboard sign in the corner of one window said "Closed." Jackie tried the door, which was edged with studs and locked. She cupped her hands against the window and looked in. A faint light came from behind the bar; bottles glowed against the mirror. Overturned chairs sat on the tabletops. She returned to the door and knocked.

Above her, a window squeaked.

"Who's that?" said a deep voice.

Jackie looked up, but could see nothing through the window. Scraps of fog swirled in front of it.

"It's Jackie, Kyle Majesky's wife."

"Oh. Hey."

"Yes, well. Hey to you, too." Talking to Hunter always made Jackie nervous. Although she had never met him face-to-face, she had experienced such awkward exchanges on the phone several times over the years, trying to reach Kyle for some minor emergency or other. Hunter was not a forthcoming conversationalist. Plus, Jackie feared she might accidentally cause him to have a flashback. You never knew what could trigger one—a completely innocent word, like "tree," maybe, or "fire."

Hunter spoke no further. Through the small of her back, Jackie felt the macaroni and cheese cooling.

"I, um, brought you something," she said. "Something to eat." What did she think he was, retarded? "Mac and cheese," she said. "With ham."

"Thanks," he said.

Jackie waited for him to come down and let her in. But he didn't. She stepped back and peered up at the window, but still saw nothing. Where had Hunter gone? Did he think that her bringing him mac and cheese, suddenly, out of the blue, was weird? Yes, it was weird, horribly so. What was she doing here? Hunter did not know Jackie from Eve.

The mac and cheese had gone stone cold.

"I'll just leave it outside here," she shouted up at the window.

Jackie set the Tupperware bowl on the pavement and rewrapped the towel. She whispered, "You'll be all right." Tears formed in the back of her throat.

"Don't forget," she shouted again.

Despair swamped her. She could not understand why. What had she lost? A bowl, a towel, some cheap ingredients, and a few hours of her time. Hunter did not want her food. So what? It wasn't the first time something like this had happened—people not wanting what she tried to give them. She would soon experience this again in spades, what with Christmas coming up and all.

But that was just it. Day in and day out, she offered, and others refused.

Of course, she was not the only one—far from it. Hadn't protestors spat on the vets when they came back from Vietnam? Didn't frustrated men beat their dogs to death for wanting nothing more than love from them? Weren't farmworkers poisoned by pesticides and women burned to death in locked sweatshops? Didn't children die of cancer while murderers lived long, happy lives? And wasn't nuclear war still just around the corner, once the seemingly amiable Gorbachev revealed his true colors and pushed the button?

In The Missing Link's empty parking lot, the awfulness of the whole world yawned before Jackie. All of human history was sadness and wild cruelty. She could not bear to live.

She ran, harder and faster than she had ever run. She had to save her child from her vision, but it was too late. The child had seen it through her eyes. Shock spread outward from her belly. Jackie ran down an alley, leapt over a concrete barrier, raced the water from yesterday's storm as it poured over trash-choked gutters. She passed the Chinese dentist's office and the vacuum cleaner repair shop. She recognized these places, but where they were in relation to her home, or where she had just come from, she could not fathom.

She had broken the grid of Morton's streets, defaced it with shortcuts and diagonals she would never have considered using before. The grid was her lifeline. It had saved her from having to pay attention to where she was while she lost herself in the bliss of running. She had only to turn left, left, right, right, etc. up to the Chevron station on the corner of Napier and Grove. She repeated the pattern in the opposite direction and found herself back home. This process had been automated months ago.

She stopped at a corner and tried to find a street sign. The fog closed around her. She checked her watch. Katie would be home from school by now. Jackie was going to have to find a phone booth and call Kyle to come and get her. But the thought of doing that was too dreadful. It meant saying out loud what she now knew to be true: she did not even know her own town, the place she had lived all her life. Wherever she was, she was a stranger.

Jackie shoved back the hood of her rain suit. She was standing in front of a large, pale-blue stucco building with a darker blue roof. It looked like a Travelodge. But the marquee sign, glowing yellow on the green lawn, said Bible Church of the Valley.

"Jackie? Is that you?"

It was Esther, whom Jackie had known and avoided since first grade. Despite her own teetering mound of problems, Jackie had always felt Esther's had to be worse—what with her overearnest manner and visible mustache. She had a way of coming up under you, like a bear cub pushing against your chin, even though she wasn't actually touching you. She also had the accent, the one Jackie's mother had stomped out every hint of in her children's own speech. Esther said "tarnation." She even, on occasion, said "them's."

"Esther," said Jackie. "I'm so glad to see you."

"Me too." The cub invisibly nuzzled her.

"Are you coming?" Esther asked.

"To what?"

"The women's Bible study. Please do join us. I just know you'll get something out of it. I've been thinking about you a long time, Jackie." Esther's accent wasn't as bad as Jackie had remembered. Come to think of it, there was no reason why accents were bad in the first place. If it hadn't been for Tessa's snobbery, Jackie thought, she would have had a much happier childhood.

"I see you at the grocery store or the gas station, always looking so sad," Esther said. "I always think, Jesus is calling out to that one there. He loves the sad ones most of all. I never dared to say it to your face, what with you being so smart and all." Esther laughed. "I've been scared of you my whole life, Jackie. But I don't need to be. Do I?"

Esther looked up at Jackie with such empathy that Jackie knew Esther could see her flayed soul. Two other women—some of those very same girls with the recipes, who had never before spoken to her—materialized with plates of brownies and chocolate-chip cookies. Jackie was starving. They led her inside.

Later she remembered hands—hands everywhere upon her, like balm on seared skin. And voices telling her she did not have to carry her burdens alone. There was nothing to fear, nothing to regret. She only had to let him in. Couldn't she feel him standing beside her? Someone stroked her hair. Someone—Esther—was washing her feet. The women sang.

Jackie's mouth opened. First a moan came out, long and low. She rocked on her folding chair. The sound became a wail. She tried to shape the wail into words, because she had so much to say. But the wail was too wide and rushing like a river. She let it flow.

Then she fell silent. Where her cries had once been, a calm, loving presence now stood. He had been there all along, waiting patiently.

"Come in," she said, and he did. She tried to stand but collapsed into waiting arms.

Then the women told her about the Apocalypse.

That night Jackie lay propped in bed, reading the King James Bible that Kyle's mother had given them on their wedding day. Kyle and Katie watched TV in the living room. They were arguing again about that stupid show. *You're saying Topper actually believes Bigfoot is real? He thinks there's some ape-man living in the forest that no one has ever caught, dead or alive?* They were all missing the point, Jackie thought—Kyle and Katie and Topper. The world was ending. Demons were emerging from hell to wander the earth, seeking one last chance at redemption. *We will not all sleep*, Esther had told her, *but we will all be changed.* What Topper needed to believe in was Jesus.

Kyle came in and stripped down to his underwear. The pink skin peeking out from under his T-shirt made Jackie's soul ache.

Jackie read aloud: "'Blessed is he that readeth, and they that hear the words of this prophecy, and keep those things which are written therein: for the time is at hand.'"

"It sure is," said Kyle, yawning and sliding a pillow under his knees. His breath smelled of beer and toothpaste.

Jackie saw what she was up against. Kyle would let even the end of the world roll off him. Just another disappointment, nothing a few beers could not take care of. And Katie? She was a punk. Punks didn't believe in anything.

What about my baby? Jackie had asked the women. This was the best time ever to have a baby, they had assured her. Babies would go straight to heaven, no questions asked. For a moment, Jackie had felt unfathomable relief. Then she realized the rest of her family's fate was in her hands.

CHAPTER THREE

When Mollie was born in late April, a hush fell over the delivery room. The doctor was the first to say it: "My God, what a beautiful child."

In his gloved hands, Mollie turned toward her mother. The expression on her face conveyed not confusion—as had been the case with Katie—but pure love. Mollie's eyes shone, blue and clear as wisdom itself.

Jackie burst into tears. All her terror, all these months, had been for nothing. Mollie brought a message, all right, but it was not of doom. It was peace. All would be well. Jackie reached out for her child.

Mollie's perfect little mouth twitched and opened. Out came a scream containing the pent-up grief of the whole world. And it did not stop.

Over the ensuing weeks, nothing quieted Mollie: not milk, medicine, proffered fingers, unconditional love, lullabies. Certainly not the handmade dolls that Grandma Tessa turned out by the bucket load. Jackie did the math. Mollie had come a full two weeks early to be born on the same day that the Chernobyl nuclear power plant in Russia had melted down. The book of Revelation said a star called Wormwood—*Chernobyl* in Russian—would poison the waters.

It was now obvious, to Jackie at least, that Mollie was no ordinary baby. She was some kind of prophet.

"Yo, Adrian," Kyle called one bright Sunday morning in May from the couch. "I was thinkin' about scrambled eggs for breakfast."

Jackie was so tired she could not feel her face. Mollie writhed in her aching arm. Jackie finally managed to place Mollie's formula in the microwave, close the door, and push "Start."

By mutual agreement, Kyle had begun sleeping on the couch so that Mollie's sobbing wouldn't keep him up. He needed all his energy for his act. When Jackie glared at him through the doorway, he grinned and pummeled an invisible speed bag above his forehead, even as he remained supine.

"If you make the scrambled eggs, Kyle, then we will have them," Jackie said.

Flummoxed, Kyle paused midpunch. "I was doing Rocky, there, Jacks. Did you get that?"

"I don't know, Kyle. To me, it sounded like you, only louder."

It seemed to Jackie that his impressions had been better before the foot thing happened. Maybe he was trying too hard because he was getting worried. It had been over two months, and Letterman's producer had not yet called back. Meanwhile Kyle had just flopped at another open-mic night in Oildale. Jackie hadn't gone, but according to Katie's terse explanation, the crowd had taken a hearty dislike to his John Wayne.

In her bedroom, Katie awakened and cranked up her stereo. She sang along, something about hating the army and the RAF. Her voice was low and off key, but oddly interesting. Still, Jackie could hardly condone the sentiments of this particular song. Katie was basically saying she hated soldiers. People like Hunter, who'd broken themselves for their country.

She pounded on the door and opened it. She caught Katie in midthrash, doubled over in her old flowered nightgown, a vestige of her prepunk childhood.

"You might not have so much hate in you," Jackie said as loudly as she could without shouting, "if you came to church with me today. The Lord helps people with that sort of thing."

Katie stood, flushed, her expression poised between amusement and rage.

"Hate is a sickness, Katie. But if you open your heart to Jesus, he will heal it."

"What if I want to hate?"

"Nobody wants to hate."

"You do. You hate anyone who's not as *righteous* as you." Grinning ferociously, Katie stretched the word "righteous" to its breaking point. "You hate Dad," she added, with a nasty smirk.

"How dare you suggest that. How *dare* you!"

Between Mollie and Katie's music, Jackie could not hear the reply.

"So you got no sense of Rocky at all?"

Kyle stood in the kitchen, drumming his fingers on the head of his hideous new cane. Had he always been this needy?

Jackie tried to rouse herself. Katie would judge every word of her answer.

"Oh, you mean *Rocky*. I thought you meant Rambo. Rocky's different. I could get Rocky from that. Sure. Why not?"

Thank God, Jackie thought, that Kyle and Katie did not go to church. At least she had an excuse to get away from them.

Today would be Mollie's first appearance at church. Jackie had wanted to take her sooner, but certain concerns had held her back. Her new friends had, of course, come to visit after Mollie's birth, bearing casseroles and silly toys. They'd all held Mollie and tried without success to soothe her shrieks. But Jackie had seen the way their eyes had combed her baby's face, seeking even the tiniest flaw with which they could comfort themselves. Of course it could not be helped that Mollie was far more beautiful than any child they themselves had ever produced. It was simply God's will. But Jackie had not found the right way to explain this to them, and so their envy, even now, seemed to lurk in every corner, ready to pounce.

Another concern weighed more heavily. Bringing this beautiful child, born on the day of the star called Wormwood, into a holy place might prove dangerous. It would be like forcing the positive poles of two magnets together. Or bringing in a bomb. Jackie had gone so far as to picture a flash of white light the moment Mollie crossed the threshold of the sanctuary. Zip—everybody gone. Except, strangely, Jackie, holding out her empty arms.

Still, the risk was necessary. Pastor Mike would recognize Mollie's true purpose and clarify the meaning of her cries. Once the world understood her message, she thought, Mollie would relax.

The white light never materialized. But Mollie disrupted the service, no question. Her screams soared over the singing and Pastor Mike's preaching. Worshippers glanced over, opening accusing eyes midprayer. Jackie patted

Mollie's back, embarrassed but unwilling to do the polite thing and take her outside. She needed validation. Surely Pastor Mike, if no one else, would see what she saw—that Mollie's grief was the world's grief, and that she was calling on everyone to . . . what, exactly? Well, that was her question for Mike.

Jackie barely heard the sermon, about UFO sightings and how those lights were lost souls trying to get into heaven in advance of the Rapture. They bounced off its boundary, the equivalent of a force field.

It came time for the anointing of the sick. This was Jackie's favorite moment in the service, because it helped her remember her own spiritual healing not so many months ago—although those months now felt like a lifetime.

First came Melba Finch, whose arthritis had flared up. Her son boosted her onto the low stage. As she crept toward Mike on her walker, the country-gospel band laid down a slow, pulsing beat.

"Melba, you are hurting," Mike said in a sort of moan-whisper, placing his palm on her bluish forehead. "Melba, you are in pain, and Jesus does not want you to be in pain. The Devil has hold of you, Melba. The Devil has you and is hurting you. But Jesus will kick the Devil out of you!" Mike's voice burgeoned, louder and faster, and the band's picking and strumming kept pace.

"Back off, Devil!" Mike shouted. "Back off and take your arthritis pain with you!"

He placed his palm on Melba's forehead and gave it a shove—a little one, but a shove nonetheless, which made Jackie flinch. Melba's eyes rolled up and she shriveled into her son's arms like a scrap of paper in a campfire. Her son laid her on the stage beside her walker, replaced the slipper that fell off her foot, and returned to the congregation. A chorus of joyful shouts rose up.

Mike raised his arms to heaven. "Thank you, Jesus!" People danced and sang. The band was really rocking now, its red-faced members grinning through their sweat. Katie ought to like this music, Jackie thought. It was as fast and thrilling as punk. She held Mollie tight as ecstatic bodies jostled her. Melba did not move, stirring a small concern in Jackie.

As usual, Jackie could not quite open herself to the Spirit. It had only happened that one time, the afternoon that Esther had first brought her to

Jesus, and she had felt him vividly enter her heart. That was the only time she'd ever spoken in tongues. She had prayed to Jesus to give her the gift again. Perhaps her one experience had scared her so much that the Lord had decided not to dwell in her heart after all. He had come to the wrong house—she was still inhabited by fear, not faith. Or was he still standing right beside her, waiting for her to notice?

All she knew was that although she loved this church, and these people, she could not stop holding herself apart. She did so not just out of fear, but the pride that Tessa had falsely instilled in her. She didn't want to look like a fool.

Mike spread his hands to calm the band as Shelly Thayer, a part-time nurse, mounted the stage. Mike had just healed Shelly last week, Jackie recalled. Hay fever, was it? Yet here she was again, in her sheer blouse, tapping the damp hollow of her throat to indicate congestion. But Jackie reminded herself that the whole world was in pain—as Mollie herself testified day in and day out. If some people needed help more often than others, who was she, Jackie, to judge?

"Let our sister breathe, Jesus!"

Shelly fell, splaying her arms theatrically. A button on her blouse came undone. Pastor Mike loosened his tie and lowered his eyelids as Shelly thrashed on the stage. Melba moved over to accommodate her. The band turned up the heat, and the praise again flew up to heaven.

Mollie shrieked into Jackie's ear, causing her eyes to suddenly, inadvertently, meet Mike's. He looked as surprised as Jackie felt, as both were thinking the same thing. Could Mike actually heal Mollie? For some reason, that possibility had never before crossed Jackie's mind. But of course Jackie wanted her to be healed. She wanted that more than anything. Mollie spoke the world's anguish, the terror and sadness of its last throes— but she had suffered enough already. Let someone else be the messenger.

As he watched Jackie approach the stage, Mike looked as though he wished he had never taken up the ministry. But Mollie's distress soon moved him to sympathy. He nodded to Jackie, and she stepped carefully over the energetically twitching Shelly.

"Child, are you ready?" Mike said. The band began to strum again, softly, building the ladder rung by rung.

Jackie held Mollie out to Mike, who dangled his hand over Mollie's face.

"Devil, back off!" he shouted. "Jesus is touching you, Mollie! You feel him burning you, Mollie! He is burning your pain right out of you!"

Jackie grimaced. She wanted to tell him not to yell, especially about things like being burned alive. But the Devil did not respond to whispers, apparently. Mollie turned beet red, her eyes wide in terror at Mike's fingers. He pressed the base of his palm against her little forehead.

"Be healed!" he shouted.

Mollie screeched. Mike pushed her again, so hard that Jackie's knees buckled.

"Don't hurt her!" Jackie shouted.

Mike paused. The band thrummed, wanting to get up and running.

Mike raised an admonishing finger at Jackie. "I am not hurting her. The Devil is hurting her." He rolled up his right sleeve and began dangling his hand again. Mollie shrieked as the hand again seized her face. "Devil, relinquish your hold on this child!"

Mollie sobbed and flung her head from side to side to throw the hand off.

"It's not the Devil," Jackie shouted.

"Beg pardon?" Mike released Mollie's face and shut his eyes in a vain attempt to hide his aggravation. Jackie knew she was breaking every protocol in the book, but she could not help herself.

"I mean . . . I think she's sad because the world is ending. I think she wants us to do something about it."

"We are doing something about it, Jackie. We are doing the only thing that matters, which is loving the Lord as selflessly as he loves us."

"I mean, she wants us to do something about the Apocalypse."

The music, which had kept on pacing impatiently, vanished like an animal into its burrow. The only sound was Mollie's crying, interspersed, Jackie imagined, with the knocking of her own knees.

She cradled Mollie against her shoulder. "What I'm trying to say is, it's sad the world is ending, isn't it? I mean, all the suffering that's about to happen. All the people—everything they've ever done and hope to do will be gone forever. Families are going to be separated—some will go to heaven, and some won't. Plus the sun and the sky, trees and dogs and cats and mountains—I just can't imagine it all gone. Isn't there some way we could get God to change his mind?"

"Jackie, we must not question the Lord's plans for us. As his children we must humbly submit to him. That's the test he has set before us, whether we will submit, or, in pride and ignorance, resist him."

"But what if he wants us to stop him? What if that's the test?"

Mike shut his eyes again and sighed through his nose. He must be reminding himself, Jackie thought, that she was still new here. Though Mike was probably no more than fifty, his eyelids hung heavy, as if they themselves bore the weight of his knowledge.

"I have been studying Scripture since I was four years old," said Mike with his eyes still closed. "It has told me in no uncertain terms that the Lord intends to destroy this world within our lifetimes. Within two and a half years, at the outside, the world we see around us now will not be remotely recognizable. And I, and most of the people in this room, will not be here to explain it to others." On the word "others," his eyes flashed open, right at Jackie. He then cast his gaze more tenderly on Mollie. "Of course your daughter will dwell with us in heaven, as she is innocent like all children under the age of thirteen. But you, Jackie, must be careful. Do not attempt to defy God's plan. Pray for the humility to submit, before it's too late."

Jackie looked at the child lamenting in her arms and again pictured those arms suddenly empty. Mike dabbed his face with his handkerchief and offered her a labored smile.

"Jackie, do you want Mollie to be healed or not?"

"I don't know," Jackie said. She burst out crying. Mollie wailed with her.

"In that case," said Mike, "others are waiting."

Jackie stepped aside and let a man with diverticulitis take her place.

CHAPTER FOUR

It was open-mic night at an obscure comedy club in Bakersfield. The small crowd seemed friendlier than the one in Oildale last month. They had even clapped and whistled for the last act, a woman who had revealed the secret life of the Jetsons' robot housekeeper. Sort of a performance-art deal, which had probably gone over their heads.

Kyle stepped onto the creaking stage and leaned his cane against the stool. He had bought the cane at the big new discount store on the edge of town, right after the doctor had told him he would probably limp forever. He had found it in a bin with a dozen other completely ordinary companions, all priced to move. Kyle's cane was black with a heavy wooden handle, carved in the likeness of an old man's head. The hair flowed straight back to form the grip as the bearded visage grimaced in either rage or triumph. People had begun to see the cane as a trademark. A man in his early forties who used a cane was distinctive, Kyle thought. And it reminded people of his accident, which had been funny. Sort of.

Kyle set his glass of water on the stool. For a moment he wished it were a beer, but reminded himself to be glad it wasn't. He was also glad this wasn't The Missing Link, where he hadn't been in months, but a room full of strangers. Though he missed his friends at The Link, ached for them sometimes, he knew they would lie to him about his talent. Whereas strangers always told the truth.

"Bogie," he said into the microphone, "eating a peanut butter sandwich."

Kyle had decided to try a new hook—celebrities doing ordinary things. Last week Katie had given him a book on screenwriting that explained why he'd bombed all his gigs so far, and why David Letterman's producer hadn't called back yet. He'd been doing shtick—as opposed to *telling stories*. Any clown could stand there repeating tag lines like *Yo, Adrian*. But a celebrity doing something ordinary, and failing at it, was a story.

Kyle, as Bogie, proceeded to eat his sandwich. "Mmmph," he muttered. "Mmmm." He stretched his face to its breaking point as the tough guy tried to hide the fact that his tongue was stuck to the roof of his mouth.

One problem, Kyle realized as he rolled his eyes in mock agony, was the lighting in the club. It was too dark. He wished he'd thought of that beforehand. His facial expressions weren't translating for the people in the back.

"What the fuck you doing, man?" said a guy in front.

"Eeng msamvch," Kyle said, in character.

"You look like you're having a seizure," the guy said. He got a laugh from the crowd, which had grown smaller. Even the Jetsons lady had left, in a breach of solidarity. "You need an ambulance, buddy?"

"Mmm, mmm." Kyle shook his head, lips still glued together. But clearly this was not the venue for nonverbal humor. A stand-up had to be fast on his feet, so Kyle transitioned to his next bit.

"Mr. T," he said, "at the dentist."

"Lame!" the heckler shouted. Others echoed with variations: "Lame-o, lame-o-rama!"

Kyle, caving, went for the slapstick. He bent over backward, mouth hanging open, his finger hooking his cheek like some gruesome dental instrument. He stumbled, and his cane took the opportunity to clatter to the floor.

Kyle collapsed on the floor and began moaning, "I pity da fool," with a mouthful of pretend Novocain.

As he rolled he glimpsed Katie at her usual corner table. Her eyes brightened and narrowed and finally closed tightly. Sitting beside her, Stick rested his hand on the back of her chair. That was as near as he could get to offering her comfort.

⁓

Jackie heard them arrive just after midnight. She came out from the bedroom to join them, holding the shrieking Mollie.

The kitchen at night was a jagged landscape with a nearby streetlight for a moon. Stick could have been the spirit of the place—a wraith under a cloud of hair. Once again, Katie's expression told the tale.

Kyle paced, jittery and intent, thumping the floor with his cane.

"The Mr. T bit can work," he said. "But I can't do it right after Bogie and the sandwich. They're too similar." Jackie got the feeling he'd been saying the same thing all the way home.

"You need a more sophisticated audience," Katie said, casting a guarded glance at her mother. "The people around here are too stupid."

Kyle paused. "Are you saying I should go on tour?"

"That's what I'm saying."

"In the Reliant?" Jackie said. All heads turned toward her.

Kyle banged his cane on the floor. "You're right, Jacks," he said. "The car's no good. I should get a van. I can sleep in it while I'm on the road. That'll save money," he added, as if that was all she cared about.

"A van would be awesome," Katie said. "Can Stick and me go, too?"

"Sure thing, Katie-did. The Patients can be my opening act."

Jackie opened her mouth to speak, but there was no point. There was no point in asking, *What about school, what about Mollie, and what about me? And what* about *money,* for heaven's sake? Kyle hadn't had a paying job since he'd quit the police force. At Jackie's repeated urging, he'd finally arranged to retire on disability. But the pension was noticeably smaller than Kyle's regular salary—better than nothing, but not enough, especially with a new mouth to feed. And not nearly enough when Jackie considered that it was July, by which time David Letterman should surely have anointed Kyle as his sidekick.

Jackie returned to bed. Between Mollie's sobs she picked up fragments of Kyle and Katie's plans. They would go to Vegas first, where Kyle, as he put it, "had people." That meant Burt and Marian, Kyle's mother, in whose whiskey-smeared vision Kyle would forever walk on water. Kyle said Burt would be able to arrange at least one gig at the Tahitian, and that would snowball to other casinos. After that, it would be on to the coast, San Diego and then LA. Letterman would be begging for him by then. Stick said nothing, but Jackie knew he was still there with the others. He would not go home until Katie told him to.

Jackie got up, turned on the air conditioner, and picked Mollie up out of her crib. She laid her on the bed and curled up beside her, her body forming a question mark around her child.

"What do you know, little one?" Jackie whispered, stroking Mollie's forehead with her thumb.

Blending with the air conditioner, Mollie's howls took on a note of sober assessment: "aaaaAAAAAAaaaaAAAA . . ."

Above Jackie's dresser, next to a wooden cross, was a framed print of Jesus. When she had first bought it, Esther had told her, gently, that pictures of the Lord weren't necessary. "You'll know him when you see him," Esther said. Tessa, of course, had snorted at the "sad-clown Jesus," with the long, sunlit locks and beseeching eyes raised heavenward. It had given Jackie a special pleasure to say: "This is the art people really want, Mother. Not random blobs of color, or a woman with both eyes on the side of her head like a flounder. They want their Redeemer."

Now she realized why she had wanted the picture so badly. She was like the unpopular high school girl who'd finally gotten herself a boyfriend and had to prove it to the world—and to herself. Good Lord, how could she have trivialized God's love like that? And yet she still liked seeing who she was talking to, or thinking she saw him. No one really knew, of course, what Jesus looked like. It wasn't like anybody had had a camera the last time he came here.

Father, in Jesus's name I thank and praise you . . .

Her body ached like a bag of stones. She wanted to get out of bed and kneel, or at least sit up. In the beginning she had stood up to pray, as she did in church, lifting holy hands; or else she had knelt at her bedside like a child. But lately she'd been praying when and where the need struck her—in the shower, in the car, at the transfer station, for heaven's sake. Also, she had skipped church for the first time last week. She'd felt awkward ever since she'd interfered with Pastor Mike's attempt to heal Mollie. She never brought Mollie with her again, and had been skulking alone in the back like a bad student.

This was why her husband was failing in his new career. Why her dishwasher was broken, why this room was so unbearably hot, even with the air conditioner roaring like a jet engine. God was angry with her. Rightly so. *Hey, everybody, let's all try to stop the Apocalypse, OK?* What kind of idiot even thought such things?

Father, I thank and praise . . .

And then the Lord spoke to her. He didn't enter her; Jackie did not rise, did not collapse afterward in tears. God spoke to her calmly, simply, precisely as he needed to in order to get the message across.

Jackie, the Lord said, *Get a job.*

"I will," she said aloud.

It wouldn't be easy, but the burdens God gave his children never were. Jackie was thirty-eight years old. She had a baby whom she couldn't stand to leave for one second, and fewer skills than a teenager. Her thighs had recurdled into cottage cheese the minute she had given up running. Her dark eyes had grown weary and suspicious. She made people nervous.

She could not work at a fast-food place. The uniforms were always orange, which made her look like death warmed over.

So, in the morning she applied at CarlsMart, the huge new discount store on the outskirts of town. The employees there wore navy-blue smocks, which were almost dignified. Carl, the chain's handsome mascot, was embroidered in white above the left breast pocket. He waved from the cockpit of his little race car.

☙

Tonight on *The Weird Frontier:* Ape-men from outer space.

A few months ago, a veterinarian named Victor Davidson went camping with his wife, Alma, in the Mojave Desert.

A lovely evening unfolded. Slowly the sky darkened from pink to purple to velvet black. The stars came out in swarms. Victor pointed out the constellations.

"Well, that's Orion. And if you follow the line of his belt, you get to the North Star. Or is it Sirius? The North Star might be over there. That's the Big Dipper, for sure."

(The reenactment, featuring Victor himself, showed him pointing stiffly into the evening sky. The actress playing Alma, a teenager recruited from the general store along the highway, nodded supportively.)

Soon, Alma repaired to her tent and fell asleep. Victor, however, remained awake, feeling unusually restless as he stirred the embers of the campfire. All evening he had had a nagging feeling that something was terribly wrong. Bringing a lantern, he moved to higher ground. He sat on a rock and watched the tent containing his sleeping wife.

Although he could see no other campers in any direction, Victor began to sense another very powerful presence nearby.

Victor paced in front of an outcrop, paused, and stared like a ship's captain into the distance.

Suddenly Victor was struck unconscious.

(Victor crumpled to his knees and lay down carefully on his side. He rested his cheek on the back of his hand, which made him look, to Katie, impossibly sweet.)

When he awoke—he had no idea how much later— he saw a horrifying sight. A creature over eight feet tall, covered in hair, stood beside the tent, cradling Alma in its arms.

(Here an actor appeared in a very impressive Bigfoot costume. The fur shone in the moonlight, as though Bigfoot had a functioning family that engaged in mutual grooming. The shoulder muscles expanded as the stuntman hefted Alma. The suit took over an hour to put on and had been borrowed, without permission, from a movie set.)

"Alma!" Victor shouted.

Alma did not respond, as she was asleep or unconscious. The creature fastened its horrifying gaze on Victor.

(There is something about Bigfoot's face that makes it extremely hard for an actor, professional or otherwise, to represent. Bigfoot is human, and also not. The man portraying him must therefore compose an expression that is familiar yet unsettlingly "off." In this case, it may have been the contrast between the human face and the realistic costume that created the effect. Whatever, it got Katie's attention. She set aside the lyrics she'd been writing and turned up the volume, to Stick's slight annoyance. He was trying to pick out a tune on his guitar.)

Victor was knocked cold a second time.

"When I awoke, it was morning. Alma was kneeling beside me. She looked wild, with dust and twigs in her hair. She couldn't recall anything after going to sleep in the tent the night before. Even now, she says she remembers nothing. She says she must have been sleepwalking—or else I was. Because what was I doing outside the tent at that hour?

"I don't like to imagine what happened to her. But I can't help it. I think she was taken to an underground facility and probed. I know what it's like to examine an animal knocked out on a table. It is my theory that Bigfoot comes from a race of ape-men from outer space. For some time, a colony of them has lived on this planet to conduct experiments on humans. I can only conclude that they are seeking ways to interbreed with us and develop a hybrid race that will one day take over the earth.

"Sometimes, Alma asks me, 'Well, if they did that to me, where were my cuts and bruises and broken bones?' I tell her they're in her heart. They took something from her, I don't know what, but she isn't the same as she was. She is broken. I can see that, even if she can't.

"Maybe it's a good thing, in Alma's case, that Bigfoot has the power to wipe memories. I often wish he would have wiped mine. Because as hard as I try to convince Alma that something terrible has happened to her, she won't have it. She tells me I'm crazy. She didn't even want me to talk to you, Topper. In fact she threatened to divorce me if I did. But I have to warn people, even if it destroys my marriage. If even one other person is spared Alma's terrible fate, our fate, it will have been worth it."

"God, that sucks!" Katie said.

"You mean my song?" Stick said. But then he saw that she was crying.

The WF's schedule expanded to seven nights a week. It turned out that Dottie Mayflower was not an isolated lunatic. Bigfoot sightings had proliferated across the nation. Brightly colored pushpins representing these events now littered Topper's map, which he displayed and updated at the beginning of each episode. The clusters of pins, he thought, formed a pattern—if only he could discern it, he would make the find of the century.

Topper had no intention, by the way, to permanently imprison or kill Bigfoot, as some nuts insisted were necessary measures to achieve proof. Nor did he care about personal fame or glory. He only wanted to haul the creature, blinking and grunting, into the light for all to see. Then he would let him go.

Work was a blessing, Jackie thought. How had she not remembered this from the old days at the IGA? It was so simple: People wanted things. She gave those things to them. They thanked her. They paid her. Then, when her shift was over, she was done until the next day. It was not like home where only the first two statements were ever true. Yes, there were downsides, like reporting to a kid almost young enough to be her son and having to entrust poor Mollie's care to Katie, Tessa, and even Kyle sometimes. Jackie could only imagine the contradictory signals Mollie's pristine soul was absorbing from that bunch. On the plus side, the experience of caring for an inconsolable baby would probably discourage Katie from becoming one of Morton's many pregnant teenagers. That was a relief, because she and Stick were spending a lot of time together. They said they were rehearsing.

Work, work, work. It was also a blessing in that it kept Jackie's mind off her husband and his upcoming "comedy tour." As promised, he had purchased a van—a real bargain, he had insisted. Dull black, except for the orange primer on the driver's door, it looked like the Devil's own vehicle. Kyle had hired Enrique, a kid from Katie's school, to custom paint the outside. Kyle wanted an underwater scene.

"Since when do you like fish?" Jackie had asked him.

"I've always liked fish."

"How come you never got an aquarium?"

"I knew you wouldn't like it."

"I like aquariums. Since when don't I like aquariums? Do you want an aquarium?"

"No."

At CarlsMart everything was clear. There were bosses and there were underlings. There were policies on hairstyles, employee parking, sudden illness (you still had to punch out, or find someone to do it for you), and the number of rings (two) after which any phone had to be answered. There was a scientifically determined location for every item in every aisle. There was no disorder or dirt, as outbreaks of each were spied instantly by closed-circuit cameras and set upon by trained personnel. There was a company word, "Incredible!," and a company greeting: "It's an incredible day at CarlsMart!" Whenever the phrase came over the loudspeaker, customers and employees paused and lifted their heads.

The store manager, Melvin, was approximately twenty-four and had a bachelor's degree in business from a nearby university. He also had pimples and aviator glasses with lenses that were supposed to get darker as the light got brighter. In CarlsMart, they stayed medium gray. Melvin proved more than happy to share his knowledge with Jackie. She spent her lunch breaks with him, soaking up information like the desert in a spring rain.

"Market research," Melvin said, as they munched hotdogs in his office overlooking the entire sales floor. "Put it this way. Do you think this CarlsMart is exactly the same as one up by San Francisco? Hell no! Here we carry guns and ammo, beef jerky, and eck-cetera. Up there they don't want any of that. They're too delicate. You know what their CarlsMart sells? Recycled toilet paper."

Jackie laughed with the appropriate shock.

"The point is," Melvin said with mustard working its way out of the corners of his mouth, "it's all about research. People there aren't like people here, and CarlsMart takes that into account. We got computer guys back in LA who turn people into numbers, and then crunch 'em all up. And out comes the exact inventory that we need for every store."

The vision of crunched people made Jackie cringe. But overall, she thought, market research sounded like a wonderful idea. What it really was, was common courtesy. Ask people what they want, and then provide it.

Jackie began thinking of ways to make CarlsMart's customers even happier. "Let's dim the lights a little in the ladies' dressing rooms," she said. "Let's put the insect spray right next to the inflatable pools. We could offer a free pair of gardening gloves with every wheelbarrow." Melvin was impressed. "I wish my mom learned things as fast as you do," he said. He mentioned that a shift supervisor position would open up soon, and why would he have mentioned that, except to indicate it would be Jackie's?

The clarity of CarlsMart stiffened the backbone of Jackie's faith. She had always been prone to overthinking, making everything more complicated than it really was. Pastor Mike was right: faith, like work, was simple. Follow the procedures. Follow them well. They would take you where you had to go. What a relief, to step into such well-worn tracks and let them lead her to her rest—whether that meant quitting time or heaven.

The parallels were so striking, one Saturday afternoon she was inspired to witness right there at the checkout stand. She had never witnessed to a stranger before, a failing it was high time she corrected.

"Are you having an incredible day?" she asked the woman in the brown sweater with the hole in the elbow. It was September and over a hundred degrees outside, but CarlsMart was air-conditioned to the point of chilliness. The woman's sweater showed that she was (1) cautious with her health, (2) a planner, (3) not wealthy, and/or (4) not vain.

"I guess." The woman shrugged and unloaded her cart. A faded beauty, she moved gracefully but hesitated. She probably felt guilty, Jackie thought. The things she bought were ordinary—facial tissue, some cough drops, lotion—but perhaps she didn't think she deserved even these small creature comforts. This made her the exact kind of person the Lord wanted—a sad one.

Jackie placed the items in three blue-and-white plastic bags emblazoned with Carl in his race car. The woman slid her wrists through the handles to make sure she didn't drop the bags. Her left ring finger was bare, but Jackie spotted the lighter skin and the indentation revealing the recent removal of a band. When Jackie handed over the last bag, she touched the back of the woman's hand. "Do you know Jesus as your personal savior?" she said.

The woman's brow furrowed. "You mean, like, personally?"

"Yes, exactly."

"How could anyone know him personally? He's been dead for almost two thousand years."

"Oh, but he's not dead. He lives right here in my heart," Jackie said, tapping her breastbone. "And he can save you, if you'll let him."

"Save me from what?"

"From . . . unhappiness." Jackie never liked to say "hell." It sounded vengeful, like she rejoiced in other people's impending punishment, and nothing was further from the truth. In fact, the idea of hell so sickened her that she assumed she had misunderstood something very basic about Christianity. She intended to ask Mike about this in private one day.

"From unhappiness in the next world," Jackie explained. "And this world, too." For Jackie believed no one should have to suffer, even in this mere shadow of paradise. She wanted to fling the woman's pain off her right this minute. *Sadness, back off!* They would watch it float away like silk in a breeze.

"Are you telling me you're never unhappy?" the woman said. "Not even a little?" The edge of her voice sharpened. She clutched her bags, the handles digging red stripes into her wrists.

"Of course I have moments when things don't seem to be going my way," Jackie said. "But as a Christian I give my problems to the Lord. He died for our sins, and—"

"You let someone else be punished for your mistakes?" The woman's eyes widened to the point where Jackie could see the whites above the irises. "Like some kind of *whipping boy*?"

Jackie had misread this person; her sorrow was a mask for rage. Jackie had seen it before, in Kyle's father, for instance—though with Burt, the rage covered the sorrow. Jackie needed to let this woman go on her way. "No" meant "not yet"—that was what Melvin always said, referring to sales. "No harm, no foul"—that was what Pastor Mike said. But she had done harm, hadn't she, already?

That picture of Jesus, Jackie thought. It was all wrong. He looked too meek. How could he possibly bear the burdens of the whole world, past and present, on those frail shoulders, already rent asunder on the cross? He ought to be a wolf with six-inch teeth that knocked you down and ripped the sins from your throat. Or she should think of him as fire, as Pastor Mike did. Not that pleading, betrayed young man.

"I only want to help," Jackie said.

Melvin's voice came over the loudspeaker. "Jackie Majesky, please report to the office."

Jackie tore her gaze from the woman's sneer and observed that the line at her check stand had grown to eight people. They peered over each other's shoulders, left and right, weighing the benefits and risks of jumping ship. Also her phone had been ringing—eight, nine, ten times.

"Sheila, take over at register four. Jackie to the office. Repeat, Jackie to the office. It's an incredible day at CarlsMart."

Miserably, Jackie climbed the stairs to Melvin's office. Not two hours earlier, she had come up here filled with hope. Tuna sandwich in hand, she'd planned to ask Melvin if he would write her a recommendation for the business program he had attended. She'd already sent for the application and was planning to take classes part-time. But for some reason Melvin had not been around. The assistant manager, alone and terrified, had shooed her out of the office.

"What's the matter with you, Jackie?" Melvin yelled. "How could you let your line back up like that? And your phone! Why didn't you answer your phone?"

Melvin was not normally a yeller. He believed in guiding employees to discover problems—which he called opportunities—themselves. There had to be some reason for his theatrics today, related to his absence at lunch.

And there was. Swiveling gently back and forth in Melvin's desk chair was the most handsome man Jackie had ever seen. His dark eyes studied her from beneath luxurious lashes as his strong high forehead furrowed in thought. The man's wavy silver-black hair, held in place by a firm yet nongreasy gel, added to the impression that he was as much a work of art as a human being. The artist had even made a small scar on his left temple—knowing that true beauty resides in flaws.

"Do you know who this is?" Melvin foamed. "This is Harry Ricker, the founder and CEO of CarlsMart Incorporated."

Ricker nodded, a smile playing at one corner of his mouth.

"Oh" was all Jackie could say. Her hands flew to her hair, and she turned to the huge window overlooking the store. Her ponytail had loosened, she saw in her reflection. It must have happened during her exchange with that awful woman. But how?

"What were you doing down there, Jackie?" Melvin carried on.

Jackie should not have turned her back on Melvin like this, much less on Harry Ricker. But Ricker's presence had undone her. He was her father, if her father had been rich and white-collar and possessed of an utterly different form of confidence. Her dad was the cock of the walk, preening; Ricker simply radiated power. She could feel him. In the window, his reflection leaned toward hers. He wanted to know what she had been doing down there, too. But what could Jackie say? She had never told Melvin about her faith. She had been waiting for the right time, but it had never quite seemed like the right time with Melvin.

Down on the sales floor, an odd, misshapen figure came into focus, ricocheting through the aisles like a pinball. It was Katie, carrying Mollie in the baby backpack. Mollie's mouth was a black hole. Jackie could hear her screaming all the way up here. She banged her palms on the window and grabbed the intercom.

"Katie! Up here, Katie!" Shoppers and employees, as one, looked up at Jackie. She beckoned frantically to her daughter. Katie rolled her eyes and trudged toward the stairs.

Jackie paced the office, unable to absorb Melvin's continued burbling. Kyle must have left for his tour, she thought, only he'd left forever, dropping a note on the kitchen table. *There is nothing here for me anymore.* That was the only thing that could have brought Katie here on her own, lugging Mollie almost four miles through the heat. Meanwhile, what could Ricker possibly be thinking at this point? Of course, he would fire her, if Melvin didn't do it first.

Jackie's world had chosen this ordinary Saturday, Chernobyl-like, to melt down. Maybe she had been expecting it. She'd been too happy at CarlsMart these past few months, and for no good reason.

Katie stomped in, exuding sweat and car exhaust, and plopped Mollie, pack and all, on the desk.

"I am officially done babysitting this monster," she said. "She does nothing but scream. I quit."

"Where's your father?" Jackie asked, unbuckling Mollie.

"Fucking around with the van, where else? It's not like he could make this kid shut up anyway. There's something wrong with her, OK? Like really, really wrong."

Jackie gathered Mollie into her arms and sat down with a sigh. Kyle was home. At least for today, he was home.

Ricker stood over Jackie and Mollie, observing the child with an expression of wonder.

"I'm sorry, sir," Jackie said. "Today just isn't my day."

"That," said Ricker, "is the most beautiful baby I have ever seen."

"Oh," Jackie giggled nervously. "Well, thank you."

"May I give her a present?"

Jackie nodded.

"Melvin," Ricker said, "get me one of those Carl dolls."

Was this some sort of going-away gift for getting fired? It did not seem so. Jackie stroked Mollie's puckered forehead and kissed it.

"What are you up to, little one?" she whispered.

Melvin unlocked a supply cabinet and produced a plastic figurine of Carl in his race car. Ricker held it out to Mollie.

Her eyes opened and fastened on Carl, and she stopped struggling. An unfamiliar relaxation spread through Mollie's limbs into Jackie's. Mollie's screams tapered to a series of grunts—more like questions than indignant responses to injustice. A final, tentative "uh?" ended in a hiccup.

Other than the buzzing fluorescent lights, the office was silent. For a second, Jackie wondered if she'd gone deaf. But she hadn't, for soon there was another sound in the room, like tiny wind chimes. Mollie was laughing.

"Oh, my word," Jackie said.

"Holy shit," Katie said.

Mollie grasped Carl with both hands and, very gently, touched his head to her lips. She giggled and kicked her legs. "Ga," she said.

"Mr. Ricker," Jackie said, "I don't know how I can thank you. Mollie has never . . . you have no idea how hard . . ." Jackie was sobbing. She also had no idea how hard, until this moment.

"I guess she likes Carl," said Katie, "better than real people."

Ricker sat in a chair opposite Jackie and Mollie with his hands resting on his knees. He smiled warmly and beautifully.

"Carl," he said, "was my son."

THE STORY OF CARL

Carl Ricker was a hard child. By age two, he'd wrenched his face into the scowl that he would wear every day until his late teens. Small and wiry, he registered primarily as a blur of fists, elbows, and legs. Children who sat next to him in elementary school came home with bruises on their shins and arms. He spat invectives in a voice as deep as a grown man's. A chair was reserved for him in the principal's office, where he invariably arrived every day right after the Pledge of Allegiance. His parents attended weekly conferences with his teachers but found that they, like the teachers, could do nothing with him. Therapists professed themselves mystified. No matter where Carl was or who he was with, he behaved as if he were locked in a cage. Once, in the middle of a vast snow-covered plain, he had roared, "Get me out of here!"

As a teenager he fought and broke windows and held up a dry cleaner at knife point. He was arrested several times, and only his father's enormous wealth and power—he was then the founder and head of Zoomburger, the fast-food chain—saved him from the juvenile justice system.

One weekend, to clear his mind in order to better focus it on his son, Harry Ricker decided to take up skydiving. He traveled north to the noted drop zone just outside Paradise, California.

On the first morning, his instructor strapped him into a harness in front of his body and bore him safely through the air down to the ground. They did it again, with the instructor literally showing him the ropes. Ricker felt like a baby bird.

On the second morning he made his first solo jump. He stood in the doorway of the plane, feeling freakishly light without the instructor attached to him. A golden field, splotched here and there by black cows and boulders and a few pine trees, spooled out below.

He jumped. The plane sailed away. The wind shrieked in his ears as he soared toward Mount Lassen in the distance. The mountain glowed purple and white, the sky bright blue. The earth looked two-dimensional, like a painting.

Ricker became terrified. Much later, he would understand why. In the sky, he had removed himself from the very elements—his home, his work, his wife and son and the earth itself—that composed him. He had become an abstraction. He pulled the cord sooner than necessary, not to slow his fall, but to feel the presence of a companion—the parachute.

The cord resisted. Above him he felt a kind of struggling, but not the thunder and snap of a chute unfurling. He reached around and discovered a horrifying mass, like a giant tumor. He pulled at the mass. It moved, but not freely.

At that point, Ricker's breath left him. His body began to spin like a clay pigeon. His vision narrowed and winked out.

He awoke hanging face down in a pine tree with his instructor shouting up at him. Some time later, a paramedic untangled him and carried him down a ladder. He was treated for a concussion and released.

The ride to the emergency room had been long, however, and during that time he mentioned his problems with his son to the paramedics. One of them, a brisk, broad-faced woman, told him about a special school in Florida called Program Alpha. The program worked wonders with delinquents, addicts, even borderline psychotics. It had helped the paramedic's daughter immensely. She was now a lawyer in Boston.

"I think you'll be very pleased," the paramedic said.

And so it came to pass that for two years, Carl disappeared into the leafy confines of Program Alpha. During that time he was permitted no contact whatsoever with his parents. The Program's protocol called for the subject to feel himself drowning in the unfamiliar, until, at the last moment, the Program threw him a line and pulled up a new person.

Released to his parents' care, Carl looked younger than his seventeen years—younger, even, than when he'd left. His always-handsome face had become open and eager. His body had straightened out of its attacking crouch, and his voice lilted with the cadence typical of Program Alpha graduates. He spoke with fascination about the most mundane matters; he offered a paean for his scrambled eggs every morning before polishing them off in methodical gulps. His parents hugged him, and, for the first time ever, he hugged them back, almost melting into his father's chest. He went for long walks in the San Gabriel Mountains near the family's Pasadena home, taking with him a magnifying glass and books on butterflies and moths.

On a Saturday afternoon, two weeks after Carl's return, Ricker watched through the door of his home office as his son passed by, carrying several bags from the hardware store. Even his son's gait had changed, Ricker marveled. He no longer stomped. He seemed almost to glide.

Carl went into his bedroom, which was large and unusually generic for a kid his age, for he had had no interests before Program Alpha, other than violence. Perhaps (Ricker thought) Carl had at last decided to decorate his room and thereby start revealing the contours of his new personality. He guessed the décor would consist of insect paraphernalia, nets and microscopes, containers with chrysalises in them, posters. The Program had been incredible. Before, any bug that had come within twenty feet of Carl got squashed unequivocally. Now Carl observed them meticulously—and such attention, Harry thought, presaged love.

Ricker hoped Carl would eventually apply his eye for detail to business and help him run Zoomburger. But Carl remained in a delicate stage. The soil of his psyche had been harrowed, fertilized, and seeded by the Program, but it was not yet clear what would take root there. It was important—so the head of the Program had explained during the graduation ceremony— that well-meaning parents not blast the green shoots of their children's new lives with a fire hose of anxious suggestion. The children had to find their own future.

Ricker set down the proposal he was reading for *Road Warrior* tie-ins at Zoomburger. From Carl's room he heard the rustling of bags, followed by the sounds of a device being assembled. A power drill screamed to life.

Ricker bent the upper right corner of the page and smoothed it out again. His wife was at work. She herself was a corporate attorney, one reason, perhaps, that the paramedic's description of the Program had sounded so good; it produced future lawyers, and he himself loved a lawyer. He wished Susan were home now, as she would have no qualms about barging into Carl's bedroom. Ricker could then go in under the guise of coaxing Susan out of there. "Let's leave Carl alone, honey," he would say, as he gave the scene a good once-over. "We've got to give him some space now."

Soon enough the drilling stopped. A chair scraped across the wooden floor. The chair creaked.

Ricker did not remember getting up from his desk or running down the hallway. He was simply in Carl's room, grasping him around the thighs and lifting him off the chair. Above them, the empty noose swung from a hook in the ceiling.

Ricker yanked the noose down and threw it out the window. He fell on his knees.

"My God, Carl. What have they done to you? What have we done?"

Carl blinked at him.

"Carl, please, come back to me. I'll give you anything. I mean it. You can have literally anything. Just, please, please, go back to the way you were before that goddamn Program."

At last, a spark flickered in Carl's eyes. He held out his hand and helped his father to his feet.

"I want," he said, "to be a Formula One race car driver."

So Ricker sold Zoomburger for a world-record profit and moved the family to Monte Carlo, where he set about assembling Team Scimitar. With his billions he could afford to hire the world's best engineers and designers—not of race cars, but of weaponry. The Scimitar would transform Carl's vengeance against both the Program and his parents into an elegant assault on Europe. While Carl took driving lessons from a French former champion, the frightening black skeleton of his car began to take shape.

The Scimitar's secret lay in the revolutionary material that composed its chassis. Developed by a Soviet defector now living in Switzerland, Scimitarium (as it came to be called) was light, strong, and flexible beyond belief. The car became more aerodynamic the faster it went. Combined with cutting-edge telemetry and a supremely powerful engine, Scimitarium made the car so responsive as to be telepathic.

Despite his training and intermittent practice on the junior circuit, however, Carl could handle neither the competitive level of F-1, nor the Scimitar. He soon acquired the nickname Le Crash. He destroyed million-dollar cars on a bimonthly basis. Fortunately, Carl was a natural-born escape artist. Time and again, Le Crash freed himself unscathed from the twisted and always burning chassis. For all its wonders, Scimitarium proved exceedingly flammable, producing aurora-like ribbons of color as it vaporized. This spectacle brought a host of new fans to F-1, aesthetes of a sort. Carl's escapes assuaged their consciences; but it could not be denied that what these fans craved was the vision of human and machine engulfed together in flame.

Susan delivered an ultimatum: the racing must stop. All Ricker had to do was pull the financial plug—no other team would let Carl near a race car. But Ricker did not dare even criticize Carl's driving, let alone put an end to it. He would rather Carl die than revert to the robot that Program Alpha had made him. On the day Susan filed for divorce, he told Carl he saw real improvement.

But as he crossed the border into his twenties, Carl actually did get better. His affinities for his car and his craft blossomed together. His attraction to detail finally found a productive outlet. He walked the track repeatedly before races, falling to his hands and knees to apply his magnifying glass to the asphalt. His preparation was not complete until he could sit in the cockpit and feel every bump and turn of the course unfolding inside him. At that point, the actual races became exercises in déjà vu. The Scimitar sprang into the lead on the first lap and never let go. Carl's nickname became Le Missile.

How did it happen? Perhaps it was the series of encounters with death, mapped onto the receptive strata of his post–Program Alpha brain. That was what his father believed, in the end. Though brutal, the Program had not been completely detrimental; it prepared the mind to take full advantage of experience. Carl was not just the likely F-1 champion of 1983. Along the way he had grown into a humble, witty, intelligent, and fine young man. He was more than his father could ever have hoped for. More important, he was happy.

At the San Marino Grand Prix, Carl started in the pole position, his accustomed spot by now. As he pulled into place after the parade lap, though, he didn't feel what he usually felt at this moment—the calm, the oneness with the car as it revved up. He felt he was somewhere very odd.

The seconds stretched into hours as he watched for the start signal. The crowd became a sea of colored lights, the engine noise distant birdsong. He saw a hand waving in his face, and he understood that this hand was a flame. It was too late for the Houdini act. Carl took one last look around him as the lights and colors blended into the aurora. He waved good-bye.

"That poor boy," Jackie said. "What an awful way to die." Who would have thought the doll's mischievous grin concealed such agony?

"His legacy drives everything I do," said Ricker quietly.

Mollie gazed into Carl's black eyes. "Carl," she said.

Later, Jackie would wonder, without urgency, if this had been just a gurgle. Maybe Mollie had said "girl." Or even "Kyle." But at that moment, the utterance was nothing short of a miracle. Mollie was only five months old.

"That was her first word," Jackie whispered. Mollie turned to her and smiled. As if she has been prepared from day one to say it and was simply waiting for the go-ahead.

Ricker did not seem the least bit surprised. He interlaced his fingers as Jackie shuddered from a sudden, fearful joy.

"Mrs., um," he said.

"Call me Jackie," Jackie managed.

"I would like to make you a proposition that involves your daughter.

If you will allow me, I will send a car for you tomorrow morning and outline the full concept for you in my office."

Tomorrow was Sunday. Jackie had wanted to take Mollie to church again, to show everyone how she had transformed. She was even going to let Pastor Mike think he had healed her, explaining that she'd gotten better over time instead of all at once, like they'd expected. But as Melvin always said, the worst sight you could ever see was opportunity in your rearview mirror.

"Certainly, Mr. Ricker," Jackie said.

"Harry."

"Does that mean you're not coming in tomorrow?" Melvin asked. No one answered him.

"Great. Sell Mollie's soul to the Man," Katie said, but no one cared what she said, either.

CHAPTER FIVE

It is impossible to describe just how much Kyle liked this kid, Enrique. "Mr. Majesky, the sea horse has to be higher up. Have you ever seen a sea horse? I have, at the aquarium. My parents took me and my sister there when I told them about this project. You should go with us next time. What sea horses do, see, is they look down, like this." Enrique tucked his double chin into his chest. "They swim vertically." Enrique clamped his arms to his sides and flipped his hands in small circles. Eyes never leaving the pavement, he trotted back and forth alongside the van. "They don't look up, see. They can't. So if we put him down too low, then he has nothing to look at."

"I see," said Kyle, suppressing a grin. What a great, great kid this Enrique was. There was no act. What you saw was what you got—total dedication.

"So here's what I'm thinking." Enrique whipped open a clean page in his sketchbook and mapped the sea horse's proposed location at the top back corner of the passenger side.

"Watching over everything, like," said Kyle. In Enrique's sketch, the sea horse's eyes were large and docile, its fins like a bird's wings.

"The male sea horse carries the babies, not the female," Enrique said. "And they mate for life. It's a very . . ." Enrique tucked his sketchbook under his arm and knitted his fingers together. "Intertwined relationship."

"Better make two of them, then," said Kyle, taking a bite of his Pop-Tart.

Breakfast was catch-as-catch-can on this Sunday morning. But not because Jackie was rushing off to church, or to CarlsMart, as had been the case lately. Since last evening she'd been getting ready for her meeting with Harry Ricker. She said his name like she was purring: *Harrrry Rrrrickerrrr.* The magic man who raked in billions every day and, incidentally, filled that gaping hole in Mollie's heart in a way her father had never been able to manage. The house reeked of Jackie's hair dye.

Katie appeared on the front stoop, drinking coffee, a sight Kyle could not get used to. She was too young for coffee. Of course he had started drinking it at age nine. Sometimes his mom had splashed in a bit of her bourbon for a treat.

Did he miss booze? Of course he did. Booze had made life easier. He didn't have to think about what he said or did; it all just flowed naturally. Now a layer of sandpaper had formed between him and the world. When he ran into friends from The Missing Link, he couldn't explain why he'd rejected them. For the sake of his marriage, he'd rejected their inescapable circle of drunken self-destruction that had once felt like camaraderie. But how could he tell them that? Hunter missed him, they said. He missed Hunter.

He remembered the first time—more than ten years ago, it had to be—that his former sergeant had taken him to The Link, to celebrate one of the rare busts (a couple of pothead kids) Kyle had not managed to mess up. At Walt's beckoning, the bartender had seemed to materialize out of the very shadows. In Hunter's massive hand, the beer bottle looked like something you'd get on an airplane. But Kyle's amazement at Hunter's size quickly gave way when he noticed the writing all over him. The man was a vast collection of words, a walking, breathing book. Over the course of many visits, Kyle gleaned the outline of Hunter's story from the regulars, but they knew very little. He'd been to Vietnam; he never went outside; the tattoos he gave himself served as memorials to the dead. Hunter himself said virtually nothing about anything, which seemed to cause others to pour their own stories into him, as if he were some kind of priest or a black hole. Kyle himself had offered such monologues on occasion, knowing that if Hunter ever said a word about his own life, Kyle's most painful struggles would seem like Saturday-morning cartoons.

"What do you think of the van?" Kyle asked Katie, pointing with his cane. "Pretty cool, huh?"

Enrique had painted the body an iridescent blue that sparkled in the morning sun. The inside remained gutted; Kyle would get to work on that once the upholstered seats he'd ordered came in. He had gone with the light-blue velour.

Katie shrugged. "When are we leaving? For Vegas and all?"

"What about school?"

"Fuck school."

"Katie. Language."

Katie's face brightened with amusement. She was not used to her dad playing father, Kyle thought. She probably figured he was trying to impress Enrique, who had such obviously excellent parents. His dad was a janitor at the high school and his mom cleaned bedpans at a nursing home. Yet they took him to the aquarium. For research.

"What about The Patients?" Kyle said.

"The guys can come with us. We'll be your opening act. We talked about this, remember?"

"You have to go to school. School's important."

"Come on."

Now picture that limousine we spoke of earlier, the distillation of Morton's collective longings. As Kyle began lecturing the delighted Katie on the importance of education, that very limo, minus the robust man, rounded the corner of the Majeskys' street. The sly reptile paused in front of every house as if in mounting disbelief: *A chain-link fence? A Camaro up on blocks? Lawn sculptures of a sombrero-wearing Mexican and his burro? This has to be a mistake.* At every pause a screen door opened, a head peered out, a bathrobe or T-shirt flashed and receded.

At last the limo parked in front of the Majeskys' place, with its ragged lawn and dying maple tree and weird hollow shell of a van. The unemployed father in a Morton PD T-shirt and cutoffs, cane in one hand and Pop-Tart in the other, gawked at the emerging chauffeur.

"Majesky residence?" the chauffeur asked, glancing at a card in his hand.

Before Kyle even had a chance to nod, the screen door squeaked behind him, and Jackie alighted on the front stoop, carrying Mollie in her car seat like a basket of flowers. She had spent the whole morning in the bathroom, so Kyle had not had a chance to notice until now—she'd gone blonde. She had piled that blondeness into a coy, tousled bun, like a bride's hairdo. She wore a yellow sundress with a white cotton sweater and teetered atop a pair of white stiletto heels. The clothes looked brand new. So did Jackie.

"Whoa," said Kyle. He wanted to say she was beautiful, but if he told her that, she'd think he hadn't found her beautiful before. He had, but in a completely different way.

Jackie threw a distracted glance at him and checked her hairstyle with her free hand.

"Coming," she sang.

The van was parked in the driveway, forcing her to wobble across the lawn. The turf was so hard, her sharp heels didn't even sink into it. Her calf muscles clenched like fists. She still had that runner's body, Kyle thought, queasy with love and what felt like impending loss. The driver opened the passenger door.

"Thank you. Thanks so much," Jackie said. "I hope this is no bother for you. It's such a long way to come, especially on a Sunday morning."

She continued expressing her thanks as the chauffeur closed the door behind her. Kyle tried to remember the last time she had directed such gratitude toward him. It was, he thought, the night they'd met in Vegas, when he'd carried her mother up to her hotel room. When she had thought he was a soldier.

The limo departed. Katie walked down to the curb. She drank her coffee as the mirage dwindled down the long, straight street.

Kyle finally finished off his "Whoa." His knees went weak and he had to lean on his cane for support.

An energy lived inside Jackie, furious as an animal, hard and metallic as a gun. When it took her, she could and would do anything. The energy had surfaced last summer, when she had suddenly developed her obsession with running. Before that, she had refused to allow athletic prowess in any form to impress her—as Kyle well knew, having taken her and Katie to countless high school football games.

No matter what Jackie now believed, football was the real religion in Morton. The whole town turned out for every game, roaring out its worship of the Marauders. Even Katie, before her recent transformation, had screamed and clapped, pigtails bobbing in blue-and-gold ribbons. Kyle had thought she'd become a cheerleader when she was older, and the thought had pleased him, because it meant that Katie would have an easier life than Jackie. Katie (it had seemed to him then) was like other people. Whereas, amid the frenzy of the games, her mother, alone, had remained seated, legs crossed, foot tapping impatiently. She'd applauded like a golf spectator, if at all.

And yet Kyle had adored this version of Jackie because he knew that he made her life richer. Without him to drag her to games or Police Activities League talent shows, where his impressions had tickled friendly crowds; without his cop stories, Vegas stories, stories of The Missing Link and its more intriguing denizens—in short, without Kyle's efforts to delight and amaze and soothe her, Jackie would have been far more unhappy. He had given her some life—some of his life—and that had made him proud.

But then came last summer. One day she was lying in bed in the middle of the afternoon, saying, as usual, that she was "a little tired." The next day she was tearing down the street in a T-shirt, pleated walking shorts, and the pair of old tennis shoes she only wore when cleaning the house. She bought magazines, Nikes specially designed for the particular type of asphalt she ran on, a yellow rain suit. She stretched elaborately in the living room. And, not to put too fine a point on it, she began to fuck like a banshee. Kyle had fantasized all along that Jackie might become more liberated in this area. In morning half-dreams, he had even cast her as a vampire and enjoyed her in this form immensely. But when the fantasy became reality, it was horrible. He could have been anyone lying there when that bundle of muscle landed on him. He was nothing but a source of friction. In fact, she could have managed the whole business just fine without him.

But here was what Kyle had meant to say to his wife that summer: he was proud of her for finally finding something she loved to do. He couldn't think of taking up running himself, because of his back, his clumsiness, and his unmanly softness, but he had no intention of letting that interfere with her joy. She was beautiful and strong. And here was what he meant to say when the running suddenly gave way to religious fanaticism: fair enough. Her Rapture fantasy was correct in broad terms. What it really meant was that Jackie was better than Kyle. If God existed, he would indeed pick her over him. However, Kyle planned—this was what he had wanted to say above all—to do everything he could to bring himself up to her level. Even if he could not believe as she did.

"She's leaving us," Kyle said, hobbling over to the curb to join Katie. "You mark my words."

He waited for her to spit out some obscene pronouncement. She hated capitalism, the Man, and his limos, didn't she? Wasn't all of this bullshit?

Katie shrugged and went inside. Enrique went on sketching sea horses. He had no idea what had just happened.

In the limo's wake, a few neighbors had been drawn out onto their lawns. Kyle waved at them weakly. Now they knew the car hadn't come for him, either.

Jackie adjusted her sundress, which had ridden up on her thighs. She sat on a white circular cushion in Harry's Los Angeles office. Per Harry's policy she was barefoot, which was just as well since those stilettos were killing her. But the sundress had turned out to be the worst possible choice for this meeting. Harry said he worked best when he was "close to the ground," even as his office was on the top of a thirty-story building. Thus he conducted all his important meetings on cushions, around an enormous conference table less than two feet high.

In Jackie's lap, Mollie babbled softly to Carl, whom she had not released from her grasp in twenty-four hours. Harry sat next to them, rather closer than Jackie might have expected. He crossed his legs loosely. Jackie was impressed with his toes. Encased in silky black socks, they were long and prehensile, not like Kyle's chubby nubs, one of which had gone grotesquely missing. On her soft cushion, Jackie felt herself tipping toward Harry's knee. Between avoiding that, keeping her dress under control, and Mollie, her mind and body had been fully occupied. Only now could she begin to absorb what lay on the table in front of them.

Jackie had never seen a scale model like this. Other models of towns, like the one of historic Bakersfield at the Petroleum Museum, were made of balsa wood or maybe Styrofoam, dusty and chipped. This model, covering the entire surface of the table, rippled with light, as if the buildings floated on a stream. Possibly these effects were reflections from the transparent dome covering the model. The dome, Jackie gathered, prevented Harry's visitors from spilling drinks on the town or poking around and maybe pocketing a house.

The houses—there must have been over a thousand—were East Coast style with shutters and peaked roofs; they were large and varied, in a range of pastel colors. In the bright yards, people a half-inch high lounged by pools or played ball with children and dogs. The homes and people dotted intricately looping cul-de-sacs, so that, under the faintly green dome, the town resembled the wing of an exotic butterfly.

Downtown, families strolled the main street under broad-leafed trees, eating ice cream and/or gazing delightedly into shopping bags. The storefronts were mostly brick with (Jackie leaned in closer; the attention to detail would have done Carl proud) white window boxes full of pansies. Hints of the blue-and-white CarlsMart logo appeared on store windows, though so subtle they could almost have been reflections. The only modern-looking building stood at the end of the main street, the expected location for the city hall. This edifice, though, was a green glass pyramid, somehow both ominous and enticing. On the west side of the town, a large park featured a golf course, rolling green hillocks with grazing sheep, and, on the far end, a lush, tropical-looking forest.

Meanwhile, outside the dome, the orange orb of the sun—in reality a lightbulb on a wire stalk—either rose or set. Its reflection on the dome was a pale flame.

"This, Jackie," said Harry, "is Christmastown."

Jackie laughed. She pictured a mall in Bakersfield the day after Thanksgiving—heaps of fake cotton snow, carols blaring, children packed in a train whose route was so short it was not even worth getting on, an exhausted Santa waiting at the end. What a terrible name, she thought, for such a nice-looking place.

"Actually it's Christmastown One, the first of what we hope will be many." Harry smiled. The lines in his cheeks framed his strong white teeth.

"It's a planned community," Jackie said, recalling a documentary she had seen on TV about a place in Arizona. All of its citizens wore matching visors with the name of the town on it. Sun something.

"Yes, but in a much larger sense. Folks always say they want their neighbors to be the best sort of people. And by 'best,' they really mean morally good. With Christmastown, we have found a way to guarantee that."

And Jackie had thought she was naïve.

"Harry," she said, "there's no way to tell for certain who's good. Not unless you're the Lord himself. Although," she added, "you can get a general idea, if you know a person has accepted Jesus as their Savior."

"And how do you know they're not faking that?" Harry asked.

Jackie shifted Mollie to her other hip and adjusted her sundress.

"That's my point, Harry. Only the Lord knows for sure who's righteous. That's why we put our faith in him. We can't know others' hearts as God does. In fact, I don't even know if I . . ."

Jackie trailed off, wishing she hadn't gone down this path. But Harry's calm eyes, and the way he clasped his supple fingers as he listened to her, made her want to be completely honest. She tapped her sternum, the top of which was exposed by the V of her sundress. The skin was warm against her fingers. "Despite what I think, and hope, and pray for every day, I myself may not be good in God's eyes."

She hugged Mollie a little tighter. There, she had said it. She had never said it aloud before. Mollie cooed at Carl. How wonderful, Jackie thought, to have everything you needed right in your own tiny hands.

"That must be hard for you." Harry laid a hand on her shoulder, which would have been bare save for the white sweater.

"That's faith," Jackie said. Her voice grew thick. "My husband," she said, "he's a good person. So is Katie, despite her looks and the things she says. And yet they're going to be punished, and I'm not. Or maybe I am. I've been doing lots of things that seem wrong lately. Or maybe I'll go to heaven but I'll be sad because my family won't be with me. Or else I'll forget them when I get there, and I don't want to do that either."

Harry handed her a sage-colored handkerchief, which matched his shirt. Jackie cried into it for some minutes.

"Sometimes I think," she said, after her breathing steadied, "that I'd like to stay with them. Even if it means eternal suffering. And other times . . . well, I wish I'd never heard the name Jesus."

Now she'd done it. She'd backslid big time, and she'd ruined Harry's handkerchief with her mascara. Harry's hand lingered on her shoulder.

As she dabbed her eyes, Harry picked up a remote control and pushed a button. The lights dimmed. A screen hummed down to cover the wall in front of them. He aimed the remote to his right, and a projector, hanging near the ceiling like a spaceship, flickered to life. Carl's cartoon visage filled the screen.

"The face of CarlsMart is and always will be Carl," said Harry, standing to formally begin his pitch. "However, because he's not with us in the flesh . . ." He paused, and Jackie pressed her palm to her chest in sympathy. "He has certain limitations as a spokesperson. That's why, for nearly a year now, I have been searching for a very special child to represent CarlsMart's groundbreaking new initiative."

With a whooshing sound, Mollie's photograph appeared on the screen. She beamed toothlessly, angling the Carl doll toward her mouth.

"Where did you get that picture?" Jackie asked. It had obviously been taken just a few minutes ago. Jackie's yellow dress was a haze in the background.

In lieu of an answer, three stars appeared over Mollie's photo and burst like fireworks into the words *Christmas, Every,* and *Day*.

"Christmas Every Day is a retail experience that will transform not only shopping itself, but America and, eventually, the whole world," said Harry. "I have brought you here today, Jackie, to ask you to consider letting Mollie be the face—the official Spirit—of CED.

"You see, for many people, consumer culture has become a source of anguish," Harry said, clasping his hands behind his back as his expression grew sorrowful again. "They say they love to shop. Yet the more they buy, the more they feel that something is terribly wrong. A gulf seems to open at their feet, and they toss purchase after purchase into it to keep it at bay. Ultimately, many fall in from either insolvency or sheer misery. Obviously, this is not a sustainable model for retail."

"It's awful," Jackie agreed.

"Nor does it bring out the best in humanity," Harry said. "You yourself just said you want to be good more than anything, and you have not yet found a successful means to prove that to yourself."

Jackie blushed. Her faith had just been disparaged, and yet she did not feel insulted. Quite the opposite actually.

Mollie's picture dissolved into fairy dust, accompanied by jingling bells. The next image was a blank screen in CarlsMart blue. Phrases in puffy white CarlsMart lettering began filling the space.

EACH SHOPPER CREATES CHRISTMAS LIST
Includes friends, family, coworkers, organizations, etc.
EACH SHOPPER BUYS ONE GIFT FROM CARLSMART FOR EVERYONE ON LIST
EVERY DAY
Bulk/advance buys OK
BIGGER CHRISTMAS LIST = BIGGER DISCOUNTS

"CED members will never agonize over their moral standing," Harry said. "Because they will be able to measure it precisely, and increase it when necessary, through their purchases. However, these are not purchases in the ordinary sense. Through CED, each item people buy from CarlsMart becomes invested with humanity's true purpose, which is giving to others. That's why we call CED members 'Givers.' Now, here comes the big payoff."

The blue-and-white screen exploded and was replaced by new words, materializing in rapid succession.

TOP 5,000 GIVERS
+ *IMMEDIATE* FAMILIES
ARE INVITED TO
LIVE IN CHRISTMASTOWN

This, Harry explained, was how Christmastown's citizens, aka the Winners, would know that they, and their whole community, were the best people possible. Their values of generosity, kindness, and self-sacrifice had passed the most stringent test of all: competition through the free market. If this year's program succeeded, CarlsMart would build Christmastowns across the country and run a new competition every year.

"America itself will become a better place to live," Harry said, "as CED promotes Giving throughout the land."

It was important to understand that CED did not simply reward the people who were able to spend the most money; otherwise the rich would be the only Winners. To join CED, Harry explained, people had to sign up for the CED credit card, which they would use for all CarlsMart purchases. To qualify, they filled out a form reporting their yearly earnings. Each Giver's purchases were then tracked through the card, and an algorithm measured the total volume and cost of purchases against income. A true democracy, CED thus gave all strata of society an equal chance to reach Christmastown.

"Naturally," Harry assured Jackie, "the algorithm will not apply to you and yours. Along with very handsome compensation, Mollie and her immediate family are guaranteed a spot in Christmastown. Which brings me to my next point. Jackie, this is your house."

Jackie's house—Mollie's, the Majeskys', whoever's—appeared on-screen to the sound of birdsong. Grasping the skirt of her sundress, Jackie stood and carried Mollie over for a closer look. Harry's carpet, white and soft as thistledown, tickled her bare feet.

The house was a tasteful pale pink with a variety of mature trees in the front yard and a walkway to the door lined with rose bushes. The myriad windows framed by black shutters gave the impression that the house had eyes and was searching for the right family to fill it. Inside (Harry clicked through the slides) Jackie saw a winding marble staircase, a spa, a walk-in steam shower with real ferns growing on the walls. Eight bedrooms. A much bigger family than Jackie's could live there, she thought, and never even lay eyes on one another.

"It's nice," Jackie said.

"It's the home I would choose for my own family. If I still had one." Harry, standing beside her, let his sleeve brush Jackie's.

She sighed and dug her toes into Harry's carpet. She felt happier already, just imagining the house with Kyle and Katie and Mollie all secure inside. And Harry next door.

"Where is Christmastown, anyway?" she asked.

"Mojave Desert."

Jackie laughed. "But no one's going to want to live there. It's too hot."

Christmastown would not work. Truly, Jackie was relieved to let go of the whole ridiculous idea before it got too comfortable in her mind. It was far too much to ask of Mollie. She was just a baby, for heaven's sake, not the Christmas Spirit. Jackie would thank Harry for his time, shake his hand (holding it for a second or two longer than necessary), and say good-bye. Tomorrow she would apologize to Melvin and go back to work at CarlsMart, if he would have her. From now on, her work, her family, and her faith would be enough.

Lightly touching the small of her back, Harry guided Jackie to the table. Reclaiming his cushion, he placed his fingertips on the dome over his model city. His touch sent faint ripples through the substance.

"This dome is Carl's legacy," he said. "His death defined the limits of the material then known as Scimitarium. Since then, my technologists have reengineered it to function as the most advanced climate-control system known to man. Through billions of tiny computer chips embedded in it, Miribilium screens out all but the most salubrious particles of air and light.

No harmful UV rays, no pollutants, no excessive heat or cold can penetrate it. Nor can wind, sandstorms, or rain. It keeps out all insects, though the more appealing ones, such as butterflies, will be brought inside manually. Yet the people living under the dome will completely forget it's there. They will see nothing but the beautiful desert sky, or a facsimile thereof, depending on the weather outside."

"But," Jackie whispered, "Scimitarium burned."

"Miribilium does not burn. Watch." Harry removed a pack of matches from his pocket and lighted one. He held it against the dome until the flame burned his fingers and he had to shake it out. "Feel," he said.

Jackie felt. The spot touched by the flame was not even warm.

She ransacked her mind for the objections she'd had only a few minutes earlier. Katie would have them for certain, carrying on about the Man and selling souls. Pastor Mike would call it a Catholic scheme—people trying to buy their way into heaven. But all Jackie could think was that Harry and his dead son had transformed the mundane burden of shopping into grace.

An image appeared in her mind's eye: Christmastown as a diamond in the jaws of a crocodile. Though small, it was hard and beautiful, and it held the jaws open so they wouldn't snap shut on the world.

PART TWO: ORIGIN

A man named Everill Gander was born in Elkhart, Indiana, in 1920. His father was an engineer and his mother a schoolteacher. He was the sixth of eight children. He often joked that his parents had given him his unusual first name so they would not forget about him completely.

He volunteered for service in the Second World War and spent time aboard a submarine in the Pacific theater. Returning stateside, he landed at the Port of Seattle, where he saw an ad on a bulletin board seeking loggers. Within two days he was on a crew, living in a company-owned boarding house in the small town of Prince, Washington. Everill relished being outdoors all day after the confinement of the submarine, and the trees gave him cover when he needed it. The submarine, you see, had made him different. He could not say how, only that at some point he had stepped outside of himself, and when he had returned, his body no longer fit him very well. He remained sturdy and powerful throughout his life but looked years older than he was. He had jowls by the age of twenty-six.

Everill started out on the logging crew as a choker setter. He fastened cables around felled logs, signaled with a spin of his index finger, and sprang away as the whistle punk delivered two blasts from his instrument. The log raced through the brush like a snake. Despite his size and apparent age, Everill's leaps to safety were a thing of wonderment. He seemed to get higher and stay up longer than was humanly possible, as if God were weighing him for future reference.

"It's because I'm free," he explained to those who marveled. "A guy can't jump like that on a submarine."

Everill's daytime world was green and scented with the benign blood of timber. It resounded with saws, axes, bulldozers, and trucks doing their duty. Trees bowed in reverence for their lost lives and crashed. Men shouted, not in terror or rage, but to confirm that all were out of harm's way. The battle with nature was titanic but orderly.

Only occasionally did Everill glimpse a thing in the forest that the others could not have been expected to see. Occasionally a red cloud rippled through the trees. Inside the cloud pale faces flashed, as if the cloud were lit up by lightning. The faces shouted gibberish that made Everill's skin crawl. Sometimes he flinched and whimpered in response, and if his fellow loggers saw him, he had to think fast.

"Whoo!" he shouted. "What a world! What a crazy world this is!" He shadowboxed and did push-ups, even a cartwheel or two, as his friends nodded, bemused.

"You're a wild man, Everill," they said.

In the evening the crew repaired to Prince's lone bar. Everill invented and danced jigs, which he called "The Gander" and "The Goose." These dances discharged the residual traces of the image from his soul. But when Everill lay in his bed and the night closed around him, he was a sitting duck. As rain pummeled the roof, the cloud spread itself across his vision until he couldn't see anything else. So most nights, Everill got out of bed. Most nights, walking functioned as sleep.

He walked fast, blinking rain out of his eyes. First Street was obsidian black. Reflections of streetlights rushed into gutters with the water. The cloud hovered a few feet in front of him. Everill swiped at it, flinging raindrops right and left as he tried to clear it from his eyes.

"Son of a bitch!" he shouted.

He turned right at the traffic signal between the diner and the gas station. He passed the farrier's, still doing a brisk business on draft horses worked to the bone from dragging logs. The pavement gave way to dirt, and Everill turned again and skirted the north end of the town past the sawmill, where the night shift was pushing screaming trees through the blades. Fingers of rain reached into his collar. The cloud rippled, taunting him. He grabbed at it, but it was as far away as the edge of the universe. He thought he heard the pale faces laughing.

One day, just before the lunch whistle, he spotted the cloud and decided to have it out once and for all.

"I'll be right back," he said to the foreman.

He was being destroyed by something that did not even exist. There was no reason he could not take these pale guys and their magic carpet, or whatever, out. He was a wild man, and what were they? Sprites at most, sickly and weak. He followed them into the forest until he was sure none of the logging crew could hear him.

"Face me," he shouted. "I'm sick and tired of this hide-and-seek game. Show yourselves. Make your demand of me. Be men, if that's what you are."

But apparently they were not men. The faces looked at him with open mouths and hollow eyes. The cloud swallowed them and together they sank into the hushed glade. Everill stood alone.

Well, wasn't that what he'd wanted? But it had been too easy. These guys weren't gone for good. They had gone somewhere to lie in wait. Everill turned and headed back to the job site, shaking from head to toe.

His senses were tender as a new wound. Everill smelled the stew the men were eating from their thermoses long before he could see them: carrots, onions, stringy cubes of beef. They poured it into metal cups and masticated, stabbed it with folded slices of bread. They laughed. Soon flickers of color appeared among the trees, hard hats resting on logs, woolen shirts. Breath mingled with steam from the cups and rose with the men's speech. Everill gathered their words like silvery minnows into a net. He was nearly back now, back with his friends.

Freddie, the rigging slinger, said, "Where's Everill? I thought he went off to take a dump. But that's a pretty involved dump, if you ask me."

"He probably wandered off." That was Everill's roommate, Charlie, the bucker. "You know he walks around town all night. He never sleeps."

"You see the way he jumps sometimes? Like he's seen a ghost? He starts dancing around to make it look like nothing's wrong." (Freddie, demonstrating.)

"He's a wild man." (Unclear who said that. All murmured assent.)

"It was the submarine," the foreman, Dave, said. "Anyone would be a little tetched after all those months in a metal tube under the water."

"I had a dream about him once." This was Stevie, the faller, who was no more than eighteen and looked like an overgrown twelve-year-old. The men treated him that way, too—gently. Possibly this was because he could wield the gigantic new chain saw all by himself.

"What kind of dream, Stevie?"

"I dreamed Everill was a tree. I was about to cut him down, not knowing it was him at first. He just looked like a regular Doug fir, only, actually, a little bigger. I fire up the saw and the teeth are just about to bite in. And then Everill bends down and says, 'Whoa there, what are you doing?' He's not mad; he's just asking, like. And I say, 'I'm doing my job, Everill.' And then he doesn't say anything, but he bends down and picks me up, and then he carries me all the way out to the seashore. And he says 'Look.'"

"Then what?"

"I saw water and waves crashing on big rocks. There was no color—everything was black and white, like in a photo. That was it. That was the end of the dream."

"You're a wild man, Stevie."

"Not as wild as Everill." More laughter.

Charlie said, "Your dream was right. He ain't quite human."

The howl boiled up through the soles of Everill's feet. His mouth opened and became a volcano, spewing sorrow for whatever he had done to cut himself off from his fellow man. It was later said, although never proved because the tree in question was cut down, that the howl caused all the needles on the Douglas fir he was standing under to fall off.

One man dropped his stew, another gasped. Charlie crossed himself twice. All stared in the direction of the howl but saw nothing except a shadow moving behind the trunk of the bare tree.

A minute later Everill appeared, rubbing the palms of his hands together.

"Sorry about taking off like that," he said. "Nobody swiped my lunch, did they?"

"Did you hear that?" Stevie asked him.

"Hear what?"

"That sound," said Freddie. "Like an animal howling, only . . . like it was trying to say something."

Everill shrugged. "Guess I missed it. But, you know, what a world this is, eh?"

The men finished lunch and went back to work. But from that day on, they were all a little jumpy. They looked over their shoulders; they stared at strange shadows, of which there were many in the forest. They paid closer attention to the stories the Indians told them at the bar, about the *See'atco*, the Lost Tribe—enormous hairy men who threw sticks and sometimes kidnapped children. Without intending to, Everill had opened a few cracks in the loggers' reality—enough, he figured, to give himself some breathing room next time the cloud showed up.

But it did not show up. It was, evidently, truly gone. Perhaps Everill's howl had banished it along with its inhabitants. His prehistoric grief had scared them off.

As time passed, Everill's wariness faded, and a peace settled down upon him. He stopped walking at night and started sleeping. He dreamed of a house, something like the one he'd grown up in, but it was new and all his own, full of rooms he had not even realized were there. In the rooms were luxurious couches, fireplaces with polished andirons, and carpets that glittered. When he bent down he found gold coins embedded in the pile. Everill woke feeling rested and curious.

The other men noticed the change in him, too. At first they did not know what to make of it. The jittery Everill who danced and boxed with the air was no more. In his place was a serenely nodding figure who seemed as wise as his apparent years.

"What's with you, Everill?" the other men asked. "You feeling all right?"

"Never better."

It was undeniable. He set the chokers as deftly as he always had and leapt away. But now the leaps were normal, earthbound as everyone else's. When Everill leaned against a tree trunk, calmly examining first the sky, then the pine litter under his feet, some tried rushing at him, yelling "Boo!" But he did not flinch. He smiled and rubbed his chin, and the man who had rushed at him slunk away, wondering what had gone so wrong with his own life that he would want to startle a peaceful soul like that.

At the bar, Everill sat by himself at a corner table, sipping from a mug of beer that lasted all evening. In truth he was a trifle unsettled. There was an empty spot in him that the struggle with the red cloud used to occupy. Something would have to fill it, but what? He watched the knot of men at the bar, telling jokes, flirting with the waitresses, occasionally beckoning to him with perplexed grins. Everill raised his glass but did not join them. Though some of them were twenty years older than he was, he had begun to think of them as children. As they played, a feeling stirred in him that he could not name.

One night Stevie came over to Everill's table and sat down. "I've been thinking, Everill," he said, digging a blackened thumbnail into a gouge in the tabletop. "I've been thinking you know something the rest of us don't. You're so calm-like. So I was thinking I'd like to know what you know."

Everill pondered for a moment. It seemed he knew less than he ever had known in his life. But he had to help Stevie. Like a forest creature, the boy saw water and gratefully bent his head to drink, never pausing to wonder if it was poisoned.

"I rid myself of an illusion," Everill said at last.

"What do you mean?"

Everill thought hard. "I used to believe the past could be redeemed," he said. "But now I know what's gone is gone. It no longer exists. You understand?"

"I think so," Stevie said.

The next day Stevie backed away from the spar tree he was about to climb and pointed skyward. "You lay off!" he yelled at the clouds. "I'm doing my best down here, and I'm fed up with being told I'm no good! Can't you ever be happy with me? How about a little encouragement once in a while? I know I've made mistakes but I always intended to do good, and I always will intend it! I don't need this crap from you anymore! I don't accept it, you hear me? You lay off me, God!" It appeared to those watching that the sky then got a little bit brighter.

That summer brought Everill the joy of his life. Myra Waltz, the youngest daughter of Mrs. Waltz, who ran the boarding house, came back home. She had been living with an aunt in Seattle while attending the university there. Everill spent many pleasant hours wondering if it was her schooling that had made her so fascinating, or if she'd been born that way.

Myra wore her pale hair in two braids that extended to the middle of her back, along with granny glasses and an expression of permanent concentration that made people stammer in her presence. Her own words were clipped, like her gestures, as she helped her mother with the cooking and washing. At every spare moment she repaired to the common room, where she folded her lanky frame into an armchair, her left arm cradling some book or other. But the cradling was deceptive; that book was not in for babying. She whipped pages back and forth in ferocious reexamination, as if they dared to conceal even the tiniest shred of insight from her. She scribbled notes in the margins, gnawing her lower lip and the pen as she scoured the pages for more secrets. Everill had never seen anyone attack a book like that. His mother, the schoolteacher, had held them in her palms like offerings.

At first he was terrified to approach Myra. In waking nightmares he loomed over her about to say something he'd rehearsed for hours—like "What's that you've got there, Myra? A book?"—when the red cloud sprang from behind her armchair and enveloped her. He yelped and pawed at her; Myra's book went flying. She bent down to collect its sprawled carcass, her braids brushing the floor. In Everill's imagination, she glared up at him over her granny glasses, and when he apologized, she groaned, "Idiot." But gradually, Everill realized that such a scenario could no longer happen.

So, one evening after dinner, when the others had gone off to the bar, Everill brushed his teeth, Brylcreemed his hair, and made his way across the creaking floor of the common room. He paused a few feet from his objective and made a show of examining the bookshelf, replete with dozens of volumes that Myra had brought back from Seattle.

"Graduated, have you, Myra?" he asked, pulling out a volume of essays by Wittgenstein. From the corner of his eye, he saw Myra raise her head. She quickly ducked back into the pages she was wrecking.

"Yep," she said, her eyes racing along lines of print.

"What are you going to do now?"

"What else? Cook and clean. I have to take this place over some day. I'm stuck here."

"For good?"

"Yep."

"I guess I am, too."

Everill had never thought this before. He had been so busy crawling through his nights toward the relative safety of daytime—with its chain saws and massive crashing trees—that he had given exactly zero consideration to what the next forty years of his life might look like. He saw now that the figure in front of him, her legs entwined under the meadow of her skirt, was his future.

"You ever read Plato?" Myra asked, holding her book up so Everill could read the cover.

"Can't say as I have." Everill decided not to tell her that the bulk of his reading, even as a grown man, amounted to *Tarzan*, H. Rider Haggard, and the occasional *Superman* comic.

"He says everything in this world is only a shadow of the real one. All we see is a kind of projection, like a movie—but we mistake the movie for the real thing."

"Hmm," Everill said. Did she want him to believe this or not? It reminded him of Sunday school in Indiana. This world was like a ladder, his teacher had said. You have to climb it in order to get to your destination, but once you're there, the ladder falls away.

"It's bull-puckey," Myra said. "What's right in front of us is all there is."

Everill said, "That means you're all there is, Myra."

Myra smiled. Her teeth were small like a child's. Everill shivered.

Does God lie in wait for us? If he does not react right away, or reacts too subtly for us to notice, how do we know that something we've done has pleased or angered him? Is meeting the man or woman of our dreams—dreams we did not even know we had—our reward for picking up that desperate hitchhiker last week? Or is the hitchhiker's theft of our checkbook a punishment for joining the playground gang that mocked the splotchy-faced new boy thirty years ago? Possibly it's for something we will never even remember doing. And what of that hitchhiker—is she an agent of the Lord or an outcast? Have her scores of similar thefts—she's been on the road for five years after fleeing her stepfather, who raped her but also once saved her from drowning—added up to a diagnosis of evil? If she and her stepfather both repent, are both of them equally welcome in the kingdom of heaven? Does God ever change his mind?

For Myra, the fact that such questions could be even asked proved that God did not exist. Early in their courtship, she set about stripping Everill of any faith he might be harboring. Everill got a kick out of the intensity of her efforts, so he provoked them as often as he could. As for God's existence, he didn't actually care one way or the other. If the past was really past, the question did not seem to matter.

"Epicurus," Myra said, tapping her toe against Everill's calf (they were at the diner, eating hamburgers), "says God is either omnipotent or good, but cannot be both."

"Then I choose good," said Everill, smiling around a greasy mouthful.

"You don't get to choose!" Myra shouted.

"Why not?"

"Look." Myra set her hamburger down so she could point at Everill with both index fingers. "Say there's a God."

"OK, there's a God."

"Let's *posit*, for the sake of argument, a God. By definition we do not control his nature. At best we can only seek to discover it."

"Who decided that?"

"Well, in this scenario, God did. You can't go around choosing what kind of God you want. You don't have that kind of power. For the very reason that *you are not God*." Myra's cheekbones flushed with the effort of getting through to Everill. A braid slid off her shoulder, its tail curled in the crook of her elbow.

"Maybe God is whatever we believe about him," Everill said. "We believe in an angry God, that's what we get. We picture a nice, loving God, we get that instead."

Myra laughed. "You're saying we make God in our image."

"That's not it."

"Then what?"

Everill aligned his remaining three French fries in order of ascending height. "We bring God out," he said carefully. "It's up to us to bring him out in the best possible form." It was just an idea.

Myra laughed again and dumped the ice cubes from her soda glass into her mouth. She crunched the ice with her little teeth, and for that alone, Everill thanked whichever God he had—possibly, inadvertently—called forth.

The wedding took place three months later at the Lutheran church with the whole town and loggers from all over the Olympic Peninsula in attendance.

Two of Everill's brothers came, as did his parents. They looked like a pair of exhausted strangers, which, in fact, they were. They had driven cross-country in their 1938 Terraplane to see Everill for the first time since he had left for the war. He'd written to them often since returning, mostly in the form of postcards—sepia photos of enormous trees with loggers posing in the undercut. *Jonah in the whale, ha ha!*, he wrote. But he didn't want to see his parents face-to-face. *I can't tell you what I did in the war*, he had explained in one card. *I mean I can't tell you because I don't know, and I don't want to know, and if I see you I might remember.* They understood, his mother wrote back. They both walked with Everill down the aisle, each clinging to one of his arms. His fear of seeing them had been absurd. They were tiny. He could have lifted them each off the floor as they walked.

At the reception, Everill asked the pastor why there was a fence around the church. The sight had always bothered him a little. The fence gave the slight suggestion of keeping something out, which seemed wrong, and there appeared to be nothing to keep in. The pastor explained that back when the church was first built, there had been sheep in the yard. Wolves had taken the sheep, all of them, in one horrific night decades earlier, but the pastor had left the fence up as a memorial. Wolves had since been erased from the Pacific Northwest, and the pastor was thinking of getting sheep once again. Everill did not mention that there were still the coyotes to consider.

"Wars of all kinds have ended," the old pastor said. "Now is a time of hope." Everill nodded, crying, and kissed his bride's hand.

Two decades rolled by in blissful fashion. After Mrs. Waltz gently passed into whatever realm she believed awaited her, Everill and Myra presided over the boarding house, welcoming new generations of loggers. Older members of the crew, Charlie and Freddie and the others, built homes of their own nearby and raised smart, mannerly children. On Wednesday evenings young and old gathered in the common room for Myra's philosophy seminar. At one time Myra had dreamed of being a philosopher herself. She would have been the itinerant type, living off the land and the alms of strangers and writing books about her experiences. But are we not all philosophers, whether wandering or confined? At any rate, thanks to Everill's encompassing love, she had apparently come to terms with life in Prince. She did not bang the pots so loudly anymore when she cooked.

Everill was promoted to faller, and then almost immediately to foreman when Dave retired. He was a natural leader. He purchased state-of-the-art equipment. He researched and taught the men new techniques for timber management. He talked headquarters into hiring a tree-planting company to replace the ones the crews had cut. The company put up signs by the highway explaining how birds thrived in second-growth forests. People seemed to appreciate that, especially the tourists. Profits soared.

In the spring of 1969, Stevie disappeared.

To Everill, it was a scene reminiscent of twenty years ago. The men gathered around a huge old stump they were using for a table and opened their pails. The smell of Myra's chicken à la king blended with the earthen dampness of the forest.

"Where's Stevie?" someone asked.

"Taking a walk," said Freddie, still with them after all these years. "Said he'd be back soon."

"He's a dreamer," said Cyril, the new bucker.

"A wild man," Everill agreed.

"'Sometimes we are inclined to class those who are once-and-a-half-witted with the half-witted, because we appreciate only a third part of their wit,'" said Freddie, who'd been attending Myra's seminars and had become a fan of Thoreau.

They ate and waited.

"Well, we'd better go and look," Everill said. He remembered, though not with bitterness, how no one had come to look for him when he had disappeared in the woods for a short time.

They walked in pairs, shouting for Stevie. They looked in and under the skidder, the crew bus, the trucks. They tramped through the forest, shouting, listening for a call or a snap of a twig. Some of the more intrepid fellows doubled over and scanned the ground for footprints, but found none they could recognize as Stevie's. His chain saw was missing, too. His boots and climbing spikes were discovered beneath the branches of the last tree he had felled.

As night descended, they collected flashlights from the trucks and fanned out in twos and threes. They walked for hours under an indifferent strip of stars. They splashed light on stumps, slash piles, ruts from skidders. The light made negatives of everything, the forest a backing peeled off a

Polaroid photo. To Everill it seemed that something was exposed in this peeling—a blueprint for the world's destruction. War had returned, spewing flames that seared people's flesh clean off. Any day a bomb could kill the whole planet.

The crew drove back to town and delivered Stevie's boots to the sheriff, who'd been apprised over the radio and was getting up a search party of his own. Then Everill, his men, and Myra went to see Stevie's wife.

Alice came to the door wearing a red shawl around her shoulders, which gave Everill a start. They sat in the living room while Everill explained how everything was going to be OK. Alice, a Quinault Indian, wrapped the shawl tighter as she listened.

"*See'atco*," she said. "Stevie told me he heard one in the forest once, howling."

"He just wandered off," Everill said. "He's a dreamy sort, as you know. He'll turn up." He wanted a shawl to wrap around Myra, Alice, himself, and the little girl—Alice and Stevie's daughter—peering at them around the corner. But not the red shawl. What was it doing here? Was this a joke? Divine vengeance? It couldn't be. Not after all this time.

Alice shook her head. "They took him," she said. "He was always like a child is why. They take children. He's one of them now."

"He'll come back, you'll see." Myra took Alice's hand in both of hers. Everill could tell from the furrow in Myra's brow that she thought the See'atco story was crazy. It would make good fodder for the seminar when this was over, but that was all. Myra still had very strong opinions on such issues. She also did not believe that a person could simply disappear.

Alice and Stevie's daughter drifted into the living room. Freddie made a bunny rabbit at her with his fingers.

"He'll turn up, I promise," Everill said.

He was wrong. Still, over the months and years that followed, he never gave up hope. In the back of his mind Everill always believed he would find Stevie wandering barefoot in the woods with his chain saw. He was fine, just a little hungry. He had only gotten a little turned around.

Early the next morning, Everill drove his and Myra's pickup as far as he could on the logging road. He parked and hiked up a ridge, wearing a pair of binoculars around his neck and carrying a rope, harness, and climbing spikes. At the base of the tallest tree he could find, he put the spikes on, attached his harness, and kicked his way up the trunk.

The top of the Douglas fir swayed gently as he leaned out, sweeping the binoculars over the forest. The air was soft and green gray. Below, logging crews were making dents in the carpet. The trees shuddered as chain saws attacked them—the firefights of the North American jungle. Here, at least, there were no bombs falling, no peasants appearing out of nowhere with machine guns. To Everill this relative peace felt obscene. It had swallowed Stevie.

He thought of all his men, young and old, as his sons, but Stevie especially. He still looked like he was twelve, and had never shed that absurdly trusting nature. And then there was that business years ago of yelling at God in the sky. In a sense, Everill had put him up to that—though he'd never believed the kind of being who would respond to yelling was up there. But he couldn't help thinking this had opened a gap in Stevie's universe, and Stevie had slipped through.

"Stevie!" Everill called, as if the binoculars could amplify his voice as well as his vision.

Down below, it was easy to forget how close the forest was to the ocean. In all their years together, Everill and Myra had gone to the seashore a dozen times at most. They loved it there. Myra spread a blanket on the sand and gathered their two English shepherds and all their provisions inside its boundaries. "Pretend we're on a raft," she said as they stared out at the silver waves. But once they got home, the ocean vanished from their memories within days. Eventually some reminder, like a TV show or a postcard from a former boarder, took them by surprise, and they said to each other: *We should go there. Why don't we ever go there?*

Now a mere tip of the binoculars filled Everill's vision with water. It was red and alive with screaming men.

Everill ignored their cries, or more precisely, he was encouraged by them, because what he was doing was exactly the right thing. The submarine had torpedoed a Japanese supply ship and surfaced in order to finish off the survivors. The commander had chosen Everill specifically for this task, because, unknown to Everill, he had been noted during training for his marksmanship. The unexpected recognition thrilled him, and he vowed to confirm the commander's faith.

Bracing himself against the swells, he seized the deck-mounted machine gun and poured bullets into the water. The men kept popping back up, thrashing and screaming, and so he moved over to the deck gun and blew one after the other to smithereens, pieces almost too small for the swarming sharks to bother with. He felt bad for the fish, their confusion whipping the water into pink froth, and he tried to avoid hitting them and aimed at men only. But after a while he could not tell what was a man and what wasn't. So he kept firing until someone pulled him away and told him, "Good job." He said, "Thanks." The air tasted of salt and iron. The swells carried him up and down.

The next thing he knew he was on a troop ship. Somewhere in the middle of the Pacific, they pinned a medal on him.

Everill vomited down through the branches. Then he lay back in his harness, facing the sky. Tears ran down his face into his hair. Eventually he decided that he could not live with himself, the self he now recognized as his. It is impossible to say how long he hung in the treetop before he came to this decision. But at some point he unhooked the harness and let himself fall.

He must have fallen like a leaf to the ground. It must have taken a very long time—a minute, an hour—for he landed unhurt, or at least unable to feel any pain. Pain is a form of memory. And the man once called Everill did not remember anything at all.

He walked for days. He slept while he walked, not noticing any difference between states of consciousness. His path was an ever-widening pattern that took him deep into the rainforest. Moss hung from branches, which became the arms of orangutans. Crocodile heads sprouted from ferns. Streams chattered; rain chattered. The whole forest conversed urgently, even though there was nothing to talk about, no one but the shell of a man passing through.

He came to the beach. Water swirled around sea stacks, dashing itself against the dumb idols. The shell-man felt the roar of the surf go through him. He threw back his head and roared with it.

In the distance, a woman in a red jacket had been walking along the narrow strip of sand. The roar froze her right in place. Everill—an oddly familiar word to the shell-man, but when he tried to apply it to himself, it wouldn't stick—waved to her. It seemed like the thing to do.

The woman's arm rose slowly from her side. Then she screamed and ran into the trees.

The shell-man looked down at his body. Every inch of him was covered with dirt and leaves. His clothes were like layers of bark; mud had soaked through them and dried partially, and more had collected on top. He must have fallen several times, slid down a slope, but he couldn't remember. He had also jettisoned his boots and socks. His feet were caked with mud. He touched his hair and discovered a miniature forest of leaves, twigs, and needles. He seemed to remember someone having a dream like this once. But he had not been the dreamer.

I must go home, the shell-man thought. "Home" was a strange word, like "Everill," but he could picture rows of windows, a passenger ship in the night. There was warmth there, and children, possibly. But the children had all drowned, hadn't they? Hadn't someone thrown them overboard as an offering to the bloody ocean? Home was not a place for the man. He could no more live there than a fish could.

He heard voices. "There! Don't get too close. Hurry up!"

The woman in the red jacket had returned with a man. That man lifted his hands to his face, and light flashed off the brim of his cowboy hat. He had taken a picture.

The man and the woman whooped and laughed. "That's something all right," the man said. "But I don't know what."

The couple's laughter made the shell-man smile. It appeared they had been fighting before. The shell-man had brought them back together. The woman tucked the camera under her jacket, and both of them ran.

A wave broke and reached the shell-man at the edge of the forest. Foam circled his ankles like a cat. The shell-man did not know what he was, either, although it struck him that he might be some sort of god. Whatever other gods there were had left this place.

PART THREE: CHRISTMAS EVERY DAY

CHAPTER SIX

December, the season of abandonment, descended. But how things had changed. Now Jackie lived in the eye of the holiday storm. Christmas, as the phenomenon was coming to be understood, depended on her baby daughter and on her.

As CarlsMart's new Vice President for Product Management and Media Relations, Jackie was charged with keeping Mollie lovely, on time, and on cue for every one of her televised appearances, photo shoots, and visits to CarlsMart stores throughout Southern California (and soon, Harry promised, the whole country, and then Canada, Japan, and Europe). Jackie engaged in constant negotiations with directors, producers, makeup artists, and representatives of the company manufacturing the talking Mollie dolls that Givers were to receive after their first one hundred purchases. She had stopped noticing whether she was in a limo, an office, a CarlsMart store, or a studio. Even her home seemed like nothing more than a darker-than-normal place she was passing through, or which was passing over her like a cloud.

For the general public, there was no escaping Mollie. For the past month, she had appeared on television almost twenty-four hours a day. First of all, there were the commercials for the wide range of affordable items at CarlsMart, meant to recruit new Givers for the Christmas Every Day "experience." (That was Harry's term for it; he disliked the word "program.") The commercials ran on every station.

In the spot for the Zenon personal cassette player (only $59.99 at CarlsMart), Mollie sat on a park bench in the middle of a raging thunderstorm (projected on a green screen in reality) intended to represent her mood. Her screaming instantly ignited viewers' guilt: *Who left that poor baby out in a storm? Why, I must have! I'm a monster! How can I become a better person?* A pair of beneficent hands reached down and placed headphones over Mollie's ears. The sky and Mollie's face cleared simultaneously as cartoon birds landed on her shoulders. "Can't you think of someone who'd love a Zenon?" the announcer purred.

Or take the commercial for Rockon sneakers ($29.99). Again via green-screen technology, Mollie sat inside a giant shoe as if she were driving a car. The shoe was an inferior brand, so it wouldn't go anywhere, causing Mollie, naturally, to scream. Dissolve to Mollie seated in the Rockon, zipping along a winding country road. Her amazing blonde curls flowed in the breeze, generated by an offscreen industrial fan, as she squealed delightedly and clapped. "Why not give someone you love a pair of Rockons—and freedom?" The announcer then recited the benefits of becoming a Giver. Of course viewers were still welcome to buy Rockons at CarlsMart, whether or not they signed up for CED. But then the Rockons would be merely shoes. "Don't you," the announcer inquired, "want something more out of life?"

The commercials pivoted on the ability to turn Mollie's screaming on and off like a faucet. Take Carl away from her and she screamed bloody murder. Give him back, or at least show him to her just out of camera range, and all was right with the world again. The whole business made Jackie a tad uncomfortable, especially as she was usually the one who made Carl vanish and reappear. But Mollie showed no signs of being traumatized or of building up a carapace of resentment. As soon as she saw Carl, her pain vanished, and everyone who witnessed the change felt cleansed.

If the commercials were raindrops steadily pelting consumers' heads, the CED Network (CEDN), also known as the Giving Channel, was the mighty Mississippi at flood stage. It ran on cable television twenty-four hours a day. Mollie appeared several times each day in taped segments, perched on the laps of various celebrities in front of a giant blinking Christmas tree. Contrary to rumor, the tree was not sending out coded signals. They were not necessary, as the actual signals were powerful enough. "Gala Microwave," chirped Mollie, whose linguistic precociousness amazed even her mother. The seven-month-old infant memorized and repeated every brand name and slogan, provided it was reasonably short, as soon as the words were spoken to her. (She had turned out to be a prophet after all, just of a different realm.) The microwave was the Gift of the Day, and it could be ordered by phone or purchased at a local CarlsMart. The celebrity beamed and nodded vehemently at the camera, as if to say, "It's true—now get cracking."

For genuine family feeling, these segments were recorded in Tessa's Victorian, the Majesky bungalow having been deemed unsuitable. Tessa concurred, noting that the nation's most adored baby could not be seen scrabbling around in that hovel like a mouse in a shoebox. Diaphanously gowned, fingers barnacled with homemade rings, Tessa fawned over the celebrities as they swept into her living room, as many as three on a given day. She had gone so far as to kiss Cheryl Tiegs's hand while escorting her to the armchair.

This arrangement increased the tension between Jackie and her mother. And this morning, Jackie once again found herself yelling at her on the phone.

"What do you mean, she should be training for the—did you just say 'the-ah-tah'? Are you British now? She's not going to be in any plays, Mom, or movies either. She's not an actress. She's the Christmas Spirit. She inspires people to become their best selves. Why can't you understand that?"

Jackie slammed down the phone and stomped into the kitchen, where Kyle sat in front of a half-eaten bowl of cereal. Jackie pretended to have forgotten something in the living room.

"Oh, fff . . . ," she whispered as she stubbed her toe on the kayak in the hallway. A man from Montana had sent it to Mollie two days ago.

CED had caught on faster than even Harry Ricker had predicted because of one factor which no one had foreseen, though in hindsight seemed glaringly obvious: the person for whom people most wanted to buy gifts was Mollie. Her beauty, her innocence, the thunderous depth of her needs combined with the evident simplicity of meeting them—now imagine all that turbocharged with the power of the media. Mollie truly was supernatural.

Which meant that CarlsMart products now arrived at the Majesky household at a geometrically increasing rate. The bungalow was already packed to capacity with toys, cooking utensils, clothing, bottles of spot remover, tires, ottomans with hidden compartments for God knew what, birdcages, three-ring binders, candy, paint-by-number kits, children's books, personal flotation devices, rifles, hats, Halloween costumes, and so on. Tessa's house and garage had been commandeered, and Jackie had arranged for a storage unit, which would soon prove nowhere near sufficient. She wished she could give some things away to charity—but that would not have been in the spirit of CED. The gifts had to be appreciated—no, loved—by their original recipients, or the whole system collapsed. Jackie could not wait to move to Christmastown. The drawings showed miles of underground storage facilities, and Harry had indicated that they'd be able to move in early.

Jackie sat on the kayak and rubbed her toe. In her mind, her feet were in Harry's lap, as she reclined on the cushions, or—even better—that ridiculously soft carpet in his office. Her shoulders, like her legs, were bare. Harry was so well traveled, he must know some exotic massage technique. Harry whispered, "I've been so alone . . ." These days if Jackie rested for even one second, a reverie like this could drown her.

She returned to the kitchen, and to Kyle. She really did not have time for this.

"How's the van coming?" she said, yanking out a chair for herself. The vinyl was cracked; foam stuffing with a dry yellow crust had seeped out. Why hadn't someone sent Mollie a new dinette set?

Kyle shrugged. "There are some issues with the kelp. Enrique's working with a new nozzle."

"Did you like the sheepskin seat covers I bought you?"

"Oh. Yeah. I'm supposed to send in a coupon or something, right?"

The Thank You Coupons were Jackie's idea. It had dawned on her that certain Givers might create a Christmas List, all right, but then keep all the purchases for themselves. And so coupons were now attached to every CarlsMart product, and recipients simply tore them off, signed them, and mailed them (postage paid) to a facility in Nebraska. Once the signature was verified, the Giver got credit for an additional 10 percent off any purchase. Harry had been skeptical of the coupons at first. He did not believe Giving should be in any way coerced. But Jackie did not want any selfish people slipping through the cracks into Christmastown. Or, to put it another way, a Giver's generosity had to mean something, and every false Giver who gamed the system chipped away at that meaning. Follow the procedures. Follow them well.

Anyway, Jackie had thought Kyle really would like the seat covers. Also the wrench set, tires, chrome wheel covers, fuzzy dice, road atlas, duffel bag, even the nice dress pants for whenever he decided to do his act again. But the Thank You Coupons were still attached to each item, along with the explanation of how they were supposed to work. All he had to do was sign and mail them, but he never did. Of course, the Majeskys were already guaranteed a spot in Christmastown, so neither the coupons nor the gifts really mattered in their case. It was just that it was such a simple action. The coupon was *right there*.

"Don't worry about it," Jackie said.

"I was thinking," Kyle said as Jackie checked her watch. The driver was coming in five minutes to take her and Mollie to the Christmas tree lighting at the Van Nuys CarlsMart. "I could do something on CEDN."

"Like what?" Jackie said. Unfortunately, she knew what.

"Like a regular gig. For Christ's sake, Jackie, I'm Mollie's father. How come she can sit on David Brenner's lap and not mine? I could do my act and plug the product at the same time. I have no moral objection to plugging products, if that's what you're thinking. And I'd work for free."

"What about going on tour?" Jackie asked. "You were going to go on tour and all. You've got your road atlas, your nice new duffel bag."

"The van's not done. And it would give me a real boost to be on television first. If you're on TV, you get bigger audiences. Nicer ones, too. They give you the benefit of the doubt if you're famous. Can you ask Ricker?"

Jackie did not need to ask Harry. She selected all the celebrities who appeared with Mollie. As VP for PM & MR, not to mention Mollie's mother, she was the guardian of her child's image, and no weirdos or cokeheads would ever get their hands on her. Still, it would have been so much easier to tell Kyle that she had asked Harry and that Harry had said no. But she didn't want to put Harry in that position.

"The thing is, Kyle, I don't think impressions would be appropriate."

"You had Fred Travalena on last week. He did Michael Jackson!"

"Yes, I know, but . . ." *Harry said no more impressionists after that . . .* oh, Lord—Rich Little had just taped a segment. "The thing is, Kyle," Jackie said, checking her watch again. "Fred's impressions are more . . . polished than yours. He's been doing them for years."

"So have I."

"But he's a professional. Listen. I used to be a runner, right?"

"You still look like one," Kyle said with a sad smile.

"But I didn't think I was Flo-Jo or anybody," Jackie said. "I was just having fun. It made me happy, like doing impressions makes you happy. And it's great, Kyle, that you've found something you really enjoy doing. Now you can do it as much as you want, because we don't have to worry about money anymore."

A strategy took shape in Jackie's mind, inspired by one of Mollie's commercials. "I mean, think of the *freedom* you have, Kyle. That's a gift that almost no one else has. Fred Travalena *has* to do impressions—they're his *job*. I bet it's no longer even fun for him. Every day he has to go somewhere and do this guy or that guy, no matter how sick of them he is, because that's what the public demands. But you—you get to do impressions for pure joy. You're lucky. No, you're *blessed*. I hope you'll see that for yourself one day."

The doorbell, at long last, rang. Jackie rushed to collect Mollie as Kyle returned to the cold slime that was his cereal.

Cars poured into the giant parking lot at the Van Nuys CarlsMart. Personnel in fluorescent vests directed vehicles along circuitous routes. One by one, the pilgrims emerged. Many stooped and picked their way through the light rain on walkers. Others pushed shopping carts or towed wagons full of offerings for Mollie. Sounds of weeping pierced the air like birdsong.

In front of the store, Mollie sat on a dais, wearing a white fur coat and hat and clutching Carl in her white mittens. The thirty-foot Christmas tree loomed up behind her. As always, Santa was banished from the proceedings as a competing brand. He represented Getting, not Giving. And as for Jesus . . . well.

The master of ceremonies, Dudley Moore, looked a trifle dyspeptic, but no matter. No one would even remember he was there. The crowd pressed against the red velvet ropes around the dais; the small contingent of store security guards linked arms with bewildered employees to form a makeshift barrier. Cameras flashed.

"Ladies and gentlemen," Dudley began. "Fellow Givers," he added quickly. "Though we are gathered this afternoon at what is undeniably a commercial venue, I would like to take this moment to reflect upon the vast number of nonmaterial gifts that we all . . ."

"Mollie!" a man cried out. "My mother is dying! Look, here she is, in this wheelchair! She wants to hold you, just for a minute."

"Mollie, I've come all the way from Colorado. I cheated on my husband. He yells at me, and I was just looking for solace. But now I feel terrible. What should I buy him to tell him I'm sorry?"

". . . that we all share. By giving to others, what we are really saying, in our own humble way, is . . ."

"Mollie, will you come to my son's birthday party?"

"Mollie, I love you!"

"Did you get the place mats I sent you, Mollie?"

Reluctantly, Moore stuck the mic in Mollie's face. She knew exactly what to do with it. "Merry Christmas," she said with the most perfect little lisp on her r's.

The tree lights came on. The crowd erupted in a tremendous cheer. Then, as if programmed to do so (and they were), the thousands surged forward. One of the guards stumbled and barely recovered. The crowd paused, regrouped, and surged again, its movements accompanied by a strange low roar.

Mollie, Jackie suddenly realized, could be in danger. Jackie lunged and snatched her off her little throne. She grabbed the mic from Moore, who was still trying to deliver his speech on the true meaning of Christmas.

"Ladies and gentlemen," Jackie shouted, "thank you so much for coming today. Mollie thanks you, and she loves each and every one of you. But now she's tired. Sometimes giving and receiving all this love makes her tired. We have to go now, so Mollie can rest up and keep doing her good work for all of us. If you'll leave your gifts in the designated area with your name and address on them, we'll be sure to send in all the Thank You Coupons. Thank you again and God bless you."

Jackie signaled to the driver to start the limo, parked right behind the tree. But they were too late. The surge hit the dais and swept everybody off. As the roar rose to a deafening level, the crowd engulfed Jackie and Mollie together. Waves of affection tossed them left and right. Jackie couldn't see above the desperate faces all bearing down on the struggling bundle in her arms. Someone yanked Mollie's coat off; someone else took her hat. The dais gave way with a crash. The tree swayed. Jackie sank onto the wet pavement and covered Mollie with her body, praying she would not crush her, as hands began pulling at her clothing and her hair, trying to get at her daughter. Mollie screamed. Jackie felt around for Carl; he was missing.

"Help!" Jackie shouted.

A shot rang out. The crowd parted. It's Kyle, Jackie thought. Kyle's here. She raised her head.

Dudley Moore stood atop a stepladder, aiming a SIG Sauer pistol at the sky. "Disperse!" he shouted. "Or I will kill all of you!"

Shakily, Jackie stood and gathered Mollie up. She found Carl under the drape that had covered the dais and snatched him up, too. "Thank you," she called to Dudley.

"Go," he shouted. "I'll hold them off."

The world was filled with unlikely heroes, Jackie thought. Covering Mollie with her coat, she hurried to the safety of the car.

It was incredible, Jackie thought, the need people carried inside them. Many of these Givers had already found the Lord. On the way in, Jackie had noted all the minivans with Jesus fish on their rear hatches. But Jesus hadn't healed these people. It was possible he never intended to. Was the wound itself somehow holy?

Givers pressed their faces to the car windows. Jackie wrapped Mollie in her coat, shielding her from the longing, hurt expressions aimed at her. Jackie nodded at the faces, trying in her own expression to convey understanding, but also that they had to back off now, or else.

Another shot rang out, followed by Dudley's cry of "Disperse!" The car lurched forward and the Givers slipped off the vehicle. Prints of their hands and faces clouded the windows.

Mollie's boots had been pulled off, and her tights were torn. There were scratches on her legs. Sobbing, Jackie dabbed the scratches with a sanitary wipe from her purse. The stinging ought to have made Mollie scream, but she seemed not to notice.

Mollie whispered, "You're OK," to Carl.

Perhaps it was better to have a Savior who was always on his way, but never—not yet—here. If he came in the flesh, Jackie thought, his people might tear him limb from limb.

"Mollie, I'm so sorry," said Jackie. "This is all a mistake. You don't have to do this. It's too much. I don't know what's wrong with these people."

Mollie's blue eyes held the calm forgiveness that Jackie so admired, though she herself could never muster it. "They're sad," Mollie said.

"You don't have to fix them, Mollie." Jackie tried to remember the last time she'd had such a noncommercial conversation with the child.

"Yes, I do," Mollie said.

The limo arrived at the Majeskys' home. What a strange place it had become, especially at night. It looked hunkered down. No lights appeared to be on inside, but that could have been because all the windows were blocked by the floor-to-ceiling piles of Mollie's gifts. Kyle's van sat in the driveway, its aquarium glow enhanced by the streetlight.

A dozen or so Givers stood on the front lawn, awaiting Mollie's return, as usual. They had picked the leaves off the poor maple sapling Kyle had been trying to grow for years. They scooped up clods of dirt for relics. In the past, none of that would have bothered Jackie. She would have allowed them to gather around and even touch Mollie. Now she stayed in the car while the driver shooed them away. She had him walk her and Mollie to the front door.

In the morning she hired a team of professional bodyguards, who went by the collective name The Wall of Men.

Kyle barely noticed when Jackie hurried past him, murmuring "you're so brave" to Mollie over and over. He lay on the couch watching *The Weird Frontier*. The show was on every night now, from dusk to dawn. Topper Moss looked exhausted as he watched a young woman, who claimed to be the daughter of Alice and Stevie, attempt to contact Bigfoot telepathically.

CHAPTER SEVEN

"This is the mansion from *The Godfather Part II*," Kyle whispered to Katie.

Their limo pulled into the circular driveway of Ricker's cabin on Lake Tahoe. In his world, a "cabin" was a giant stone castle surrounded by half a dozen guesthouses. Snow rose in head-high drifts, glinting blue in the sunshine. Kyle assumed Ricker had arranged for that effect.

"No, it's not, Kyle," Jackie said.

If Kyle had been in a different mood, he might have pointed out that Jackie did not know what she was talking about. When he had taken her to see the movie—Jesus, that must have been twelve years ago, he thought—she had hidden her face in her hands the whole time. Kyle, who had seen the movie once already, had promised to warn her when any violent scenes were approaching. But she hadn't trusted him to remember.

The Majeskys had just flown in on Ricker's private jet, along with Tessa, to spend Christmas with the Great Man and a few hundred of his closest friends. They'd come a day early to get in some sightseeing and to soak up as much of Ricker's universe-crushing success as possible. Jackie and Mollie would be busy with meetings (and Ricker). Katie wanted to stay in her room and write lyrics. That meant Kyle got to escort Tessa to the casino.

"Isn't it wonderful," Tessa chattered as they meandered through Harrah's, searching for a slot machine that felt "lucky" to her. "To think, last year was the most horrendous Christmas imaginable. And now we're on top of the world."

Kyle had repeatedly apologized to Jackie and Katie for last Christmas. It had been his fault. He should not have rolled his eyes when Jackie gave him and Katie each a copy of *The Late, Great Planet Earth*. He should not have pointed out that Tessa didn't get one. Didn't Jackie care, he asked as a joke, that her own mother was going to burn in hellfire? Above all, he should not have given Jackie oven mitts. He had bought her other things, too, nice things, including a watch with a white-gold band. But she got hold of the mitts first.

She set them on the arm of the sofa. After a minute, she started crying. "You don't know anything about me," she sobbed.

With great drama, Tessa had wrapped her arms around her daughter. "See what you've done?" she'd hissed at Kyle.

Tessa found a slot machine she liked. "Why don't you go get a drink or something," she said, waving a dismissive hand at Kyle. "You'll bring me bad luck."

It was not lost on either of them that the last time they were in a casino together, Kyle had carried Tessa up to her hotel room to sleep off a bender. He was tempted to hang around the slot machine for the sole purpose of ruining her luck. But he decided he would rather have a drink. Unlike Tessa, Kyle had always been able to handle alcohol. He had only given it up to impress Jackie, and she was clearly not impressed at all.

Sitting down at the bar, he felt his bones settle, the same way they did whenever he was in Vegas. Home was where you sank in. I belong at a casino bar, Kyle thought.

Besides, a casino was where the worst night of his life had suddenly become the best one. He could still picture Jackie climbing onto the bar stool with her beaded belt while trying to hold her low-buttoned shirt closed. Back then she had been so—what was the word?—deferential. Shy, but determined to draw him out. To shoulder a portion of his grief, which she'd mistakenly believed was a noble one.

He ordered another and silently toasted his wife: *Thanks for trying, anyway.* After two more, he moseyed over to the gift shop, where he saw this amazing black fedora on a mannequin in the window. He decided to wear it to Ricker's party that evening, along with his new tux. Ricker probably had heard he was from Vegas. Let him wonder if he was a mobster.

Kyle and Katie picked their way down a buffet table longer than a city block, piled with sensuous fruits, exotic cheeses, desserts straight out of a fairy tale, and parts of every known animal cooked in every imaginable way. Reflected in the massive bank of windows overlooking the lake, the bounty became a landscape. Father and daughter paused to admire a full-size ice sculpture of a Christmas tree, complete with minutely carved tinsel and ornaments. Just standing next to it made them cold. Katie, a glass of Champagne in one hand, employed the other to stuff an éclair in her mouth.

"Isn't this bullshit?" Kyle said, elbowing her.

"Bvlsh," she agreed. She wore a floor-length black dress with a bunch of shreds down by the ankles, like Morticia Addams, along with her new leather jacket. Her mother had given her the jacket for their Christmas celebration that morning—a bribe so blatant that even Kyle was shocked. It was not even from CarlsMart, but some Italian designer with a thing for fringe and studs. Then the woman from Ricker's staff had appeared with the huge bouquet of white lilies, which Kyle had ordered for Jackie. It had gone over pretty well until Jackie realized the flowers were from him and not Ricker. At least she had done a better job of hiding her disappointment this year.

Heather Locklear breezed by and gave Katie a once-over. "Great look, girl," she said.

"You too," Katie replied as if they were old friends.

Nearly every guest, including Heather, was carrying the night's most slobbered-over party favor, the brand-new talking Mollie doll. The doll was slightly smaller than the real Mollie, but otherwise a perfect likeness. Especially through the prism of six or seven glasses of Champagne, the effect of hundreds of Mollies all talking at once was hallucinogenic. "It's Christmas Every Day!" "See you on CEDN!" "What will you give today?"

Kyle grabbed a glass of Champagne from a passing waiter's tray, threw it back, and hobbled after the guy for another. He then revisited the buffet.

As he hovered between the roast buffalo and the ostrich, and considered asking the server for a slice of each, The Wall of Men came bearing down on him. The Wall parted to reveal an even more horrific sight: a perfect family. Most of which had once been Kyle's.

Ricker, tall and placid, occupied the center. Just in front of him was Jackie, in a silver gown that could have doubled as a negligee, holding

Mollie. The guest of honor wore a sparkling white dress and a thin gold band around the top of her head. Kyle did a double take to be sure this was indeed Mollie and not one of her clones, since they all had on exactly the same costume. The dinged-up Carl doll in her hands confirmed authenticity, as did the beatific smile that appeared when she caught sight of Kyle. This wasn't a special smile for her father though; she did it for everybody she encountered. When she looked at Ricker the smile grew even lovelier.

Tessa held Ricker's left arm in a vice grip. She would not let go until the whole world had seen and acknowledged that she was with him. But this purple-velvet burden did not disrupt Ricker's pace in the slightest. Ricker guided Jackie past the well-wishers, his right hand lightly resting on the small of her back. The smile on Jackie's frosted pink lips looked like a kiss.

"Kyle," Ricker's hand, fresh from caressing Jackie, offered itself. "I don't believe we've been properly introduced. I'm Harry Ricker."

"I'm Kyle," said Kyle, feeling the clamminess of his palm against Ricker's dry one. "And this is Katie."

"We've met," said Katie. "Great party, Harry." She did not appear to mean this sarcastically.

"I'm sorry I couldn't greet you personally yesterday. No rest for the wicked this time of year," said Ricker.

"Don't I know it," Kyle said.

He should fight this guy, he thought. Strip off his jacket and challenge him to fight right there in front of the ice sculpture. Ricker was tall but not noticeably strong. He'd spent his whole life in offices and airplanes, not out on the streets running after hoodlums. Kyle was handicapped, but he still had his police training somewhere in his system.

Unfortunately Kyle felt an even stronger urge rise inside him—to be liked.

"We didn't mind at all, Harry," Tessa said. "The servants have been perfectly wonderful."

"So what line of work are you in, Kyle?" Ricker asked.

"Show business, actually," Kyle said, absorbing the fact that Jackie hadn't told Ricker even this basic information about him.

"What kind of show business?"

Kyle adjusted his fedora. "Uh, comedy. Impressions."

Jackie's eyes sparkled with alarm.

Famous faces clustered, waiting to greet Ricker and his entourage. Kyle picked them out like Easter eggs on a lawn. There was Louis Gossett, Jr., Deborah Winger, Linda Evans, and Sly Stallone. And interspersed among them shone the polished anonymous faces of the truly powerful.

Ricker smiled like a snake about to swallow a mouse. "Show us," he said.

"Well, I don't really—"

"Gather around, everybody," Ricker called out. "We've got a show for you."

A space cleared around Kyle. Eager faces glistened at him. Obviously Kyle could not do Rocky or Rambo in Stallone's presence, or Mr. T, either. Gossett might think it was racist.

"Lots of love!" a Mollie doll piped up.

"Come on, Kyle, don't be nervous," said Ricker. "Let's give him a hand to get him started."

The crowd applauded. At least they were not booing him like at the last open mic night he had been to. When was that, last summer? He was out of practice. He couldn't remember a single bit from his act.

Jackie was not even pretending to smile now. Glances darted around the room like sparks. The really bad news, Kyle suddenly remembered, was that he was drunk.

Finally, a desperate, but really appropriate idea came to him.

He cleared his throat, trying to bring up some phlegm. "I will make you," he said, "an offer you cannot refuse." He puffed his cheeks and gestured with his fingertips.

Ricker cocked his head. "Cagney?"

Christ, Kyle thought, it's the fedora. Cagney wore a fedora.

"I'm a superstitious man," Kyle continued. "If some unlucky accident should befall you, if you should get shot by a police officer . . ."

Jackie's mouth dropped open.

"If you were to get shot . . ." Kyle rubbed his fingertips together and eked out a strangled sigh.

Now the crowd looked genuinely scared. Jackie shook her head violently.

"Edward G. Robinson," said Ricker. "Sidney Greenstreet?"

"Bogart?" someone yelled from the back.

"Brando," Katie shouted. "It's Marlon Brando in *The Godfather*. Jesus."

"Ah," said Ricker.

"Ah," said a few others.

"It's the hat. It's confusing," Kyle said, pointing to it with the handle of his cane. For a second, his face was side by side with the carved grimace of the strange old man.

"Yes," said Ricker.

Jackie looked ready to faint. Tessa burst into hysterical laughter as the crowd drifted away.

"Just a minute," Ricker said. "I'd like to propose a toast." A waiter arrived with Champagne. Ricker took a glass and raised it.

"On this Christmas night, we gather to celebrate our many blessings. First of all, let us express our gratitude to America. Because it is only here, in this big-hearted, brave, and brilliant country, that human beings are allowed to reach their full potential. Our free markets spur us to innovate, continuously and fearlessly. In this country nothing holds us back. So we hold nothing back, either."

"Hear, hear," the crowd murmured.

Tears welled up in Kyle's eyes. Not because of what Ricker was saying, which Kyle had always sort of believed, although he wasn't so sure anymore. It was Jackie's expression as she watched Ricker. Once, she'd looked at Kyle that way.

"Christmas Every Day," Ricker went on, "has shown beyond a shadow of a doubt how fundamentally good the people of this country are. We are not *consumers*, a word which I have always found disgusting. We are Givers. Now, through this outpouring of our love for one another, America itself is flourishing. CarlsMart has already opened twenty new stores and added over two thousand new employees nationwide, many of them from deprived backgrounds. Our stock price has soared, and those profits are being reinvested to create even more opportunity for all. There can no longer be any doubt that doing well and doing good are one and the same.

"The goodness of the American people has touched me to the core. I truly wish that Christmastown One could accommodate more than five thousand families. But know this: we will soon break ground on Christmastown Two in northern Michigan. For those who do not make it this year, all is not lost. Indeed, all has just begun.

"For that glorious promise, as well as for everything that we've accomplished so far, we have not only America to thank. We have Mollie."

The crowd cheered. Many raised their Mollie dolls above their heads and pushed their buttons over and over: "Watch me on CEDN!" "Giving makes me happy!" "I love you!"

"Merry Christmas," the real Mollie said, on cue as always. Radio chatter spurted from The Wall of Men's earpieces. But the crowd did not surge, and The Wall stayed put, in a loose circle around Mollie and her retinue.

Kyle wiped his eyes with his shirt cuff. Fortunately not a soul was looking at him, not even Katie.

"Now, before I let you all get back to dinner, and before Sting comes out and plays some Christmas music for us, there's one more person I want to recognize." Ricker turned to Jackie and raised his glass. "Jackie, without you, none of this would have been possible. Your courage, your tireless work, your ideas, and your faith have been an inspiration to all of us in the CarlsMart family. But most especially to me. Thank you, Jackie, and Merry Christmas."

Jackie bowed her head and touched her glass to Ricker's. At the other end of the room, Sting's band started tuning up. Kyle couldn't hold back the tears any longer. He mewled like a baby.

"What is it, Dad?" Katie said, tugging his sleeve.

"Hold on," Kyle shouted. He gulped and steadied himself, for he had only one shot at this.

The crowd paused, turned.

"I also want to thank my wife," Kyle shouted. "That's right, Jackie's my wife. And she's a hell of a woman, don't you agree? She has to be to put up with me." Scattered applause. Someone squeezed Kyle's elbow. That was Katie, trying to stop him.

"You see, I'm the guy," Kyle said, "who did this." Leaning on his cane, he bent over and untied his shoe, took his sock off, and waved it to and fro. "I'm the cop who shot myself in the foot." He lifted it, forked and ugly and not completely clean. "Remember me? That's right. I'm the dumbest guy on the planet."

Katie squeezed harder. Kyle actually wanted to stop now, but he couldn't.

"I have no talent. I'll never make anything of myself. Jackie knows, even though she won't say it to my face. But she won't forsake me. No matter how much she wants to. I know she won't. Ever."

"Thanks, Kyle, that was terrific," Ricker said, gesturing over his head to Sting.

The band cranked up a sultry and very loud version of "I'll Be Home for Christmas." Katie stood frozen, one hand covering her mouth.

Kyle wiped his eyes with his sock and looked around for a waiter. Amid the blurred, laughing faces, one visage suddenly appeared in perfect relief. There was the familiar, gap-toothed grin, both wider and tighter than it appeared on television.

"Dave!" cried Kyle, lurching over to him. "Great to see you. You were going to call me, remember? Or your producer was. Anyway, the answer's yes. I would be thrilled to be on your show. I don't even have to do impressions. I'll do whatever you want. I'll wear a costume. Interview weirdos on the street. Whatever you need, I'm your man."

Letterman shrank from Kyle's hand, which still held his sock. The grin faded to a thin rectangle. "Sorry, man," said Letterman. "Your act is too gruesome for me. Try cable."

Jackie gave Mollie to Tessa, and The Wall of Men closed around them like a camera shutter. Shaking with rage, Jackie clamped her hand on Kyle's wrist.

"How could you? How could you?" she repeated, marching Kyle across the parking lot to the guesthouse. The words rose in clouds toward the stars. Jackie's shoulders were glazed by moonlight. She must have been freezing. Kyle's right foot sure was, since his sock and shoe were back at the party.

"I'm sorry," he said.

Jackie dropped his wrist and rubbed her arms. Her eyes seemed to fall on Kyle's jacket. He slipped out of it and handed it to her as he opened the door to the guesthouse.

"Never mind, Kyle," Jackie said. "I'm going right back."

"Are you sleeping with him?"

"How *dare* you. I am doing my job, Kyle. I'm a public figure now, like it or not. Maybe you could keep that in mind next time you get drunk in front of hundreds of influential people."

"I am sorry."

Jackie shivered as the warmth of the guesthouse and its anonymously tended fireplace reached out to her. "What you said back there was wrong," she said, folding her arms tightly. "I do forgive you. I will always forgive you."

That wasn't what Kyle said. He had said she would not forsake him. Jackie slammed the door of the guesthouse behind him.

Alone in the living room, the fire crackling, Kyle peered out the window into blackness. Somewhere, not far away, was the lake, deep and mysterious as a Mayan well. Somewhere, he'd heard there were bodies strewn across the lake floor, drowned for centuries but preserved by the frigid water. Eyes staring, hair shifting. The bravest divers would not venture a look.

CHAPTER EIGHT

Katie's job was to send in the Thank You Coupons from every gift Mollie received. She also had to generate a personalized note to every Giver, and had a cool new Macintosh for that purpose. But Mollie should be able to write her own fucking thank you letters by now, Katie thought. At one year old, the kid already spoke in full sentences. True, they were mostly lines from her commercials—but that was how most people talked anyway. At least Mollie made the words meaningful.

"Think of your family. Then think Roadcrusher tires," Mollie said, instead of "bye-bye," as Jackie hauled her out to the limo.

Saving her work on a floppy disk, Katie picked her way out to the living room. Through a chink in the stack of gifts behind the couch, she could see out the front window. Her dad stood in the driveway, in his uniform of T-shirt and cutoffs. The back of his neck reddened in the evening sun. Leaning on his cane, he bent to examine Enrique's latest airbrushed addition to the aquarium. The artist, a mask over his mouth and nose, paced behind him and gesticulated.

A group of neighbors had gathered to watch the work unfold. It was nice, Katie thought, that they had come to see her dad, or at least her dad's project. They weren't trying to catch a glimpse of Mollie or yanking leaves off the maple tree (not that there were any, anymore).

Katie had to admit, Enrique was a genius. He'd created a complete underwater world on the van. The more she looked, the more she saw: sea horses, angelfish, snails, an electric eel, coral, sand dollars half buried in the ocean floor. Kelp fronds swayed through beams of refracted light—how had he done that? The van was no longer a machine. It had turned into something organic.

Katie made a mental note to buy her dad a set of Roadcrushers. Her mother paid her ridiculously well for her work. She could afford the tires, plus they were on sale this week at CarlsMart. She'd get them even though her father was never going anywhere. The van was a coffin for his dream, and the endless painting was Kyle's way of pushing the dream underwater, over and over, until it finally drowned. To tell the truth, Katie was glad. Life was bizarre enough these days. She could not imagine it without her dad around, or what was left of her dad.

She returned to the computer in her bedroom to craft a response to this letter:

> April 22, 1987
>
> Dear Mollie,
>
> My husband and I have been trying for years to conceive a second child. Our son, now four, has been acting out in nursery school, time and again I have been called to take him home, that is the extent that he is disruptive. But once at home he throws things and besmirches the walls, and we know it is all because he is lonely. Yet no other infant has been forthcoming—until now. When we saw you in that commercial for the Solarus 5000 riding lawn mower (which my husband Gave to me last Tuesday, I love it!) we knew instantly <u>you are the child we were meant to have</u>. That is why I have been barren, our son disconsolate. You know it, too, it's why you said "Solarus 5000" directly to us, knowing we needed a bigger lawn mower for our soon-to-be larger lawn, which will naturally come with our larger house for our larger family. You will make our family complete! Please accept this Bonka Dump Truck, a token of our undying love, and come to us, long-lost daughter!!!
>
> Love and more love,
>
> Mrs. Virginia S. Wiggerman, + husband + son

Dear Weirdo (Katie typed),

Thanks for the truck. As a feminist I am glad you ignored stereotypes about girls when you chose a toy for me. I don't like it, but I am forced to send in a thank you coupon anyway. Don't spend it all in one place—no, actually, do.

About the problems with your son, did you know it's now legal to leave unwanted kids out on the curb to be picked up? It's called recycling. Think about it.

As for me, I'm afraid I can't join you in your love nest as I am about to be made president of the United States. But here is an autographed photo that you can shove under your son's nose every time he misbehaves, so you can remind him how inadequate he is.

Lots of Love and Keep on ~~Trucking Shopping~~ Giving,

Mollie

But Katie could not bring herself to send this letter. These people were so sad, they could have been on *The Weird Frontier*. A body blow from Mollie would have killed them.

Instead, she printed out the standard form letter:

Dear _____,

Thank you ever so much for the _____. I love it and will treasure it always. Your Thank You Coupon is in the mail. Please enjoy your additional discount at CarlsMart, and be sure to tell your friends and family about the benefits of joining CED.

Lots and Lots of Love,

Mollie

She signed the letter in crayon and then boxed up a talking Mollie doll for Mrs. Wiggerman. She had no idea if she'd made the requisite one hundred purchases, but Mrs. W. clearly needed the doll now.

"I love you," the doll said as Katie dumped packing peanuts all over its exquisite face.

Later, Katie rehearsed with The Patients in Stick's grandfather's garage. They were performing her new song, "Stupid Cake."

> *I'm not going to eat your stupid cake.*
> *I'm not going to eat your stupid cake.*
> *I'm not going to eat your stupid cake.*
> *I'm not going to eat your stupid cake.*
> *You can have some if you want to.*
> *Go ahead, you giant pig.*
> *Have some more; here let me help you.*
> *Let me shove it in your face.*
> *But I'm not going to eat your stupid cake.*
> *Stupid cake.*
> *Stupid cake.*
> *Stupid cake.*
> *Stupid cake.*
> *Stupid stupid stupid stupid.*
> *Why don't you go fuck yourself right now!*

With the unseen, seething neighbors as her only audience, she stalked her imaginary stage, waving her mic stand like a weapon. She wrapped her head in her arms and crouched as though under attack.

She gave Stick a playful karate kick to show that it was time for his guitar solo. She had decided to allow him one solo per set, though this flew in the face of everything she was trying to do with the band. The idea of *less* meant nothing to him, but the effort of containing him was simply too much. He shut his eyes as his Flying V moaned and sighed and wailed. Katie knew it was speaking to her, saying everything that Stick himself could not say.

That was usually what happened, anyway. Tonight the kick prompted nothing. Stick stumbled and then stopped playing altogether.

"What's your problem?" Katie asked him gently. She was learning to be more gentle with him, probably inspired by all those pathetic letters she had to read.

"You," Stick said, never taking his eyes off his guitar.

The bassist, Oliver, rubbed the fingerprints off his Star Trek communicator badge. Mitch slipped out from behind his drums to, as he put it, "make use of the facilities."

"How am I the problem?" Katie asked. She felt oddly tickled. Maybe Stick was standing up to her at last.

"You, like, look happy. You got a big old smile on your face, and you're bouncing around like a kangaroo."

"That's not what I was going for."

"Maybe you should face facts. You don't mean what you're saying in that song. You're rich now. You got a piece of that big old cake, and you like it. Just like you like that leather jacket."

At this point Oliver decided to "make use of the facilities" also.

"You're jealous," Katie said, surprised that she actually believed this.

"I care about the quality of the performance is all. You're the one who's always carrying on about us being real."

"So I should be unhappy then? Like you?"

"I'm not unhappy."

"Bullshit. You're a doormat. It drives me fucking crazy. Just tell the world to fuck off, for once, why don't you? Why don't you tell me to fuck off? I deserve it, don't I? Well, don't I?"

"Fine," Stick said to his guitar. "Fuck off."

"Not like that. Come on."

He raised his head. His green eyes narrowed. "Fuck," he said. "Off."

"That was pretty good," said Katie.

Stick extricated himself from his Flying V and left it and Katie stranded in the garage.

After several minutes, stunned and impressed, Katie went out to the driveway and got in her car, a brand-new black Charger. It was from her mother, a sixteenth-birthday present—although her dad had claimed at the last minute that he'd helped pick it out. To his credit, he had also tried to teach her to drive in the Reliant, during the rare times Enrique was unavailable for van painting. But his concentration had sucked. He kept staring out the passenger window like he was looking for treasure along the roadside, even when she drove over a curb onto someone's lawn. So she had learned to drive like the other kids, from the assistant football coach. He had slathered on the compliments and then passed her with flying colors, even though she was a menace to public safety. She had brought him to the house to meet Mollie.

This new life did have its advantages, Katie thought. She loved her jacket and her car and the piles of other things Jackie had given her, like black nail polish and a watch cap like a robber's. Who knew Jackie had such good taste? Amazingly, she was proud of her mother—not only for climbing the corporate ladder faster than anybody she'd ever heard of, but for understanding Katie, and life, far better than she'd ever let on. Still, if Katie was not careful, she'd end up like Jackie: a religious fanatic with capital as her one true god. Jackie said money—at least their money—was a sign of God's grace and nothing to be ashamed of. Katie was far from ashamed. Too far.

The Charger roared into the night.

At the far end of the bar, Katie thought she recognized Walt, Kyle's former sergeant, grown reedy and old. But if he recognized her, he did not want her to know it. He lighted a cigarette with the dying ember of the last one.

"Can I have one?" Katie asked, clambering onto a bar stool.

The man slid the pack over to her.

"And a light?"

The man dug a blue plastic lighter out of his jeans pocket and flicked it. Katie stuck the cigarette in her mouth and leaned in. Tonight she would become a smoker, she decided. This was the first step in getting her soul back. The smoke raked her throat.

She asked the man the world's stupidest question: "Is Hunter here?"

"Over there."

Deep in a corner, a shadow moved. A massive, mottled bicep flashed.

Katie remembered sneaking a look at him through the front window, years ago, on one of those strange midnight trips with her mother to The Link's parking lot. In the dim light he had looked green and scaly, like an alligator. Even back then, the thrill of that vision had worried her.

He stopped wiping down the table. As he lifted his head a handlebar mustache came into view. A thin black ponytail hung to the middle of his back.

This was the kind of man Jackie would never understand, Katie thought. He was the opposite of Harry Ricker—the Man himself—who Jackie was head over heels in love with. Whereas Hunter could even be some kind of Indian.

Hunter nodded to her.

"I'm Katie," Katie said.

"Kyle's daughter." He knew.

"You know he quit drinking, right? That's why he doesn't come here anymore," Katie said quickly. She didn't mention that he'd started up again.

Apparently that explanation amused Hunter, or pleased him, because he smiled. His teeth were heavy and ragged, like he'd been chewing on metal objects.

"Ow," Katie said. Her cigarette had just burned down to her fingers. She dropped it and stamped it out with her motorcycle boot.

Hunter pulled out a chair for her and sat down at the table facing her. He removed a lighter from his pocket and lighted the candle on the table. Inside the dirty red glass, the flame jumped and lunged. Words on Hunter's forearms came into focus: RIVERMAN, BARKER, JD. Some letters looked thick and blurry, like they'd been gone over several times.

Katie wrapped her jacket tighter. She had a small notebook in the pocket, which she used for writing down lyrics when they came to her suddenly. She'd take it out once she got him talking, she decided, casual-like.

"Why are you here?" Hunter said.

He was direct. That was good. Much different from certain other people in Katie's life.

"Did my dad tell you I'm a musician?"

"He said you liked punk."

Katie wondered what else her dad had told Hunter over the years. He probably knew a lot about her, but all warped through her dad's perception. He thought she was still a little girl.

"I'm in a band, and we're writing some new songs," she explained.

It was hard to tell if Hunter had heard what she just said. He seemed far more interested in simply looking at Katie. But he didn't stare at her moronically, like Stick. He took her in. Collected her. She sensed the tingle of an approaching lightning storm.

"So, anyway," she said, "you've had some interesting experiences." She reached for the notebook, thinking she'd just lay it on the table to get him used to it. "We want to sing about real stuff. The world is so fake, you know?"

"I'm not material, hon."

"Oh, no. I didn't mean . . ."

On Hunter's left hand, in the V between the thumb and forefinger, he had tattooed "ML." A lover, Katie thought. He dug at the spot with his thumbnail. Katie reached across the table and touched his wrist.

"But I thought," she said, "I mean, you have all those tattoos. Why have them if you don't want to be asked about them?"

Hunter's eyes were gray. Katie had never heard of a person with gray eyes. Only wolves.

He took a pack of cigarettes out of his pocket and offered one to Katie. She took it and lighted it in the candle flame.

"You just killed a sailor," Hunter said.

"I'm sorry," Katie said.

"You're very pretty," Hunter said.

Hunter took her hand as she tried to bring it to her mouth to smoke. The cigarette fell on the table. He held her hand in his, palm up, like an embryo.

"You are welcome here," he said. "But I have no stories for you."

She did not sleep. Her bedroom spun as if she were drunk. She threw herself from one side of the bed to the other, trying to catch up with her rushing thoughts—or escape them.

She staggered like a zombie though school the next morning. She did not respond to greetings; she forgot to hand out the beaded CED bracelets she had promised all the girls. The kids at their desks all looked soulless, like workers in a movie about the future.

In the evening she could not process the thank-you notes. The words on her computer screen morphed into tattoos. Life felt like a dream she had a week ago.

At ten p.m. her dad, as usual, lay on the couch watching TV. Topper Moss sat on a rock holding a large empty net. It wasn't clear whether he was lying in wait or if what he was waiting for had just eluded him. Topper and Kyle both looked miserable.

"I'm going to Stick's," Katie said to her dad.

He nodded, or maybe he didn't.

Hunter's hand made its way across the table. Katie put her cigarette in the ashtray. She placed her hand on top of his. Her thumb lightly stroked "ML." She didn't dare look in his eyes.

"That feels good," Hunter said.

"You don't hurt yourself, do you?" said Katie, slowly tracing the M and the L. "With the tattoos?"

At the bar, one of the regulars, Francine, came up behind a man named Chuck and slid her hands up under his shirt. Chuck spilled his beer. Francine let out a guffaw.

"Fuck, Francine," said Chuck, mopping the beer off his pants.

"Your place or mine?" Francine said, running a finger around his collar. She had to be over forty, Katie thought, with long graying hair and flapping upper arms like slabs of uncooked chicken. Everything about her was loose, including her grin. The other six people at the bar, all men, laughed at her.

Jackie would have called Francine a slut. It was a word she used to utter fairly often, like when they went to the mall and saw a girl with big boobs bouncing along in a tube top. Jackie would whisper it so Katie alone would hear—the word hissed like a spatula on a pan. At such moments Katie felt Jackie setting a trap for her, trying to make her an ally in her war against the rest of the world. Katie had always made a point of never agreeing outright; although, in the case of Francine, she could see what her mom meant. She reminded herself never to become that desperate.

"My father's dying," Katie said to Hunter.

"Is he sick?" Katie liked the sound of alarm in his voice—usually so low and calm.

"Not physically," Katie said. Hunter nodded, his face relaxing, as Katie savored her power to offer him this small relief. Then she reeled him back in. "I mean, my dad's dying inside."

ML—who was ML? The letters were small enough that Katie's thumb could hide and reveal them again in one stroke.

"At least he's not working for the Man anymore," Katie went on. "He never liked being a cop. He did it for my mom. But she didn't even care."

Francine tried to climb onto Chuck's lap, wet spot and all. The regulars all kept laughing, egging her on. Chuck pushed her off, but weakly. It was clear she was going to get her way—if not tonight, then soon enough.

Katie jerked her head toward the scene. "Francine ever do that to my dad?" she asked Hunter.

He shook his head and pulled his hand away. Katie's chest tightened. She shouldn't have said that. She definitely should not have hoped, if only for a second, that it was true.

Shame—that was what Hunter made her feel sometimes. But that was what she wanted to feel.

Kyle examined his stubble in the bathroom mirror. The permanent five o'clock shadow was in style now, he thought. Made you look tough, like Don Johnson, who was so tough he could wear a pink jacket. But Kyle was not the type to pull it off. His beard had a peachy cast and made his features even more indistinct.

Stubble or no stubble, he was fading. Nobody saw him anymore; his wife, Katie, Mollie—they all looked right through him. *Have you seen my purse? Oh, there it is, right behind you.* At this rate he'd disappear completely in a few months. He couldn't remember from the movies whether invisible men could walk through walls. That could be fun for a time. But if walls were permeable, why didn't the men fall through the floor? Maybe they did after a while. At the center of the earth writhed a huge knot of invisible men who'd fallen. They grasped and groaned and stepped on each other's faces, trying to climb back up. But if they slid through the floor, why not right out the other side of the planet? That made the most sense. At this moment, the millions drifted through outer space, floaters in God's eye.

Kyle soaped his face and dragged the plastic razor down his cheek. He had to stop feeling sorry for himself. He was a man of leisure, as Jackie said. He had the type of life his father, for instance, would have given his right arm for. No more standing at a table like a robot, throwing cards at people you would rather see drop dead than win a dime. Kick back, watch an old war movie, have a margarita. Buy a boat.

In Christmastown, Jackie had promised, Kyle would have a soundproof room all to himself. He could practice impressions to his heart's content; no one would ever hear him.

Kyle finished shaving his face. Not too bad, he thought. He still had something like a jawline. He soaped the neglected thatch of hair on top of his head. The razor mowed it off. The scraping sounded like static electricity.

Fully shaved, his head looked intentional. He no longer let hair grow on it randomly, a result of inattention as much as anything. He had policed his hair. He thought about waking Katie up to show her, but decided against it. By his calculations, she had only gone to bed three hours ago.

Enrique's airbrush hissed in the driveway. Eight a.m. The kid was right on time as usual. He'd work all day, through the barking July heat, just to push his vision one step closer to reality. What a great kid. Kyle couldn't stand the thought of leaving him in a few months, but he had no choice. Enrique's parents weren't Givers. Kyle hurried outside to show him his 'do.

"Looks awesome, Mr. M," said Enrique through his mask. "It's really you." The air smelled of paint, which had become Kyle's favorite smell.

"I'm really gonna miss you, E," said Kyle. "When we go to Christmastown, I mean."

"Me too."

"Are you sure your family doesn't want to come? I bet they could get on a waiting list or something. I'll look into it if you want. I know the management," he added with a wink.

Enrique picked at a hangnail on his pinky. "My parents don't want to live there," he said.

"Are they worried about jobs?" Kyle said. "There will be lots of jobs in Christmastown. Especially . . ." He was going to say "for unskilled workers" but stopped himself.

"It's not that," Enrique said. "They said . . . I'm trying to figure out how to put it in English." Kyle couldn't read Enrique's expression through the mask.

"What did they say, E?"

"They said CED is a lie."

"Everything is a lie," Kyle said. "When you get older, you decide to believe some of the lies anyway."

"Which lies do you believe?"

Kyle thought. "The ones about family," he said.

CHAPTER NINE

J ackie answered the front doorbell and almost passed out. There, seeing her soon-to-be-ex-house for the first time, stood Harry Ricker. She watched him conquer his initial expression of shock, deciding not to mention that the mountains of junk in the living room were partly his fault. Jackie had been given to understand that her family would move into Christmastown early. Or at least their stuff would. But Harry had said that the storage facility was still not completed, nor, more importantly, was the dome. Without the dome, life in Christmastown, he had assured her, would be hell.

Harry wore a loose-fitting white shirt with the sleeves rolled up, revealing lightly tanned forearms. A gorgeous smog-enhanced sunset spread out behind him.

Jackie had just returned from a two-week swing through the Midwest with Mollie. Her suitcase lay open on her bed, and she was still wearing her travel clothes—designer jeans, a little sweaty from sitting for hours on the corporate jet, and a sleeveless top. As luck would have it, she'd just tossed aside the matching blazer, and now she saw, through a discreet rolling of her eyes, a dark half-moon of sweat below each armpit.

Harry said, "I want to take you to Christmastown."

"Harry, no," said Jackie, giggling unexpectedly. "I'm not in any shape to go now. Besides, it's off limits, isn't it?"

Since ground had been broken, access to Christmastown had been strictly controlled. A private security force patrolled the perimeter day and night. Press and cameras of any kind were strictly prohibited. Construction workers were frisked upon entering and leaving each day. To prevent industrial espionage pending the erection of the dome, the airspace overhead had been designated a no-fly zone.

"Not to us, it isn't. Come on. It's a beautiful night."

A silver BMW convertible was parked in front of the house. The driver's seat was empty.

"Just you and me?" Jackie asked. "No chauffeur?"

"Get Kyle to watch Mollie for a few hours. He'll do that, won't he?"

In the driveway, Enrique gathered up his equipment for the night. Kyle, in a paint-splotched T-shirt and cutoffs, squatted beside him, studying a sketch. His newly shaved head—Jackie would never know what had possessed him to do that—reflected the evening.

"Absolutely. No problem at all. Kyle!"

Harry drove with confident ease, the way he did everything. He steered lightly with his left hand, his elbow resting on the windowsill. His right hand, only inches from Jackie's knee, cupped the floor shifter. He drove fast, overtaking lesser vehicles like semitrucks and Toyotas as his sculpted hair mocked the wind's attempts to ravage it. He pushed the car into overdrive, and they crested the mountain pass.

What did they talk about on the way to Christmastown? First, Jackie's trip. The shortage of membership applications at the Springfield, Illinois, event. The throngs bearing gifts, the hunger to see Mollie and to touch her. Jackie feared the throngs less now, thanks to The Wall of Men. But The Wall itself was a shame.

"I wish we didn't need them in the first place," Jackie said. "The Wall, I mean."

"The Givers mean no harm. You should trust them."

"Easy for you to say. You haven't come to any of these events."

This was a sore point with Jackie. Not just because Harry didn't believe her about the Givers. But she could not mention the other reason: all the nights, lying in her vast hotel bed, yearning to hear a discreet but determined knocking at her door. Is that . . . ? Yes. There it is. She opens the door to find Harry looking left and right down the hallway. He says, "I couldn't stay away." Jackie whispers, "We shouldn't," as he slips inside.

"The Givers are not happy, Harry. I thought Giving was supposed to make people happy."

"Jackie, it's time you understood something. Happiness isn't sitting on your ass all day and smiling. It means striving. The Givers have a goal, a purpose in life, so powerful it all but devours them. Believe me, that's what every human being wants more than anything."

"But they're afraid. They think they're going to be left out of Christmastown."

"Fear is part of growth."

Jackie had an idea. "The Givers feel connected to their purpose but not to each other. There are too many of them to be a community. What if they met in smaller groups, like once a week? They could go to each other's houses and review their statements. Have cookies. Figure out what they have to do to get into the top Giving Percentile, or maintain their position if they are already there. That way, they'd be supporting each other, not just trying to beat each other out. We could call them Giving Groups."

"Interesting. Make CED even more central to people's lives."

Jackie blue-skyed. They would mail out a Giving Group Kit to all registered Givers. It would include tips on finding other Givers in the area (obviously the local CarlsMart would be the best bet), suggestions for festive foodstuffs (available at CarlsMart) that they could serve at meetings, and ways to buck up any Givers who mused about quitting. "Don't give up on Giving!"—that sort of thing.

"I don't know where you get your instincts," Harry said, "but if you ask me, you're worth a whole roomful of MBAs."

Jackie liked that word, "instincts." It made her ears lie back.

"I want Giving to be fun for people, Harry."

"It should be fun. It's all a game in the end."

Good Lord, Jackie thought, was that true?

Had the mob in Van Nuys been a fluke; had she magnified its monstrousness through the prism of her own still-unconquered fear? Perhaps Givers did not want to devour Mollie to quell some deep spiritual hunger. Perhaps, like the rest of America, they just wanted to bask in the glow of fame. To them, Mollie was merely another celebrity.

Well, what if she was? What if Mollie was nothing special at all?

Jackie had the sensation of something flying off her into the wind, like a scarf. But she wasn't wearing a scarf. Something she hadn't realized was bothering her suddenly, briefly, wasn't.

But she couldn't bring herself to wonder what she might have lost or gained, not with her heart and lungs and stomach all screaming for joy as the BMW plunged down the pass into the night. Ricker's hand brushed her knee as he downshifted. Jackie kicked off her sandals and pulled the lever beside her seat. She dropped onto her back and saw the stars.

"There it is, Jackie. Look."

She sat up, reluctantly bringing her seat back up with her. Rocks and scrub flashed by, overexposed in the BMW's headlights. In the distance, mountains bled like ink into the sky. Then Jackie saw it: a fissure of light.

"The construction crews are working mostly at night now," Harry said. "It's too hot during the day." He turned onto a dirt road toward the fissure.

At the gate a guard met them. Harry showed his ID, which the guard scrutinized briefly. He asked for Jackie's driver's license. The guard looked at the license, at Jackie, at the license again.

"Your hair," he said. "It's different."

"It's an old picture," Jackie said. In fact, it was an old life. She laughed, recalling that awful DMV photo—staring eyes, lips pressed as thin as a paper cut, hair like molasses poured over her head. How odd that this portrait of unhappiness remained her official identification.

The guard waved them through. Jackie noticed several other guards watching them pass. All were dressed in short-sleeved khaki uniforms and armed with pistols. One cradled a high-powered rifle.

"It won't always be like this," Harry said. "Once the dome is up, the security won't need to be so . . . palpable."

They headed downtown. Jackie's first impression was that everything in the town was white. But that was an illusion, caused by the huge spotlights blasting every surface—for security purposes, and so the construction crews could see what they were doing. Workers toiled on roofs, behind the wheels of growling vehicles, framed in the crossbeams of unfinished buildings. The noise was tremendous. The car, shaking along with the jackhammer, edged around a road crew. They passed a smooth pale-blue building with a peculiar spire shaped like a rocket ship. Ribbons of red neon wrapped it. At first Jackie thought it was a church, but neon letters on the spire spelled CINEMA.

"The architecture of Christmastown is what you might call retrofuturist," Harry shouted over the hammering. "It looks both forward and backward. That spire captures the kind of innocent hope the country felt at the dawn of the space age. Space travel meant we could live on other planets. We didn't have to depend on this one. The human race could exist forever. We had no limits. Maybe we didn't even have to die."

When they reached a quieter part of the street, they parked and strolled along the wide brick sidewalk, inscribed at regular intervals with circles of dirt. Harry explained that that was where the trees would be planted. They were bringing in full-grown magnolias—no sad, spindly saplings with rubber rings holding them up.

Jackie smiled, picturing the street full of families, kids eating ice cream, mothers pausing to look in store windows. Everything would be just like the model in Harry's office. Christmastown would come true.

Harry touched Jackie's forearm. "There's City Hall," he said, pointing to the green pyramid, huge and otherworldly in the floodlights.

For the first time, Jackie wondered who exactly would be in charge of Christmastown. Harry? But there would have to be elections, for Harry was anything but a communist. Then again, elections were so unpleasant, campaigns so vicious. In the past, though she did have her preferences, Jackie had never even voted. She didn't want to dip her hand into a nest of vipers. But in Christmastown, she had to believe, things would be different. The people here would all share the same values. They would cast ballots joyfully, all for the same candidates, not because they had been brainwashed, but because Christmastown would take the discord out of freedom once and for all.

"The living Christmas tree will be planted in front of City Hall," Harry said, pointing at the extra-large ring of dirt. "It will be decorated all year round, but only lit up at Christmastime."

Lit up by Mollie, Jackie thought. That was Mollie's job.

She had begun to notice an odd lack of specifically Mollie-related décor in Christmastown. Shouldn't there at least have been a statue in the town square? True, Mollie was growing, and a statue would freeze her in time as an infant. This way, Christmastown could accommodate her growth. Still, what would happen when she turned eight, twelve, twenty, thirty? Wouldn't Mollie have to go to school, have friends, a husband, kids? Perhaps she'd become an American Princess Diana, a fairy-like beauty who traveled the world, bestowing beneficence. If she wanted to, of course. Surely Harry had given some thought to this.

"Harry? What, exactly, is Mollie's future going to be?"

"We can't know the future," said the man whose son had burned up in a race car. "That's why we have to seize the moment." He made a fist and smacked his palm with it. "We must do it today. Do it now. Hold nothing back, not for a single second."

The lines in Harry's face darkened. His eyes softened. Despite his exemplary vigor, he was not a young man, Jackie knew. He was at least ten years older than she was, and his life had been both fuller and harder than most people's. Christmastown was to be Harry's legacy, his pyramid.

"Come on," Harry said. "Let's go see the Green Space."

They drove for half a mile toward what appeared to be a luminous cloud. Harry parked the car. Jackie followed him, tottering in her heels over the rough ground, to the lip of an enormous pit. Jackie swayed, and Harry clutched her arm.

Deep down—dizzyingly far down—pipes tangled incomprehensibly, like the viscera of the very earth. Some looked wide enough to accommodate a car. Smaller ones branched off, festooned with crank wheels and gauges. Tiny men crawled through the maze, attacking at apparent random with drills and blowtorches. A smell rose up, made of earth, metal, and smoke.

"The irrigation requirements for a tropical forest in the desert, not to mention the meadow and the golf course, and the everyday needs of the community itself, will be extraordinary," Harry yelled over the noise. "That's why we'll be diverting a significant amount of water from the Los Angeles Aqueduct, as well as several previously protected lakes and rivers. This is an engineering feat on the scale of the Hoover Dam. Fortunately, regulations have recently become more favorable to business interests. Let's just say I have friends at the Department of the Interior."

Jackie stared into the pit. "That's a long way down."

"That's not the half of it. The facilities for storing gifts will be underneath all of this. So they can be expanded if and when necessary—

all the way to the center of the earth." Harry winked, though it was not entirely clear if he was joking.

"I never realized," Jackie said. "This is such an undertaking."

Harry laid his arm across her shoulders. "Anyone can have ideas," he said. "But only a few ever change reality. You and I are among those very few, Jackie."

"I want this," Jackie said. "I really, really want this."

"I know. Now let's go see your house."

Jackie's heels echoed on the hardwood floor. She removed her shoes and left them in the vestibule beside Harry's.

The house was silent, construction in the residential areas having ended weeks earlier. The security spotlights outside turned the walls pale blue. Jackie ran her fingers along the wallpaper, a tasteful pattern of intertwined roses and lilies of the valley.

Everything looked exactly like the drawings Harry had shown her: The gorgeous kitchen, in which a personal chef who knew how to make hollandaise sauce from scratch would bustle about. The living room, whose sunken floor hinted at mild decadence. The spa-style bathrooms filled with exotic plants. The dining room, a chandelier with lights shaped like tulips. Bedrooms with dormers and window seats, where a person could curl up and read good books, if a person felt inclined to do such things. Jackie had been meaning to get to *88 Reasons Why the Rapture Will Be in 1988*.

More bedrooms. Jackie tried to keep track of them in her mind. That one could be Mollie's; that one Katie's; that smaller one could be Tessa's (if she came); and the bigger one Kyle's. He would need a room of his own, of course. For his work.

"The master bedroom," Harry said, turning the crystal doorknob at the end of the long hallway. "I'll warn you," he said mischievously. "I took a liberty here."

He opened the door onto a vast field of white. What appeared to be snow, two or three inches deep, twinkled in the bluish light. Had Harry created an interior winter wonderland for Christmastown's first family? No, he had better taste than that. That magical whiteness was, in fact, the same carpeting Harry had in his office. The thistledown.

Jackie shrieked and ran into the room, pirouetting like a child. The thistledown tickled the soles of her bare feet.

"I thought you might like it," he said. "I had the builders put it in. It's Miribilium, you know, spun very fine."

"I don't like it," Jackie said. "I love it."

Harry joined her in the center of the room. Taking her hands in his, he leaned into her. She backed away. Then she paused. Carefully, she placed his hands on her hips and slid her hands up his chest and onto his shoulders.

"Do you want this?" he said, his lips brushing her neck. He smelled like the desert, of sage.

Jackie pulled him down into the carpet.

The Majeskys' bungalow hunched in the predawn as Jackie stepped out of Harry's car. Kyle's van shimmered weakly in the driveway. Seeing no one around, Jackie dove back into the car for a final kiss, which Harry provided in abundance.

She slammed the door and regretted not having closed it quietly. She looked around again. Only then did she notice the square of blue light poking through the picture window of the bungalow—someone seemed to have made a gap in the gift tower. Harry gunned the engine and roared off.

Jackie decided to go through the front door, head held high, damn the consequences. She paused on the stoop to slip her shoes on. Now she knew how her older sister, Pam, must have felt years ago, climbing through her bedroom window to find Tessa and Jackie waiting for her in their bathrobes. Jackie's body hurt all over, each ache a memory. Her lips were raw. She undid her ponytail and shook her hair out, as if that could hide the bruises on her neck.

Trembling, she slid her key into the deadbolt. It was unlocked already.

Kyle lay on the sofa, watching *The Weird Frontier*. The show was terrible. Jackie couldn't fathom why no one had put a stop to it by now. Look at that poor lunatic in his pith helmet, holding up a hunk of fur in a plastic bag like he'd found a piece of the True Cross. But Kyle was addicted. He apparently enjoyed watching a fellow human being unravel.

Kyle lifted his head as Jackie closed the door behind her. She'd never noticed before: with that rounded nose and slightly protruding lower lip, Kyle was a dead ringer for his father.

"Can I get you something?" she asked Kyle. "Some coffee?" She didn't know how to make coffee. Coffee was Kyle and Katie's thing.

What had happened had nothing to do with Kyle. He did not cause it, nor could he have prevented it. The events with Harry could only be explained as God's will. Sometimes grace came in forms that looked, from the outside, like sin.

From the TV came the sound of panting and crunching footfalls. Topper Moss was running through a forest at night, carrying his film camera. Trees lunged precariously at the screen.

"Nearly . . . have him . . . ," the poor, insane man huffed.

"No thanks," Kyle said.

Jackie couldn't remember what she'd just asked him as waves of memories from last night washed over her. That cool, soft Miribilium on her naked back, and Harry's warm tongue. But if she could have given her happiness to Kyle, she would have. Even if that meant she herself could never feel it again.

Kyle sniffed and rubbed his nose. Oh, yes, he knew. That was obvious. He had suspected it months before it had even happened. Telling him now would only rub salt into the wound.

Besides, it was not like Kyle would be cast out. They were still family. He would still live in Christmastown and play a significant part in his daughters' lives. Jackie could arrange to have a substantial cottage built on the grounds of her mansion, or else she would locate a house for him within walking distance. She made a mental note to look into doing one of those two things.

Also, there was the publicity to consider. Jackie's divorce and remarriage to her boss would seriously taint CED's family-friendly image—especially if it all happened too quickly. The process had to be managed in just the right way. Jackie made a mental note to schedule a meeting with the PR boys.

PART FOUR: THE ROBOT

CHAPTER TEN

Burt flipped a card, a bush-league mistake he had not made in over two decades. Humiliation rose in his throat, but he crushed it with his molars.

"Misdeal," he said and collected the cards. The players knew better than to say a word, though one of them, the big one, smirked.

Burt was the smoothest dealer on the floor. Everyone knew it. For as long as he could remember they'd called him The Robot because of his precision. Also for his demeanor. He was formal in his work. He didn't get all friendly with the players like other dealers, as he didn't see the point. It wouldn't change the way the cards fell.

But though they remained silent, the three people at his table—as well as the guys behind the Eye in the Sky—now had evidence against him. Word would get around. The younger dealers would mock him for a mistake that they themselves made constantly without the slightest compunction.

"What's the matter, Burt? Got the yips?" they would say.

"There was gunk on the table," was his planned reply. "You may have noticed the hygiene of our clientele has deteriorated over the years. We are no longer attracting the caliber of people as we did. In my opinion the Tahitian is going down the toilet."

In fact, the misdeal wasn't his fault, but he couldn't risk explaining the real reason, because the pit boss was looking to elbow him out. He wanted to bring in another one of his young cousins, and Burt's relatively ancient ass was in that cousin's way. If the other dealers found out, they would say Burt had gone senile or that all the booze had finally caught up to him, though it was his wife who drank like a fish, not him. Or they would remember all those times that Burt (like an idiot) had talked about failing the eye test, the only thing that had kept him from combat in World War II. His eyes, they would say, were giving out for good. A half-blind dealer presented an obvious liability.

But the truth was, just for a second, Burt was certain that he had seen his son. As if almost twenty years had not passed, and the kid still worked there at the Tahitian, if you could call what he did "work"—standing there with his tub of dirty dishes, staring across the casino floor at his father. Burt had gotten him a busboy job at Smuggler's Cove, the Tahitian's fanciest restaurant. He had pulled some pretty big strings, which he really had not been in a position to pull. He had thought Kyle would finally stop dreaming and get his life moving, once he had a path laid right in front of him. Over time, Burt dreamed, Kyle would move up to waiter, then maître d'. He'd wear a suit, usher the high rollers to the VIP table. Who knew? Kyle could even run the hotel one day. He wasn't really so stupid.

But, given a foot in the door, what had the kid done? Stood there day after day like an ape in a tricorn hat, gaping at Burt. Like he couldn't believe this was his father—a heterosexual man in a purple shirt, with a parrot embroidered on the pocket under his name tag. The name tag that assured people they need never call him mister or sir as long as he lived—just Burt will do fine, thank *you*, sir. During the big war, when he'd worked as a file clerk in the basement of the air-force training center, he'd also worn a name tag and called everybody sir. There, they had called him "The Troll."

At least Kyle had not been one of those hippie college kids, protesting instead of going to the classes their fathers had worked their butts off to pay for. But in his own way, Kyle had thrown (and still threw) his privilege in his dad's face. It never occurred to him that others had to fight for things, or that others' lives had not turned out they way they'd hoped. Instead, Kyle dreamed. To this day, he dreamed.

A boy lay on the pavement with his face turned away. His left arm lay under him. The feet were oddly positioned, like blocks of wood. That was how you knew the kid was dead, from the feet. Also a girl, a hippie, knelt beside the boy, waving her arms to the heavens. Making a show out of it. She was a runaway who didn't even know him. That was what *Life* magazine had said anyway, in the article that went with the picture. Almost twenty years ago now—Jesus, Mary, and Joseph, how time flew.

The arm tucked under, and the feet—so strange. So uncomfortable to lie that way on a street. Burt had heard that the boy did not bathe as a matter of hippie principle. His body had stunk up the ambulance, so they had to open the doors when they drove him to the morgue. But how could they drive with the doors flapping open like that? Some exaggeration had occurred in that story, no question. Burt could never forget the way the other people in the photo just moseyed along in the background. Strolling, chatting. No urgency. Typical day on campus, a guy lying there with his arm tucked under, and a girl, who didn't know him, screaming.

For months he stared at the photo, day after day, in the break room. His obsession embarrassed him, so he hid the magazine inside *Road & Track*. He sweated and ached as he stared, as if at pornography, and after he returned to the floor he thought of the picture and how many minutes it would be until he could see it again. A part of him gloated about the boy's death, while another tried to figure out how to breathe life back into him through a magazine page.

As the image smoldered at the edges of his mind, month after month, Burt tightened the clamps of his self-control. He spoke only in single words or mere gestures if he could get away with them. He joined his wife in a glass or two of whiskey before dinner, shielding himself from conversation with his trusty copy of *The Rise and Fall of the Third Reich*. He learned to tune out the TV, the newspaper, Marian's laments on affairs both foreign and domestic. Nothing provoked him. No one, least of all Kyle, knew what his mind contained. His mind was a fire.

In the autumn, through an exercise of will that would have astonished his juniors but was no big deal for men of his generation, Burt had personally carried the magazine out of the break room and lobbed it into one of the massive dumpsters by the loading dock. The magazine fluttered down like a shot bird. After that, the fire in Burt's mind dwindled. He covered the mental image of the dead boy with the stars and stripes, waving in front of a blue sky. Once in a while, he still shook his head and muttered "dumb kid." But if anyone witnessed that, they had to figure he was just thinking about Kyle.

And then, one night, Kyle had appeared at his table, hunching his shoulders, waving peace signs—no, V signs. "Hello, gamblers, it's me, Tricky Dick Nixon, in the flesh! Back for you to kick around once again."

All his life Burt had been a tin can—sealed, compact, under pressure. Kyle's mockery of Nixon, his heedless joy in mocking the president whom Burt admired and understood so deeply he sometimes felt they shared the same soul, punctured the seal. Burt had exploded at his son in front of everybody. That had been a mistake; he could have controlled himself. Still, everyone knew what happened to tin cans in the end. They were thrown in the garbage. Meanwhile, those who mocked their country and its leaders were beloved and remembered and wailed over by girls.

He redealt, zinging the cards out of the shoe. One, two, three. His wrist was a precision-tuned delivery system, applying just enough force so the card glided to a halt one inch above the player's betting circle. Pushing seventy, Burt remained capable of the finest degree of motor control. Let the Eye in the Sky record that.

The dark spot had moved to the other side of the casino, by the bar, where Kyle would have taken his break. Of course neither Kyle nor the spot was really there at all. The spot existed solely in the corner of Burt's left eye. He stuck a finger under his glasses and rubbed at it. The spot stayed, clearly not his son, for his son had not stayed. The same night Burt had lost his control, Kyle had fallen ass over teakettle for that crazy woman, Jackie, who promptly hauled him off to a hick town and destroyed him.

Jackie wore Kyle down as dripping water wore down granite. She was cold. She was critical. She made no effort to make a home for Kyle, who was, after all, doing an important job as a cop. Even Marian kept a cleaner house. She covered the good chairs in plastic and vacuumed several times a day, not to mention she cooked Burt dinner every night, all while soused out of her gourd. Whereas on Jackie's watch, dust bunnies escaped from under the couch and roamed freely. Later, after she became a religious nut, she'd had the nerve to tell Kyle he was headed for hell. In Burt's opinion, he was already there. He was a whipped man. No wonder he had shot himself.

And yet the old Jackie was a cream puff compared to the one that had recently appeared on the cover of *Forbes* magazine. (The break room now offered Forbes, as all the young dealers thought they were going to be rich someday.) *Mollie's Mom Is Harry Ricker's Right Arm*, said the headline. Bossy, blonde, and absent for weeks on end—Jackie was a wife in name only. Why Kyle couldn't or wouldn't see that, Burt would never understand.

"How about hitting me, there, Burt? You blind or something?"

"I'm sorry, sir. I will hit you."

"Jesus. You're like in outer space."

What the hell was this black spot? Was he going to have to go to the doctor? The doctor would find cancer, and then Burt would collapse like an old barn. Undiscovered cancers never hurt anybody, but once they were seen and given a name, watch out! The doctor would gouge his eye out and put it in a little jar.

"Hey, asshole, you gave me two cards. I asked for one. That's it. I'm getting the manager."

The man snapped his fingers as if for a waiter. He was maybe thirty-five, dressed in a shiny shirt with cuff links. He had one of those punk haircuts, spiked in front and shaved close to his ears, but down to his shoulders in the back. The guy was also sizable. Burt possessed a keen awareness of his own height, five feet seven inches, formerly five-eight, but the years behind the table had taken that inch from him. Still, time had given him one compensation: his boundless reserve of rage.

"Here comes the boss," said Mr. Shiny Shirt. "Now your ass is grass, old man."

With the acuity of an international assassin, Burt focused his rage to a laser beam and hit Shiny in the sprig of hair right between his eyebrows. "Get out."

Shiny's grin fell into a stunned frown. "Well, I . . . hold on a sec. Just let me talk to—"

"Get out."

Shiny raised his palms, glistening with sweat. He backed away, stumbled, and disappeared into the bright confusion. Approaching from the right, the pit boss felt the edge of the laser beam singeing his skin. He turned and left without a word.

The game, as it had for over thirty years, went on.

CHAPTER ELEVEN

Katie waited for Hunter at their table. Tonight she wore her Black Flag tank top to show Hunter her unmarked shoulders, neck, and arms. If he suggested giving her a tattoo, she wasn't going to say no. What did she want? A rose with thorns, or a scorpion. But Hunter didn't do pictures. She liked his name. Maybe he could write it, HUNTER, on her lower back.

He brought a bottle of Jack Daniel's and two glasses. She threw down a shot and let it burn her throat. Hunter filled her up again. She lighted a cigarette.

Over by the bar, Francine selected a song from the jukebox, "The Gambler." Hips swaying, she made her unhurried way to the bar. She slipped her arm around Walt, Katie's dad's former sergeant. Good for Francine: she never gave up. Katie raised her glass to her, and she winked back.

Katie had been coming to The Link almost every night for two months. The regulars had long since accepted her. She'd slid easily into the rotation that brought Hunter's meals, did his errands, and helped clean up the bar. No one asked what was going on between her and Hunter. Here, everyone had secrets.

Katie stroked the back of Hunter's hand, a charred-looking landscape of runnels and ridges. One letter on each finger of his left hand spelled out ROACH. Fanned along the tendons were DELTA, FNG, MERCY. And ML, small, down by the thumb.

"Sometimes you make me feel so stupid," she said to him. Francine bopped around Walt, who feigned disinterest.

"How do you mean?"

"Just by sitting there and listening to all the shit I tell you about my life. I sound dumb. Mean."

Hunter said nothing.

"I don't love him, you know."

"Who?"

"Stick."

Hunter poured himself another shot. Katie knew he remembered who Stick was. Everything she'd ever told him lived safely inside him.

"Sometimes I feel like a fake," she said. "Like I can't really feel anything. I'm just pretending. I wouldn't even know how to fake it, except I've seen someone acting sad or happy on TV, and when I think I should be feeling that way, I imitate that person. But none of it is really me."

Katie felt on the verge of tears. But whose tears were they? Who were they for? Did she even believe what she was saying?

And why was she saying it?

In the candlelight she detected a hint of a grin on Hunter's face.

"Closing time," he said.

"I don't want to go home," she said.

"It's time, hon."

"No."

Hunter took hold of Katie's hand. Reflexively she pulled it back, but he did not release it. A glass fell to the floor and shattered.

"This cannot be a game," he said.

His ragged teeth flashed on that last word. Katie shuddered. But she knew what he meant. For all his tattoos, Hunter seemed to have no skin. He felt more pain, more deeply, than everyone else—and he was putting himself in her hands.

"I don't play games," she promised.

On the stairs to Hunter's apartment, his body closed off the space behind Katie, driving her upward.

The apartment was filthy, redolent of something wild and animal. In the darkness Katie saw a mattress on the floor and a wad of rough-looking bedclothes on top of it. At the other end of the room she made out a desk. A towel hung from a nail beside an ancient-looking sink. Three canning shelves groaned under rows of tattered paperbacks: *Being and Nothingness*, *The Brothers Karamazov*. She had no time to see anything else.

Hunter shoved a pile of books off the footlocker at the end of the bed and flipped the lid open. Out came a coil of climbing rope, like a charmed snake.

"Jesus," said Katie.

"Don't worry," Hunter said. "The rope's for me."

Katie saw at once how the fumblings with Stick, the backrubs with the wandering fingers that she'd half hated, half enjoyed, had been literally child's play. They did not even count as a learning experience. What was about to happen was all new.

"Do you trust me?" said Hunter.

"Yes."

"I don't want to hurt you. That's the last thing I'd ever want to do."

"You wouldn't," she said.

"Tie me to the chair."

Katie tied him, following his instructions.

"Now you can do what you want," Hunter said.

It turned out that what she wanted, first, was be looked at. She undressed slowly as her captive watched. Goose bumps rushed over her body in the wake of her hands. She turned so he could see. She danced toward him, swaying her hips like Francine. She lifted his T-shirt and read his tattoos aloud. Then she kissed each one. Some were so faint that she had to pull his skin taut to read them.

Later she slept under Hunter's rough blanket, like an Indian. He stayed tied to the chair by the bedside. He couldn't take any chances, he said.

During the night Katie had a bad dream. She reached out for Hunter. She felt his calf, hard yet compliant in its bonds.

"ML is My Lai," Hunter said. He had been awake the whole time, watching her.

"Who's that?" Katie whispered. She whispered low and flat. Even half asleep and rattled from her dream, she realized this was the most important moment of her life. The moment she would learn the truth about the world. The slightest hitch, the smallest hint of desire or anxiety or excessive interest would seal Hunter's lips forever.

"It's not a person. It's a place," said Hunter.
Katie said nothing. She didn't move.
He told her what he had done there.

CHAPTER TWELVE

November. Moving day, or rather, the last of five moving days. The Majesky family had finally been cleared to settle in Christmastown, one week ahead of the masses. Kyle had underestimated the number of moving vans they'd need. Mollie's stuff had been so tightly compacted in the bungalow that removing the first few items had caused a kind of explosion, like spring snakes popping out of a can in a magic act.

Enrique came over to say good-bye. He and Kyle shook hands. Kyle assured Enrique they would stay friends and that he could come and work on the van some weekends, or else Kyle would drive over to his place. Lie though it was, Christmastown was not that far away. Enrique wiped his eyes with the sleeve of his T-shirt. Kyle teared up, too.

The eighth van departed, and still significant piles of guilt-inducing unused products remained. But slowly, the original bungalow had come into view again. For the first time in a year, Kyle saw the stain on the living-room carpet where he had once upended a plate of spaghetti. The sight filled him with an almost painful relief. His old home had not changed; it had lasted.

Then two movers came and hauled the old furniture out to the curb for the Salvation Army to pick up. Absently, Kyle followed the couch outside and sat on it, facing the street.

So there he was. It was winter and foggy again, and he reminded himself that fog was a cloud that had come down to earth. He wondered if this was what heaven was like—people floating around on clouds. That would suck. No wonder Jackie hadn't wanted to go there, at least not alone.

Katie, evidently done with her own packing, came out and sat beside him. Her leather jacket reeked of smoke. Stick's grandfather smoked, she'd told Kyle, and he'd chosen to believe that lie for the time being. She had never exactly worshipped the sun, but now she looked so pale as to be transparent. Her blue-black hair and black jacket made matters worse. She appeared haunted.

She twisted something around her wrist—a sweatband.

"I think we'll like Christmastown," Kyle said, "better than we think we will."

"I'm not going," Katie said, twisting. "I've decided I should finish out the school year here. Also, there's the band. We have gigs scheduled here in town. I don't want to be driving back and forth constantly."

"Gigs, eh?"

"So I'm going to live with Stick's family. It's all arranged. His grandfather's fine with the whole thing. You don't even need to check with him."

"I wouldn't think of it."

"I'll come to Christmastown on weekends. Whenever I'm free. I promise."

"Did you tell your mom about this?"

"I was hoping you would."

Kyle laughed. Like he had any influence.

"It makes sense, you know," Katie said. "Morton High's a shitty school, but I'll have continuity. That's important for a good education."

"Who gave you an idea like that?"

"You did."

"Bullshit."

Katie laughed, and for a second she looked like Kyle's real daughter. "Look, I just don't want to go right now, OK?" Twisting, twisting. "I mean . . . you know what it's like to be in love, right?"

Kyle wasn't ready for that one. He started coughing and couldn't speak for about a minute. "I do," he said.

"I'll be careful. I'm being careful. Safe. You know."

"That's good." Kyle couldn't find a coherent thought in his head. "Stick's a good guy," he said.

"That's true," Katie said. "He is a really good guy."

Kyle's dead maple sapling still stood there on the front lawn. He thought about digging it up and taking it to Christmastown. But it was nothing but a trunk, streaked with scabs from its dismemberment at the Givers' hands. Christmastown could not perform miracles. The tree would still be dead at their new place.

The Salvation Army truck came so they had to get up off the couch. Katie said she had a rehearsal.

"Katie-did," Kyle said.

"Yeah?"

"I'll miss you."

"I'm not going anywhere. Not really."

The Prisoner

Possession is nine-tenths of the law.
And so I guess you own nine-tenths of me.
I didn't know I wanted to be eaten.
I'm sinking in the quicksand of your soul.
Take me down with you.
Take me down with you.
You promised me that you were dangerous.
You said the past was more than you could stand.
I said I'll take whatever you give me.
I said, you'll bury me, I'll carry you.
Take me down with you.
The hardest thing I've ever done is give up.
And say I'm lost and don't want to be found.
Nothing matters anymore, nothing.
As long as you own me,
I'm yours.
Take me down.
Take me down.
Take me down.

Katie dropped the microphone, all wrung out.

"That's one fucking hell of a song," Stick said.

PART FIVE: CHRISTMASTOWN

CHAPTER THIRTEEN

Givers were storming the gates of Christmastown. It was December 1. The contest winners had been announced yesterday, and the town had officially opened for move-in day. As promised, five thousand households were admitted, a total of 24,287 people. But at least that many people had arrived already, and a large portion of them were not supposed to have come at all.

At all six entrances, haphazardly parked cars and moving vans jammed the lanes. People streamed out of vehicles brandishing credit-card statements, Mollie dolls, their own children. Cops in riot gear pushed them back from the security gates. On the other side of the boundary, mobile command units, like huge unfestive RVs, formed a final barrier. The police had made dozens of arrests already. Helicopters circled above the fray: the big ones were Christmastown security, the others media.

Jackie, sad to say, had anticipated all of this. CED may have been a game, as Harry had said, but certain people had proven themselves extremely poor losers. These were the sort she had hired The Wall of Men to deal with. They had killed the little maple tree in the Majeskys' front yard; they'd hacked chunks of vinyl siding off the bungalow. They had clawed Mollie's legs that horrible afternoon in Van Nuys and stolen her coat. Jackie had begged Harry to ensure that Christmastown was fully prepared. So, thanks to Jackie, this assault would ultimately fail. It was only a matter of time.

Still, it appalled her, this outraged and groveling humanity. The CED system really did screen the wrong people out. One needed only to witness the behavior of those with the proper credentials, waiting patiently as the police cleared a path for them. They'd followed the procedures, done their duty, and now humbly claimed their reward.

Jackie sighed with relief as she realized that once they lived among Winners only, she could at last dispense with The Wall of Men.

She and Harry watched the spectacle on a bank of monitors at police headquarters inside City Hall. The feeds came from tiny cameras embedded in the dome, so powerful they could focus on individual faces nearly a quarter mile beneath them. More cameras, along with microphones, swiveled above the gates and atop officers' helmets. The mics picked up the cries of the crowd.

"Look at my statement from last month! I was in the ninety-ninth percentile and I've increased my Giving twofold since then! There's no way I didn't make it!"

"We've already sold our house back in Texas!"

"Where's Mollie? She'll help us! We sent her a bathing suit and she wrote a letter to us personally! She knows us!"

Jackie recognized Shelly Thayer, waving a sheaf of statements in a cop's face.

"I'm in Jackie Majesky's Giving Group! She promised me two weeks ago that I was a shoo-in!"

Had she promised? Jackie tried to recall. She must have said something like "I'm sure you'll make it," but she had said that to everyone. The purpose of Giving Groups was to provide support. At their final meeting before the announcement, Jackie had wanted to offer everyone hope, regardless of standing. In the end, Jackie always chose hope over truth.

Two officers placed Shelly in bright pink plastic handcuffs and escorted her into a command vehicle. Jackie nodded with sober satisfaction. The police and their guns, like the dome itself, didn't just keep the wrong people out. They shored up the hearts of those inside the dome, which were subject to softening.

The crowds dispersed after a couple of days. The Losers (not the official term) had exhausted their energies. They headed into the country's vast interior or perhaps returned to their previous lives. Of course, many had already erased those lives, quitting jobs, uprooting children from their schools, and settling scores that would otherwise have remained in flux. In their hearts, Jackie thought, they had to know it was all for naught. Winners had received packets by registered mail, containing computerized ID badges which would be scanned at the gate. Those without them had no hope whatsoever of getting in. Yet huge numbers had come anyway, convinced they were, despite the metrics, the exception. Their quest embodied a certain nobility—that special American optimism that carried with it a belief in miracles. That optimism would pay off eventually, Jackie told herself. Christmastown Two was officially under construction in the Upper Peninsula of Michigan.

Once at peace, Christmastown basked in its own glory. The temperature was a heavenly seventy-two degrees every day. When the sun shone outside, the dome stayed clear, and the Christmastown sky was the actual crystal blue of the Mojave. If more than a predetermined number of clouds appeared, the dome turned the same color blue to blot them out, and an artificial sun made a timed arc across the vault. Then, whether real or simulated, the desert sky at night presented the greatest planetarium show on earth.

In those early days, the Winners spent most of their time outdoors, simply marveling. Jackie passed them on the multipurpose trail that looped through town. She had taken up running again.

Pastor Mike, heading toward her on his bicycle, dinged his bell and waved. Jackie waved back, her pace quickening with a certain pride. She felt like the fisherman who'd landed the big one. She had worried Mike would disapprove of CED as a form of works righteousness. But as it had turned out, Mike could not resist a competition. His urge to win was so strong he had even forgiven Jackie for interfering with his attempt to heal Mollie. He had shown up at every Giving Group meeting, calculator in hand, and never even mentioned that Jackie had stopped coming to church. Truth be told, she had not yet made it to his new church in Christmastown either. She simply had too much to do.

Well, there was another reason. Now that she actually lived here in Christmastown, Mike's promises of heaven had come to seem a little paltry. Heaven represented an end, a vague, pale place where untroubled people did nothing but worship God. Whereas Christmastown, Jackie had to think, was a beginning. Thousands of people, their character honed by the unflinching fires of consumer capitalism, had joined together in one inspiring place. Who knew what this new, superior civilization might accomplish? The Winners might cure cancer. They might solve world hunger or invent an entirely new form of music. They could build a rocket ship and reach the stars. By contrast, heaven looked, well, like people sitting on their asses smiling. Or like death.

"Hi there, Pastor Mike," she called out as they passed.

"Beautiful day, isn't it?" Mike shouted.

Like all the Winners, he always tacked on that "isn't it?" at the end. The tic reflected amazement bordering on disbelief. *Can every day really be this beautiful?* the Winners asked themselves. Or, perhaps more to the point: *Will I always be here to say "beautiful day"?* The answer to both questions was yes, provided, of course, that they remained Givers in good standing. Coming to Christmastown did not mean leaving the requirements of CED behind—far from it. But maintaining their status would present no problem for the Winners, who were here because they loved Giving above all. For them, not Giving would have been like not breathing.*

In fact, it was officially Jackie's job to keep these faithful and trusting Winners safe and sound, so their Giving could go on unhindered. Because Jackie was now Christmastown's mayor. Harry had quietly considered the appointment for months, but Jackie's prescience about security matters had finally convinced him. Unfortunately, her instincts remained necessary. Christmastown still faced a weak but constant threat from would-be interlopers. Some demanded entry for political reasons. These people knew perfectly well they hadn't Won; most had never even signed up for CED in the first place. Nevertheless, they filed lawsuits. CED, the suits

---

* This remains the case today. By now, former Winners have scattered far and wide, and are not always easy to identify. They rarely even recognize themselves as part of a distinctive movement. To them, their practices seem as ancient and basic as the wheel. Anthropologists have recorded interviews with some of the original residents of Christmastown, and their mercantile homilies sound so much like English, they seduce the researchers into an illusion of comprehension. The professors scurry back to campus to transcribe the recordings only to see their meanings dissolve as soon as they hit the computer screen. The scholars shake their heads in baffled admiration: once again the Winners have told them *nothing*.

said, discriminated against those whose cultural traditions did not include the celebration of Christmas. Jackie could not believe the inanity. CED discriminated only between the truly generous and the less so. People had a *choice*: they could either Give, or not.

Soon a tent city sprang up at the edge of Christmastown's land. Most of the town's guest workers took up residence there, as traveling to and from their real homes proved too arduous. Primarily landscapers and nannies, they carried ID cards with chips that alerted the authorities if they stayed inside the dome after their shifts ended. But already some workers had been caught holding cards with altered or disabled chips.

And so, due to these factors, Jackie quietly stepped up surveillance. She hated having to do this; it felt like The Wall of Men all over again. Still, she had the dome's precision cameras programmed to record all public activity and ordered the bank of monitors to be manned day and night. She increased the number of foot patrols inside and outside the dome. She authorized security personnel to stop anyone who looked suspicious and demand—in the nicest possible tone—identification.

Perched atop the backseat of a red convertible, Jackie waved to the crowds that had gathered along Commerce Street. Mollie, wearing a tiara and her Christmas Spirit sash, blew kisses and brandished the golden wand she would soon use to light the Christmas tree in the town square. In front of them, the marching band from Christmastown High (the kids had had only had two weeks to practice, bless them) played carols. Winners ducked in and out of shops. Smoke rose from the barbecue tents. It was a beautiful evening for a parade, like all evenings in Christmastown.

For the Winners' first Christmas season in their new home, Jackie had decided to dispense with the usual celebrities in favor of small-town warmth. The parade before the tree lighting affirmed the values of generosity and family that had brought all these people here in the first place. Jackie had thought of the idea after noticing that many Winners carried their Mollie dolls with them wherever they went and dressed them in various themed outfits (angel, baseball player, professor) available from CarlsMart. These people, she figured, would like nothing better than showing off their Mollies at Christmastime. Thus the first annual March of Mollies was born. Jackie heard the marchers behind her, singing "Good King Wenceslas" along with the band. The dolls cried out Christmas greetings. Along the route, large Christmas-tree-shaped jump houses ingested children and swayed wildly.

As she and Mollie reached the town square and mounted the dais, a mild fear ruffled the wings of Jackie's pleasure. Several thousand enthusiastic Winners moved toward them, holding replicas of Mollie above their heads. Still, as Jackie smiled and waved to them, they waved back in a seemingly friendly manner. These people had made it, Jackie reminded herself. They were the opposite of the desperate seekers who had overwhelmed her and Mollie in Van Nuys. Jackie appreciated the police officers lined up in front of the dais, their hands clasped in false repose behind their backs. But resurrecting The Wall of Men would have been overkill.

The artificial sun set, and streaks of colored light spread across the western half of the dome. The streetlights and the stars came on. Winners spread throughout the square, still singing. They waved at Mollie and Jackie and pointed to their dolls as if for approval. Jackie pointed back and gave them the thumbs-up and OK signs.

Yet, in the twilight, the strangeness of the Mollie dolls became apparent. It turned out they were not only wearing the outfits offered by CarlsMart. Quite a few Winners had gotten "creative." Jackie saw Mollies dressed as Farrah Fawcett, Charlie Chaplin (complete with a little Hitler mustache), Alexis Carrington, and animals. Lots of animals. Lions, bears, domestic cats and dogs, even birds with brightly painted beaks. What exactly were these people doing to Mollie? And why?

The police chief, standing behind Jackie, leaned in and reminded her to start the ceremony.

She glanced at her notes. "Friends," she said. "Givers. Winners. Citizens. Welcome to Christmas in your brand-new home." A hearty cheer went up, reminding Jackie that this was indeed a moment to celebrate. "I am honored and humbled to greet you this beautiful evening as your mayor. Your generous support of the CED movement has resulted in prosperity, not just for the thousands of us here tonight, or for CarlsMart LLC, but for millions across our great nation. A rising tide does lift all boats, and wealth does trickle down—or rather rain down—from above. By giving to your loved ones, you have given to your country as well. Giving is patriotic, and it is good. I know you all know that, but I want you to take a moment to be proud of what you have achieved."

The Winners cheered again and waved their dolls—a bit recklessly, Jackie thought. Evidently they didn't see these dolls as real. Or, judging from the animal costumes, human.

"You are the heart and engine of this nation," she went on. "More than that, you are pioneers on the next frontier of civilization. Make no mistake—the world is watching this experiment very closely. The world looks to us—to you—for an example of how to live in peace and in prosperity. Today we are the first, but we won't be the last.

"So let us commit ourselves tonight to fulfilling the limitless promise of Christmas Every Day and Christmastown. Let us never stop Giving. Let us never stop striving to be better. Let us always think of others before ourselves. If we do these things, I promise you, our new city will thrive forever and ever.

"Thank you for coming to this celebration tonight. Please enjoy your city. It is yours. You've earned it.

"God bless you," she added. She'd almost forgotten.

Jackie nodded to Mollie on her throne.

"Merry Christmas to the Winners!" Mollie said.

Jackie lifted her up and she touched a branch of the tree with her wand. The tree burst into light.

The cheers exploded. The crowd undulated, and Jackie tensed. But as the artificial fireworks detonated beneath the dome's vault, the sea of Winners calmed, entranced by a wonder as ancient as fire.

Afterward the sea broke into harmless streams, branching toward the barbecue tents and the shops. The jump houses swayed, emitting screams. The country-western band started up, and the Winners danced in the street.

Jackie wished Harry were there to dance with her. But she had not seen him since move-in day, when they'd slipped away from monitoring the melee and stolen a half hour atop the desk in the mayor's office. On the phone, he'd been vague about when he was coming back. He was on a mission, he said. He said he missed Jackie. She reminded herself that she loved him for his questing nature. He never stopped looking for moments to seize.

Kyle had not come to the ceremony either, deciding to stay home as usual. So Jackie danced with the police chief, a muscular man but very stiff, like a reject from The Wall of Men.

CHAPTER FOURTEEN

During one of his increasingly rambling philosophical interludes, Topper Moss had once said something about a butterfly flapping its wings and causing a hurricane halfway around the globe. Of course the butterfly had no idea what it was doing. It was an insect. It was just living its life. It did not mean to wipe out that island village, all those poor people.

What if Kyle had never shot himself in the foot? What if he had not had that last beer at The Link before the Lions Club demo, trying to dull his awareness, on the eve of Valentine's Day, that his wife no longer lived in the same world he did, but in a terrifying hell where she was always on the verge of losing half her family? What if he had tried harder to reassure Jackie about the meaning of the Challenger explosion, so she hadn't jumped every time the refrigerator started loudly to defrost itself, clutching him or a nearby table as if to beg the Lord, "Not yet"? Going even further back, what if he'd taken up running with her, so she had not gotten lost on that foggy afternoon and wound up in the hands of Esther and company?

He could have, at least, told Jackie from the get-go that he accepted Jesus and made Katie tell her the same. What would have been the harm? Some lies were better than the truth. Jackie would have relaxed, and then Kyle could have relaxed, too. Then he might not have shot himself or, inspired by his fleeting fame, quit his job. Then Jackie would never have gone to work at CarlsMart. She would not have met Harry, learned what a real man was at last, and fallen for him. Without Jackie and Mollie, CED would have never gotten off the ground. Harry Ricker had said so himself at his Christmas party. Had Kyle not shot himself in the foot, this insane city might never have existed.

Was it possible? Was Kyle the butterfly of Christmastown?

These days the butterfly spent his waking hours, and actually his sleeping ones, in the game room. He was pretty sure Jackie had designed it herself to make him feel at home. Like a casino, it was a noisy place, with flashing pinball machines and blooping video arcade games along with a pool table, ping-pong table, and dartboard. Rows of shelves held decks of cards, board games, and *Mad Libs*. It wasn't clear who he was supposed to play these games with. Jackie tried to encourage him nonetheless.

"Kyle, have you tried the pool table?"

"Kyle, didn't you use to like to play darts?"

But he was not interested. He had given up. On everything. Kyle's beautifully painted, lushly upholstered van sat inside the five-car garage next to Jackie's new gold BMW. (The Reliant had gone straight to the Malpaso Junkyard in Morton with only a stifled groan from Kyle by way of farewell.) Even his hair had grown back into an untended smear. The shaved head had suggested purpose, and he had none.

So, as the arcade games flashed and pinged all around him, Kyle lay on the couch watching TV. *The Weird Frontier* was now on twenty-four hours a day. Like CEDN, it had become a channel, a universe of its own. At the moment, Topper was showing a live feed from a Bigfoot convention in Boise, Idaho.

In his thick accent, Klaus Lorentz, the avid tracker, set the ground rules for the next panel.

> "There is to be no discussion—none—of outer space, telepathy, astral projection, sexual probing, subterranean machinery, robots, or spores. The search for Bigfoot is a scientific endeavor on par with finding and identifying the now well-understood platypus. Cryptozoology is a branch of zoology, and it is past time for it to receive respect as such. We have had far too many crackpots at this event already. I hereby say no to crackpots. We will confine our discussion to the science, and the science only."

On cue, a man rose from the audience. This meticulously groomed person wore a tailored white shirt and navy-blue pressed slacks and could have lent the enterprise the credibility that Klaus so desired. The only hitch was the short purple cape draped over his shoulders and fastened with a gold chain. "I see nothing wrong with exploring the paranormal aspects of Bigfoot," said the man whose name did not appear on screen.

"You wouldn't," said Klaus, who obviously had dealt with him before.

"We now know that the Apocalypse is coming any day now, and this increased Bigfoot activity cannot be a coincidence. The so-called paranormal events that accompany this activity may well signal the operations of a superior intelligence with telepathic and other powers. Might we surmise that Bigfoot is the next stage of mankind's evolution, who will take over once we are all gone?"

"NO!" Klaus roared.

Professor Bud Zeeb of the University of Eastern Northern California, a man so conflict-averse that his trembling was visible from thirty feet away, stood carefully.

"Bigfoot is most likely an earlier stage of human evolution, or rather a dead-end branch thereof. A Neanderthal or Gigantopithecus that survived the last ice age, perhaps by dwelling in underground lava caves. The fossil record suggests—"

"Damn the fossil record!" said Cape Man.

"Damn you!" Klaus pointed at Cape Man from the lectern. Cape Man was held back from rushing the lectern by his cape.

"Your time is over!" Cape Man coughed as his gold chain tightened at his neck. It was unclear whether he meant Klaus's time on earth or merely the time allotted for his remarks. Clutching his neck, Cape Man turned and shoved the man who was trying to restrain him. Both staggered and fell into a stack of folding chairs. The melee escalated. Klaus hurled a pitcher of water from the stage. Suddenly the camera began moving, following behind as Topper, who had been resting in the back, swam through the rows of shouting men.

(For Topper the past year had felt like twenty. His complexion had taken on a yellow cast. He had lost his deadpan demeanor—which some thought ironic— entirely. Only his cockeyed pith helmet identified him. His pursuit of Bigfoot had led him to two inescapable conclusions: [1] this was the most important story of all time, and [2] absolutely no one else was capable of grasping why.) Pausing just below the lectern, he waved a hortatory finger at the fuming Klaus. "Klaus Lorentz," he shouted, his voice high and quavering. "You are a person who has consistently failed to appreciate the power of myth."

"Myth?" Klaus sputtered. "Myth?"

"You believe that if something is a myth it cannot also be real. I say nothing is more real than myth. At this very moment, around the world, people are flagellating themselves in the name of myth. They are starving or singing, or building statues or skyscrapers or bombs. They are deciding how to live their lives based on mistranslated stories that are thousands of years old. We make myths out of human beings, call them celebrities, and throw ourselves at them, craving their attention and their blessing.

"This nation is perhaps the greatest myth of all. America is a story we tell ourselves. I told it to myself as a child in England—someday I would go to a land of unlimited promise, where people reinvent themselves over and over. Where the past is not entombed in stone monuments, but light and flexible, like film, like the very future. Now here I am, living right in the middle of the story and helping to compose it at the same time. We are living in this story, you and I and all these people here"—

he waved his arms frantically over the crowd—"and out there, too." He flailed toward the camera. "What you are missing out on, what you are destroying for everyone, Klaus, is *wonder.*"

"Topper Moss, you and your disreputable show treat the truth as a dog treats a fire hydrant."

Klaus did not so much launch himself into the crowd as bounce into it, his barrel-shaped head leading him straight to Topper. With a cry of "TRUTH!" he grabbed Topper around the waist and tried to tackle him. Topper's pith helmet fell off, revealing a bony pate ringed with a sad gray fringe. Cape Man hit Klaus in the back with a folding chair. Bud Zeeb tugged weakly at Cape Man's cape from behind, succeeding only in spinning it sideways. Topper extricated himself and struggled, gasping, toward the camera.

"All of you out there. You understand, don't you? It's not just science. It's not just myth. It's the irrepressible pull we all feel toward the unknown, the unsettling, even the impossible. That's what makes us human. Don't you see? I have been trying to show you people *your own humanity.* I beg you, tell me my work has not been in vain."

Kyle could have sworn Topper looked right at him with his golf-ball-sized eyes. But what could Kyle Majesky, of all humanity, possibly do to help Topper? He could not even get off the couch, let alone reassure a man who lived on television that his whole existence had not been a waste. Poor Topper, he thought. No one listened to him. He had met the fate of all prophets, which was why most kept their mouths shut.

On the other hand, Kyle thought, I just won my bet with Katie. Topper really did believe in Bigfoot, though not exactly in the way Kyle expected.

He dialed Stick's number, but as usual got his grandfather's answering machine and its slow, confused greeting. He left Katie a message to call him. If precedent held, it would be days before she did so.

He set the phone down. He missed his daughter. Daughters. He missed Mollie, even though she was right in the next room with her new nanny. Despite Kyle's utter lack of engagements, pressing or otherwise, it had somehow been assumed that he was not to be a major part of Mollie's life. Well, he didn't deserve to be, did he? Look at him, and then look at Jackie. Who was the better example for a child to follow?

Through the doorway, Kyle watched his wife direct the rearrangement of the living room. Having somewhat overcome her fear of crowds, she had decided Mollie would receive visitors at the house on alternate Saturday mornings.

"Mollie," Jackie said to the police chief, "will sit in an armchair on the far side, with an empty chair beside her for the visitor. I will sit on her other side. My assistant will keep an eye on the time and arrange for the disposal, by which I mean storage, of the gifts people bring her. A police officer will check IDs at the door, and one will be stationed at the far end of the room. I want plain clothes for both. There is no need to appear unwelcoming. The rope line will go from the front door into the sunken area, here."

Jackie jabbed her pencil toward the living room. The chief nodded, and Jackie resumed yelling into the telephone in her other hand.

"Listen to me. Mollie's snowsuit is to be plain white, with white mittens and a white scarf. No ears. No tail. Mollie is not a *creature*, understand? Now, about the hotel in Winnipeg . . ."

Next week Jackie and Mollie would leave for a tour of Canada, a nation smothered in snow. Jackie had received assurances that the weather would not affect turnout at Mollie's events: Canadians did not even notice snow. So now she was making plans to film CEDN spots with Mollie on a toboggan, with a snowman, etc.

The poor girl was nothing but a puppet, Kyle thought, a corporate ventriloquist's dummy. This was as much his fault as Jackie's. He had had major doubts about CED from the beginning, but he'd squelched them, partly but not only for Jackie's sake. He'd thought he could do his impressions on CEDN.

And now look at him. He hadn't done a single impression since, God help him, Tahoe. Jackie had told him the home recording studio was his whenever Mollie wasn't using it for CEDN. It was state of the art, but

Kyle was not an artist. He was a piece of furniture, a chair that drank beer. Even now, he could somehow not lift a finger to save his baby daughter's soul. What would it take to get him to do his duty? Maybe nothing short of the Apocalypse.

Kyle had sunk so low, he even wished Tessa had agreed to move to Christmastown with them. But, as it turned out, she had refused Jackie's almost-sincere invitation. She said she was happy where she was. Which had surprised Kyle, until it occurred to him that she was still waiting for her husband, Leo, to come home. After all these years, she wanted to make sure he knew where to find her.

In Calgary, perched atop a stuffed moose in front of a newly opened CarlsMart, Mollie dropped Carl into a snowbank. She started shrieking immediately. The assembled crowd began to wail with her. Arms futilely reached for her as The Wall of Men shoved the would-be consolers back.

The cries erupted: "Help her!" "Please, she's so sad!"

Jackie patted the air with her gloved hands and smiled. "It's all right," she told the crowd. "It will all be over in a second."

An underling plunged his arm into the snow and retrieved Carl. He handed him back to Mollie, whose enraged face glowed like a ruby set in the white-fur trim of her hood.

"No!" Mollie shouted, and smacked Carl back into the snow.

Jackie picked Carl up herself and inspected him. He was filthy and deeply pocked with teeth marks, but he had looked like that for quite a while now. He had, however, gotten wet, so Jackie dried him carefully with her scarf.

"Here you go, sweetie," she said to Mollie.

"I don't want it!" Mollie roared.

"But it's Carl, sweetie."

"I don't want it! I don't want it! I don't want it!"

Eventually Jackie persuaded Mollie to gather Carl to her heart once again. But she held the figure with indifference, his head hanging below the wheels of his race car.

The crowd grew subdued and even nonplussed. A few people drifted away, taking with them the presents they'd brought for Mollie. Her face still blotchy, Mollie smiled for the photographers and TV crews.

Unfortunately, they already had far more interesting shots than these. Most had already rushed off to file their reports on Mollie's meltdown in the frozen north.

Back at the hotel, a local doctor was summoned, a man whose "o's" were so round you could have strung them onto a necklace. He checked Mollie's temperature and looked in her mouth. She stayed quiet, observing him with an expression of tolerant suspicion. This nuanced mien bothered Jackie. Mollie was not one to conceal or complicate her emotions.

"I see nothing wrong," the doctor said after nearly half an hour of poking and palpating. "She could use a little more exercise, but she's otherwise quite healthy. I'd say she's just being a little girl."

Jackie's laugh came out as a snort. Did this man not own a television? Had he never been to a CarlsMart or left his office except for this one time? He had no idea that what he'd said made no sense. Mollie? "Just" a "little girl"? Then again—worst case scenario—what if she were?

There went that lifting sensation again—that scarf blowing off. Instinctively Jackie reached for it around her neck and felt nothing.

As soon as the doctor left, Jackie called Harry in New York, or maybe it was Pittsburgh, to give him a full report. You could say she was making a preemptive strike. Harry had not yet seen the breaking news on CNN.

"Mollie had a rough couple of moments out there," Jackie said. "It turns out she has a cold. She's not used to this harsh weather. But don't worry. The doctor gave her all kinds of medicine, and she'll be fine by tomorrow."

"Sounds fine," said Harry.

"Really?"

"Sure. These things happen. She's just a kid, isn't she?"

Jackie did not know what to say. It was one thing for a Canadian doctor to believe this, but Harry?

"If you want," Harry said, "You can cancel the remaining stops on the tour. There's no sense pushing things beyond their limits."

For Harry that kind of statement was sacrilege.

They finished the tour according to the original schedule. Most of the other stops went just fine. Only occasionally, Mollie's eyes narrowed as she spotted an object in the middle distance—a toy, a store window, a person cooing at her and approaching—and she turned away with a look of disgust. Her voice sometimes lapsed into singsong, as if she'd finally realized that she'd said this line, or something like it, well over a thousand times.

Also, no matter how often Jackie handed Carl to her, Mollie continued to bat him away, even after they'd returned to Christmastown. No longer a comfort, he seemed to tip Mollie's precarious mood into misery. So, after a few weeks, Jackie sent Carl to the underground Storage Facility. After all, children did outgrow their toys.

Maybe, Jackie allowed herself to hope for a brief moment, Mollie would outgrow her job, too.

CHAPTER FIFTEEN

The multipurpose trail was one of Christmastown's many urban-planning marvels. By design, no residence was more than a quarter mile away from it. The trail wove between yards along the newly flowing river, where willows wept and cherry trees flowered to welcome the spring. The path then looped around the entire downtown area, past the reflecting pool behind City Hall and the depot for the Downtown Giving Train, with its outdoor food court. Most people tended to step off the trail here, but not Jackie. She was once again the kind of runner who, once she started, did not ever want to stop.

After this, she was due at a meeting with the city council to go over Christmastown's eviction policy. Jackie believed the current one was too harsh: one month of not meeting your Giving Goal earned you a warning; another month, and you and yours were out on your behinds. There was no appeals process as such, because metrics didn't lie. But when he'd first drafted this policy, Harry had not recognized all the possible impediments to Giving, even in Christmastown.

For instance, some people insisted on keeping their former jobs, back in what many now called the "real world." This, despite Christmastown's excellent job placement service. The polity still cried out for salespeople, accountants, computer technicians, and security personnel, not to mention nannies and landscapers and maids—positions Jackie would really have liked to wrest from the guest workers. Other families drove their children hundreds of miles to outside schools, rejecting Christmastown's top-notch educators and their uplifting, free-market-oriented curriculum. Such baffling choices had led to commutes of over three hours each way for some residents, who afterward found themselves in no frame of mind to Give. And what about vacations or other extended travel to the remaining places on earth where there were no CarlsMarts? True, the town's leadership could strongly discourage or even ban such travel. But then Christmastown would resemble a communist regime, and it was the opposite of that.

Jackie's footfalls reverberated through the wooden bridge over the river. Running helped her think, and also not to think. Considered this way, it was a form of prayer. If Jackie's experiences this past year had taught her anything, it was that the Lord's ways were not only mysterious, but downright mischievous. Praying for something would indeed bring you that something, but inside out, upside down, so belated and disguised it could take you ages to understand. This was a recipe for frustration. On the other hand, if you found a way to truly forget what you wanted, you would soon have it. Running provided a way to forget.

It dawned on Jackie that the overstressed commuters might gladly hire others to do their Giving for them. If necessary, guest workers could fill the bill, but so could many residents who loved to Give and had extra time on their hands. This was a good idea. Harry would love it, as would the council. There—one problem solved already. But, oh, Harry . . . Jackie shook her head and ran harder.

The trail wound alongside the golf course and then steered the runner toward the soft hills and rhythmically moving sheep—animatronic, to cut down on pollution and the possibility of disease—of the Outer Green Space. Jackie thought of Katie, in school back in Morton, living with Stick. The girl had not made bad choices—even if Jackie couldn't bring herself to admit that on the rare occasions when they talked on the phone. Finishing out the school year in Morton made sense, though Christmastown's schools were vastly superior to Morton's, with required courses in business ethics, computer science, and architecture. Katie's decision showed maturity. Also, Katie did not want to leave the boy she loved.

So now she was gone. Not really gone. But yes, gone. Gone.

Was Harry gone, too? He'd been on the road for months. Like Katie, he had turned into a voice on the telephone, first once a day, and lately once every few. Jackie had begun to forget what he looked like—was the face she saw in her mind the real one or a figment of her imagination? But she didn't have a photograph of him, even on a magazine cover; she didn't want one, because too much precision in memory could be dangerous. How could their love be the same when he came back, when their bodies had been apart for so long? They would fold together awkwardly, elbows and knees. They could not be as they were—and so she must forget the past, even as she anticipated a better future.

Because this was not the end for them. Harry had pried Jackie open, filleted her, and left her splayed. You could not do that to someone and then leave. You owned that exposed soul, which you made raw to your touch, and to your absence. You could not abandon. You could not say, "Let's not push things." What in the hell did that even mean?

Jackie turned her thoughts to Mollie. Dear, resilient, beautiful Mollie. Day after day she rose to meet the impossible expectations heaped upon her by adults, many of whom expected far less of themselves. Mollie still had that edge of weariness about her that had surfaced in Canada last month. But no one else had noticed, not even Caridad, Mollie's wonderful nanny, who was not a guest worker but a certified Winner. Mollie just needed a little rest. Jackie had cut back on visiting hours at the house. Also, for the past several weeks, CEDN had shown reruns of Mollie's daily appearances. No one had seemed to notice that she was not live. Perhaps she had stopped being "live" a long time ago. Jackie's heart clenched. She ran harder still.

The trail bent into the Inner Green Space, which is to say, the forest. Jackie now found herself completely alone. Christmastown's other residents hardly ever came to the Inner Green Space, possibly because of its darkness, though it was still considerably lighter than most forests. But the rest of the town was an unusually bright, orderly place. The forest may have seemed too much of a contrast. The air tasted green and damp.

Jackie's sneakers crunched on the dirt track. A parrot screeched in the canopy. Everywhere else in Christmastown, if you listened closely, you could detect the background hum of the dome doing its work. It worked here in the forest, too, but the trees absorbed the sound. For the most part Jackie found the silence of the forest refreshing, but she could see why others might have felt a little scared. At the upcoming council meeting,

Jackie decided to call for additional birds to be placed in the canopy. Also a few discreet vendors along the track, to put people more at ease. There. Another very good idea. She was a good mayor, if not a good mother.

Jackie breathed deep through her nose, inviting the calming forest air into her body. Instead, a terrible stench slammed into her like a wall. She stopped and leaned against a wrought-iron bench, gasping and wiping her eyes. It smelled like some large animal had died nearby. But, except for the birds, there were no real animals in the forest.

Jackie heard a growl, very close. She gasped and, before even looking around her, instinctively checked the sky. Surely the surveillance cameras in the dome could see her—or could they? The canopy was thick, the dome only visible in splotches. Why had no one in Green Space Management realized this and cut the trees back? Did Jackie have to think of everything around here?

The growl came again, followed by a soft whistling. That was no growl, but a snore. Jackie peered into the shadows.

Under a nearby oak tree, a large, filthy creature slept. Its head rested on a backpack as it lay curled in a semifetal position with its back to Jackie. The creature wore a tattered khaki vest, the kind with a million pockets, and dirt-encrusted jeans. Twigs and leaves matted its long gray hair.

"Hey!" Jackie shouted at the sky. "Do you see this? Do you see this thing down here?" She unclipped her ID card from her shorts and waved it at an open spot in the canopy.

Minutes went by and no cops arrived on their electric scooters. Call boxes, Jackie thought. They had to put emergency call boxes in the forest. No, that was absurd. There should be no need for call boxes anywhere. The whole point of Christmastown was that Winners could always trust one another.

The monster—or was it an enormous, crazed old man?—snored on through her shouting. Jackie looked around for a stick to poke him with. She stepped off the path and kicked around under the ferns. Unfortunately the Quality of Life squad had just conducted a debris sweep, and nary a fallen stick nor even dead leaf remained. Finally Jackie picked up two of the smooth gray river stones that delineated the path. It felt like a terrible breach, breaking the line. But this was an emergency. With a stone in each hand, she tiptoed toward the heaving, stinking heap.

Out of nowhere a thought struck her. Was this her father? Had he somehow crept back to her in this ruined form, seeking forgiveness? She hadn't seen him in almost twenty years or heard from him in ten. She'd never responded to the birthday cards he used to send each year, always pink with sparkles, like she was forever his princess, that stupid little girl. So he'd stopped sending them.

He had to be alive still. If he'd died, his latest wife or girlfriend would have found a way to get in touch. She would have felt some trace of responsibility. Or maybe not. Maybe she was as selfish as a person would have be to take a man from his family.

It would be almost funny, Jackie thought, to meet him like this. He had broken her heart, so she would break his head. Methodically, she would pound it, first with one stone, then with the other.

Of course she would refrain from violence. She would only employ the stones for self-defense. Besides, this being was much larger than her father, and much less human. Resting on his thigh, his hand, covered in gray fur, was the size of a skillet. With every snore his back surged, broad as a boulder. Clutching her stones, heart pounding, she dug a toe between his shoulder blades.

"Hey," she said. "You. Get up." Where, she wondered, had she learned to talk like such a bully?

With a rumbling that made Jackie jump three feet in the air, the creature, or man, began to move. The head turned. The eyes opened, wide and blue as the Christmastown sky. Faint cloud-like forms seemed to undulate through them. Those clouds were time itself.

Inside the thick, filthy beard, the desiccated lips began to move. A word formed.

But Jackie did not stick around to hear it. Shrieking, she raced out of the forest, ignoring the cries of "beautiful day, isn't it?" that came at her left and right.

Back at her office, gulping air, she set the two stones, which she had forgotten to let go of, on her desk. The damp shadows of her hands faded from them.

In the old days Jackie would have believed she'd seen the Devil himself. She would have called on Pastor Mike to heal the city, perhaps even to lay his hands upon the dome. But life in Christmastown had modified her views. Oh, she knew the Devil existed. He was chaos, the maw that chewed up humanity's best intentions and spat them out as disasters. She also still believed in God. But he, like the Devil, did not appear and disappear magically. Both worked through systems. Through programs and technologies. That was how the battle for Christmastown would be fought.

She dispatched the police, and also Animal Control, to the forest and ordered a complete security sweep of the city.

Over the next three days, patrols fanned out through and around Christmastown. Helicopters inched like hummingbirds over the dome, looking for breaches. The guards at the gates questioned those who entered and exited, and were questioned themselves. Security tapes from the past week, and then the past two weeks, were reviewed. The guest workers' tent city was raided. No one seemed to know or have seen any large, extremely creepy man or animal. He had left no trace of himself in the forest. There was maybe a dent at the base of the oak tree where he'd slept, but Quality of Life could have made that during their rounds.

At police headquarters, one floor below the mayor's office, Jackie met with the chief. Blueprints of the city sprawled on the table in front of them. Jackie remembered the first time she had seen the scale model in Harry's office, how radiant and placid Christmastown had looked from above. How impenetrable. But the blueprints told another story. The maze that was the underground Storage Facility extended well beyond the boundaries of Christmastown proper. On the blueprint, the dome looked like the yolk of a fried egg.

"This is a weakness," said Jackie, tapping her pencil eraser all over the egg white. "The dome's surveillance system can't reach down here. This— man—could easily have tunneled in from outside."

The chief shook his head. "The Facility's encased in concrete."

"But a tunnel could start miles outside the boundary," Jackie said. "It would be easy to hide an entrance—in a cave, or under a bunch of brush. We don't have all these areas covered. An individual or group of people could tunnel up to the wall and then blow a hole in the concrete with dynamite."

"That's unlikely," said the chief. "We'd notice an explosion like that, even if it were underground."

"How? Do we have cameras that far out? Or sensors in the retaining wall itself?"

The chief looked at the floor.

"I thought so," Jackie said. "And once someone has gotten in there, they'll be extremely hard to root out. Talk about a place to hide. The Facility is a labyrinth. Plus, think of all the buckets of caramel popcorn and pretzels that people have stored down there. A person—or anything—could live for months."

The chief rubbed his chin. "I suppose that's possible," he said, "in theory."

"I don't like theories," Jackie said. "I want to see for myself."

One of Christmastown's most popular amenities was the Gift Storage Service. Every Tuesday, families placed the items they needed stored that week out on the curb. Trucks collected the items and transported them to the Facility, where they were labeled and arrayed on numbered shelves in the family's designated area. The items and their shelf numbers were all logged into a database. Families could visit the Facility to view or retrieve items at any time, but hardly any had taken advantage of this option. They received weekly updated lists of their stored items in the mail. Jackie sometimes read the list of Mollie's gifts to her at bedtime. It was a story without end. But most people didn't even open the envelope. And Jackie herself, to her embarrassment, had never been to the Facility, either.

With the police chief and the commissioner of storage, she descended in the buzzing elevator. Down, down—even farther down than she expected, beneath the vast and mysterious server farm that kept the dome running, below even the water and sewage systems. The elevator seemed to get smaller as it plunged, and the air thicker. Jackie rubbed her bare arms and tried to smile at the commissioner. His name was Roy, but he preferred being called Commissioner. As a former accountant, he had never in his life believed he'd have such a title. Christmastown had given it to him.

At last, the elevator came to rest with a gentle bounce. The doors opened and revealed a clerk sitting at a neat desk, wearing a green jumpsuit and familiar-looking gray glasses. It was Melvin, Jackie's old boss at CarlsMart. She'd heard he had made it here, but she had no idea he was *here*.

"Welcome!" Melvin shouted and leapt up from behind his desk to shake hands. "I'm so glad you've come for the tour. This is an excellent Facility, a state-of-the-art Facility. Hell, it's more impressive than the dome, if you ask me. Yet nobody ever comes down here. Do you think people even know about the tours we offer? Maybe we could print up brochures?"

Melvin had made it all the way to Christmastown, Jackie thought, just to spend his days underground. Could he really like working in the Facility this much? If he didn't, CED, in a sense, had failed him.

Melvin asked his visitors to sign in, helpfully clicking the ballpoint pen for them. He offered them earplugs like the ones he was wearing, which resembled orange circus peanuts. The constant roaring, he explained, was a combination of industrial-strength dehumidifiers, air conditioners, and fans. These state-of-the-art technologies ensured that all nonperishable items would remain in perfect condition for centuries.

"You will find it a little cool in there, if I may suggest," Melvin said, eyeing Jackie's bare shoulders. She accepted a green Facility jacket from him. She was glad Harry couldn't see her now, in stiletto heels, hunched into what looked like an army jacket, orange peanuts poking out of her ears.

Melvin punched a code into a keypad, and the two steel doors behind his desk drew slowly open. The roaring, which the earplugs did little to mitigate, poured into the anteroom like a fire.

"Go on in," Melvin shouted. "Don't forget the map. The tours are self-guided, though you of course have the best guide of all." He nodded to the commissioner, who offered the barest nod in return. "I suggest you use one of the electric carts there," Melvin said. "It's a big place. Damn, I wish I had time to go with you. I never get tired of the Facility—it's different every time you go in." He offered a jaunty, slightly uncontrolled salute, and the doors closed behind the band of travelers.

Electric minitrucks hauled trailers up and down the aisles, wide as two-lane streets. But rather than storefronts or houses, these streets were lined from floor to ceiling with objects of every possible color, shape, and size, on huge industrial shelves that merged at a vanishing point in the distance. The map showed a grid of these streets, but instead of poetic names like Angel Street, where Jackie's family lived, they were designated by letters and numbers that corresponded, the commissioner explained, to the axes of the grid. A family's gifts might reside at the address BB27: GGG621: Level C11. Mollie's gifts alone, the commissioner noted, occupied twenty entire blocks. Row upon row of circular lamps blasted light down from the high ceilings, and yet the overall impression was of darkness.

The cart glided down aisle D. Jackie sat beside the commissioner, who drove. The police chief sat behind them, facing backward. If either of them spoke, Jackie didn't notice. The roaring consumed her attention. She began to imagine that the sound came from the gifts themselves. Colors, shapes, noises, and textures blended into a mural, like one might find inside some foreign pagan temple. Banished, the gifts had become vengeful deities. She suddenly felt the need for Jesus's protection. *Lord, can you see this?* she asked. *Can you see this down here?*

Shockingly, more than a few Mollie dolls occupied the shelves. Their plump little arms reached out toward the yellowish light, offering embraces that were not returned. This had to be the result of an error. No Winner would intentionally treat Mollie so callously. It was all Jackie could do not to jump out of the cart and grab all the dolls off the shelves. But she had nowhere to put them. She would come back tomorrow, she decided, and note which families had discarded, or rather stored, their Mollies. She would have her assistant call them and offer to bring them back up.

Jackie pulled her jacket up around her neck and pushed her earplugs in farther. She forced herself to remember why she'd come here in the first place. As mayor, she was responsible for her people's safety, which also meant their integrity. Christmastown's legitimate residents had literally given their all to live here. The interloper in the forest might have intended no harm, but any intruder represented an attack on the Winners' good faith and hard work. Jackie had sworn to keep Christmastown's promise to its chosen people—that their citizenship meant something. This was not like other places, where just anyone could live. One *earned* one's home here. If the Winners doubted that promise, Christmastown was history.

And Jackie? She would crumble with the city.

The bright lights overhead created deep shadows. Jammed together on the shelves, things morphed obscenely into other things. Was that a stuffed tiger looking down at them or a human face? Was that motion some battery-powered device winding down or a hand closing around a weapon? Was that guy way up on the ladder a real Facility worker? A hundred monsters could be perched on the high shelves, planning an invasion. Plus, with all the noise, you could set off ten bombs in here and no one would even hear them.

The commissioner leaned toward Jackie and shouted, "I think of this Facility as Christmastown's foundation. Without this, you know, the town wouldn't exist. This stuff—I mean these gifts—is the reason we're all here."

Jackie shuddered. The Facility was chaos, draped in a feeble mesh of order. And what about earthquakes? What if the water pipes above them burst? The Facility could swallow the dome, and everybody under it, in a heartbeat. All these gifts wouldn't keep the town afloat. And why should they? The gifts, bearing the love of thousands of Givers, had been forgotten.

The police chief turned around from his front seat. "I agree with Commissioner. And it's because of you, Madame Mayor. All this is because of CED and you."

It took Jackie a minute to realize that the chief was not accusing but thanking her. Like the commissioner, he watched the passing cacophony with a smile on his face.

At last, mercifully, the self-guided tour ended. The travelers emerged from the elevator into blue sparkling Christmastown.

"I want cameras at all intersections down there," Jackie said. "And twenty-four-hour security patrols in the aisles."

"The police will all have to do double shifts," the chief said. "And we'll have to bring in more, um, nonresident workers. Otherwise we won't have the manpower."

"Do it," said Jackie. "Screen the you-know-what out of those guest workers."

The head of engineering, whose name was Yuri, worked in an office above a candy shop on the corner of Commerce and Prosperity Streets. As Jackie spoke with him, the heads of geraniums bobbed in the window box outside. She recalled, vaguely, that the flowers were supposed to be pansies.

"The dome's not picking up enough activity," she said. "It's my understanding that it was designed to be more sensitive."

The slight flexing of Yuri's waxed mustache showed that he was ruminating.

"Well?" said Jackie.

"Design and execution are two different things, Madame Mayor," said Yuri. "Some of the systems remain in the prototype stage. For instance, motion detectors, both inside and outside buildings. We could turn them on, but—"

"Great. What else do we have?"

"We can increase the sensitivity of the microphones," he said. Jackie waited. "And enable infrared detection, which would pick up heat. However, apart from the concerns for people's privacy and a certain unknown radiation risk . . ."

"Yes?"

"In our tests these systems have proven difficult to calibrate. As of now, anything that gives off any heat and moves in any way will be recorded. So will nearly every sound. Cats meowing, trees rustling, sleepers groaning in their beds. Cars, telephones, TVs. There will be a flood of data. The poor dome will not know what is significant and what is not. It will take a tremendous amount of power to calibrate and cross-reference the information. In the meantime, literally everything that happens will appear meaningful."

"Do it," Jackie said. "We don't know what we're dealing with at this point, so we must have as much information as possible. By the way," she added, as Yuri reluctantly wrote down her last order and underlined it, "let's not mention this to anyone who doesn't need to know. We don't want folks to get paranoid."

Jackie had the forest razed. At least those trees wouldn't confuse the dome with their rustling. Besides, the place had been a security nightmare from the get-go.

The death of the forest finally brought Harry back to Christmastown. He marched into Jackie's office unannounced, dragging his impressively compact rolling suitcase—his black box.

Jackie threw her arms around him and wept.

"Harry. Thank God. I've missed you so much."

Harry, she couldn't help noticing, had not let go of his suitcase. With his free hand, he patted her on the back, as one would a tolerated relative.

"I'm not staying long. Shall we?" He gestured toward the conference table. Evidently he did not mean to "take" her on top of it.

Jackie sat across from him and folded her hands in her lap. Harry removed two manila envelopes from a pocket in his suitcase and set them significantly to one side. He formed a pyramid with his fingertips.

Jackie remembered when she'd first met Harry, his quiet smile as Melvin excoriated her. This time he did not smile.

"You cut down my forest," he said.

"I told you on the phone. I came across an undocumented, uh, person."

"So?"

"Harry, this is not the usual guest-worker problem. This was a very weird individual."

"Did he say something? Point a gun at you? What was he doing?"

"Sleeping."

"Jesus Christ, Jackie. That is literally the least threatening behavior in the world. What is wrong with you?"

"What's wrong with me? I am trying to protect this town. I am trying to keep it intact while you are out gallivanting all over creation."

"Is that what you think I've been doing?"

"I have no idea. All I know is you're never here. It's like you don't even care about Christmastown anymore. Now that it actually exists, you're on to the next thing. You've forgotten us."

By way of response, Harry opened the first envelope and handed over a stack of printed spreadsheets. "I assume you're familiar with CarlsMart's current financial picture."

"I am," said Jackie with a shrug. Her familiarity was not of an intimate nature.

"As you may recall, CarlsMart, along with every other business in the country, took a major stock-market hit last fall. That means Christmastown took a major hit, too, just as everyone was moving in. While many other businesses are now recovering, we are still in a hole. We spent a ton on security for the move-in. Since then, those expenditures have only risen."

Harry tapped a manicured fingernail on a column, which Jackie pretended to look at. "And in the past week," he said, turning a page, "they have gone through the roof." The new page showed a full column of numbers in bold font, all with minus signs in front of them.

"I believe in sparing no expense when Christmastown itself is at stake," Jackie said.

"Christmastown will indeed fail, Jackie, if you continue to spend it into the ground. The logging crew alone cost a quarter million. And they did a crappy job. Secondly, there is the matter of the dome itself. Yuri tells me it is not built to provide the level of ongoing surveillance that you are asking of it."

"You've been talking to Yuri?"

"I'm his boss."

"Since when? I'm the mayor."

"Now hear me. I want you to scale back on the security. Take the dome back to its normal level of activity, and get rid of those helicopters and the extra patrols. The citizens are getting nervous. A couple stopped me on my way into the building just now and wanted to know if there had been a communist infiltration. I'm counting on you to restore the people's confidence and get our stock price back up. Understand?"

"Sure," said Jackie. She'd decide whether or not to obey him later.

Harry's face relaxed, and for a moment Jackie saw the calm, handsome, loving man she had longed for all these months.

"What's in the other envelope?" she said, by way of reconciliation.

Harry glanced at it, then at his watch.

"I think we've had enough for one day," he said, "Let's take this up again in the morning. I'll call you." Harry slid the envelope back into his suitcase.

She stood, hoping for a hug. She didn't get one.

"Harry," she said, following him to the door, "when are you going to move into your house in Christmastown?"

A flicker of regret crossed Harry's face—or maybe she imagined it.

"I don't have a house in Christmastown," he said.

PART SIX: CHRISTMASTOWN LOST

CHAPTER SIXTEEN

From the window of his private jet, Harry Ricker looked down on Christmastown. The dome was clear today. He could see inklings of the town inside, although the Miribilium distorted the view. His city looked like a bowl of tiny colorful fish. Jackie was in there, still waiting for the phone call he'd promised her yesterday.

After a restless night in his Pasadena mansion, the home he loved because it made him sad and lonely, he could not bring himself to tell Jackie what was in the other envelope: photographs of Mollie's replacement. He thought she had understood from the beginning that the Christmas Spirit was not a permanent position. Innocence tarnished; Ricker had seen it and seen it. Mollie's decline had begun right on schedule, what with the blowup in Canada and those scowls during her live broadcasts. Even the Winners had begun to weary of her. The fact that they dressed their Mollie dolls up as other people or animals plainly indicated that they wanted someone else.

After traveling the country for months, Ricker had found that someone else: Jessie, a baby girl who had fallen down a well and been brought up three days later, unscathed. Mollie was pretty and she had a way with words. But Jessie was miraculous. People demanded nothing less than miracles these days.

He would tell Jackie after his trip to Minnesota, where he was going to sign the papers with Jessie's family. This time the contract spelled out

179

the terms explicitly. Two years maximum, with a possibility—though an unlikely one—of renewal.

The question now was what to do about Jackie herself. Ricker had fired thousands of people in his lifetime, including people he had slept with. But never anyone he had loved. He figured he loved Jackie, because the idea of firing her devastated him. She wouldn't forgive him for that, even on the off chance she got over the Jessie business. She had taken to government like Carl once took to his race car, with a deep and dangerous passion. And she trusted him—even now, unaware that he had already betrayed her. But left to their own devices, she and Mollie would destroy Christmastown.

Ricker felt a powerful urge to let it all go. He was getting too old to fight the combined forces of Jackie, nature, and the free market. Why not retire, pick a nice house in Christmastown, and golf amid the robot sheep? Tolerate the regime's modest encroachments on his liberty—after all, he was not the sort of person the system sought to root out. And if Jackie spent Christmastown into the ground or drove its citizens mad with paranoia, so what? Utopian schemes (Synanon, the USSR) failed all the time. Perhaps human beings were not designed to live in harmony, but to relentlessly thwart any plans laid out for them by men or gods. Besides, he would have a golden parachute no matter what.

Speaking of parachutes.

Ricker's previous skydiving trip had nearly killed him. But it had also reset his mind, altering the equation of his life forever. And so, instead of taking him to Minnesota, Ricker told his pilot to turn around and head toward Paradise.

Ricker leaned back in his seat and clasped his hands behind his head. In just a few hours, he would see the world entirely differently. He couldn't wait to strap on a parachute and climb into that rickety old DC-9.

PARADISE
A minor epic
by J. M. "Topper" Moss

Of Harry Ricker's last day in the sky,
His vanishing from life—or his rebirth,
Sing, Muse.

Say first how Ricker opened the plane's door
As he had that fateful time before,
And looked down on the town of Paradise
Unfurling toward the pasture where he'd land.
Beyond it lay the cinder fields, blue lakes,
And snow-streaked mountain peaks of Lassen Park.
The engines roared. He took a breath and leapt
Into nothingness. Then suddenly,
He thought that he should pray. He hadn't prayed
Since he was a boy, but it might be
A way to link himself to Jackie, to see
Life as she saw it: as God's creation.
Oh, Lord, I throw myself upon your mercy.
I ask you to catch me by my ripcord,
And set me gently standing on your Earth.
He pulled the cord.
He heard the pleasant thunder
As the chute deployed, and his fall slowed.
Thank you, he said to God. *And now perhaps*
You could tell me what I ought to do
About the woman I once loved, and may
Love still. In truth I don't know what love means.
Do I owe her? What do I owe? Does she
Not have enough now, more than she could want?
Could you help her understand the market
So she will know why all things have to change?
He drifted past a cinder cone and saw
The reddish ring around the crater's rim.
That placid peak is going to blow again,
He thought; *that lake nearby is going to boil*
Someday. But not today. Not in my time.
And then he noticed he was going up.
It seemed a wind, a river of air,
Had taken him. Just then he passed through
A small cloud like a spider web, which broke.
The air, he noticed, had gone thin and cold,

Yet he still breathed, not struggling at all.
He felt no concern, just mild interest
In his predicament. A plane screamed by.
He saw astonished faces in the windows,
And he waved. He thought of Carl, his son,
As he flew higher, never to be seen
Again by the eyes of mortal men.

"He'll turn up," Jackie said to reporters, to Givers, to anyone who asked during those first few weeks of Ricker's absence. Wagging her finger dramatically, she explained, "Harry's a very resourceful man and also a mysterious one. He's going to surprise us all with the brilliant new idea he's working on. The skydiving was a ruse so he could sneak off to hatch his plans in secret. He's in a cabin somewhere up in the mountains, or even in a cave. Probably meditating." People laughed knowingly, although they didn't know Harry Ricker from Adam.

Kyle watched Jackie from the game room after that day's batch of reporters had left. She moved jerkily, as if in an old movie with some frames missing. Her shoulders slumped. She sat at the foot of the marble staircase and palmed her forehead. Caridad approached, holding Mollie, and Jackie waved them both away. She held her knees and rocked from side to side.

Kyle's beer tasted loathsome. He held a mouthful, wishing he could spit it out. Instead, he forced it down. Let that be his last experience of alcohol forever.

Jackie checked her messages again and put the phone down. She bit her lip and paced. Kyle came up behind her. When he placed his hands on her shoulders, she jumped.

"What are you doing, Kyle?" she asked as he gathered her into his arms.

They sat on the couch in the game room. Jackie rested her head on Kyle's shoulder. He put his arm around her and held her close. The tabletop *Ms. Pac-Man/Galaga* game burbled in the background as Topper Moss, now nothing more than a phantom himself, pursued his impossible goal.

This hour we meet Myra Waltz Gander of the Northwest Sasquatch Information Center. Myra believes her husband,

Everill, was murdered by a Sasquatch nearly twenty years ago.

The center used to be a boarding house for loggers, which Myra ran, just like her mother before her. Upstairs, the rooms remain exactly as they were when each boarder left them, in a hurry, for the last time. Beds are unmade, the impressions of young sleeping loggers still in them. Their forms have filled in with dust.

The common room now houses the center's library and exhibits.

"These are needles that fell off that tree when the Sasquatch howled." Myra removed an envelope from a glass case and shook the needles gently into her palm.

"Here's some footprint casts I made. I took them just outside the house by the kitchen window. Every three or four months there are some fresh ones. Sometimes I leave food out for him, some fish, some pie sometimes. It all gets eaten."

"You say 'him.' Does that mean you think there's only one?"

"That's the conclusion I have come to."

"How can that be? There are Bigfoot sightings all over the world."

"There are also many hoaxers in this world, Topper. But that's not a bad thing. I believe the Sasquatch knows about them, and they please him. They make him feel less lonely. Because these hoaxes show him that other people really want to be like him—to *be* him even. He wishes they could, too. Imagine being the only one of your kind."

"Forgive me, but . . . your concern for Bigfoot surprises me. Didn't he kill your husband?"

"Killed and ate him. Even ate his bones. He left no trace."

"I'd think you'd want revenge for that."

"At first I did. Every day I went into the woods with a rifle and a crossbow and a hunting knife long as your arm. I offered a bounty for the Sasquatch's head, until the sheriff told me I couldn't do that. I begged the boarders to come out with me at night and look. I stopped making their beds and cooking for them. I barely ate anything myself—just scooped stuff out of cans when I thought of it and left them out on the counter. So the boys all left. I can't say I blame them.

"But over time I got to thinking: everybody has to eat. We are creatures of this world, all of us, and we eat each other. Humans, animals, plants. That's how it is. So what's the point of being angry?"

Topper laid his head on Myra's enormous dining room table and burst into sobs.

"Now that," said Kyle, "is what I call forgiveness."

Jackie burrowed her face into Kyle's chest. Kyle wished he had changed his T-shirt, this week of all weeks. Just like you didn't want to be found in dirty underwear if you got hit by a bus, you also should always be prepared for your wife to cry on you—even about another man.

Kyle didn't quite allow himself to hope that Harry's disappearance was permanent. But he had begun to think that things might finally change. Even in Christmastown.

"We could leave, you know," Kyle said to Jackie as her warm tears soaked his shirt. "Mollie's older, and she's getting restless. I know you've seen it. Everyone has. Maybe this is a good time to, you know, try something else." He braced himself for a rebuke. *You don't understand. You've never understood. Why would you want to leave the most wonderful place on earth?*

Instead, Jackie cried harder. "I wish we could," she said. "Some days I want nothing more than to go back to that little bungalow, you know? We could just raise our kids and work and eat and go to church. Or not go—I don't even care about that anymore. We could just be normal and happy, like we used to be."

Perhaps if Kyle's jaw hadn't dropped open and stayed that way for several seconds—if he'd been able to form words right then instead of gaping in astonishment—he might have convinced Jackie to act upon this desire. It would have been so simple. They could take Mollie and go this minute. They could leave all this crap behind—the steam shower, the game room, Mollie's gazillion unopened presents. They didn't need any of it. And the bungalow, he happened to know, had not yet sold.

"But we can't," Jackie said, sitting up and blowing her nose. "Otherwise Christmastown will fall apart."

"So what if it does? It's not even a real place. It has no history. Is there even a cemetery? The whole town is completely artificial. People won't miss it, believe me. They'll just move on."

"That's not true, Kyle. This place is all about faith. In America. In our basic, common goodness. And in me. As mayor, I represent this place, maybe even more than Mollie does. Don't you see? If I run away, I'm stomping all over people's faith."

Whether this was a delusion of grandeur, or a deeply humbling willingness to give one's all for others, Kyle could not say. He only knew he loved his wife. And that, if he wanted to get Mollie out of Christmastown, he'd have to do it without Jackie.

CHAPTER SEVENTEEN

In May, one month after Harry's disappearance, Jackie met with CarlsMart's legal team in her office. The meeting concerned the future of the corporation in light of the CEO's protracted absence.

Jackie had long had the distinct impression that she was second in command of CarlsMart LLC. But the attorneys informed her of a wrinkle she had not counted on—Harry's ex-wife. Some time ago, Susan had reinvented herself on the heels of grievous loss by starting the hugely successful, if relatively unknown, CarlsBad Holdings. It now emerged that she and Harry had been "in talks" over the past several months on the subject of CarlsMart's financial future. Harry's disappearance had then triggered some obscure clause or other, and CarlsBad had snapped up CarlsMart for a song.

Jackie gathered that the governance of Christmastown under CarlsBad was to change. Mollie's role was also being tampered with. Mention had been made of an infant by the name of Jessie. Was she to become Mollie's sidekick? It was all very murky.

"I will speak to this Susan in person," Jackie told the lawyers. This Susan had to realize that Jackie was not just going to hand the whole shebang over to her vulture company. Jackie intended to go down fighting for Christmastown.

As the lawyers left, she stood at the window, gazing out over her city. Through the pyramid's green glass, downtown bustled with Winners as always. The residential section crawled with landscapers and parents and/ or nannies pushing strollers. In the Green Space, golfers golfed, sheep animatronically grazed. As mentioned, the forest had been cleared away, if indeed more haphazardly than Jackie would have liked. It was hard to get skilled logging contractors on short notice, especially in the desert. The slash piles, jagged stumps, and heaps of dead vegetation remained eyesores. But fixing all this meant more money, which obviously presented a problem right now. Someday, Jackie wanted to replace the forest with a water park.

Meanwhile, no more strange, leafy ape-men had shown up in Christmastown. As the only witness to that one appearance, occasionally Jackie wondered if she had imagined the whole thing. However, it was more likely that the increased security had scared off any other would-be invaders. Corroborating that theory, arrests of guest workers with altered ID cards had gone down. The workers now entered and left the city limits in full accordance with the law. When they knew someone was watching them, people behaved.

Which was why Jackie had decided not to follow Harry's orders. Now more than ever, Christmastown was her city. With Harry gone, she alone was responsible for its well-being. She had kept the dome's security systems running full throttle, and if it emitted some odd noise or other once in a while, nobody cared because the noise meant they were safer than ever before.

"All is well," Jackie whispered to the city. For the first time in as long as she could remember, she believed her words. She pushed the button on her intercom. It was time to draft her counterproposal to Susan.

As she waited for her assistant to arrive, a greenish light suddenly burned through the sky's blue canopy. The light was about the size of the planet Venus, but much brighter, plus Venus didn't come on until evening, and it was two o'clock in the afternoon. On the streets, shoppers paused to look up at the spot. Multicolored rays spread outward from the bright center, glistening like the fibers of Jackie's bedroom carpet. The green shape rippled as it spread.

Jackie dialed the police chief.

"Do you see this?"

"We do," the chief answered. "It's beautiful."

It was beautiful. And of course the police chief wouldn't know what this thing was. Jackie's assistant, now standing beside her at the window, gawked like a mental patient.

"Get me Yuri," Jackie told her.

The circle had grown to at least five times the diameter of the sun, pulsing gently, as if someone were pushing a fingertip into the dome from above. Then, just as Yuri answered the phone, the circle collapsed back into a point and vanished.

"What in the holy H was that?" Jackie shouted into the phone.

"We don't know for certain, Madame Mayor," said Yuri. "It looks like some circuits overloaded." Yuri's Russian accent, tinged with Swiss German, reminded Jackie that he had been the original designer of Scimitarium, the coffin in which Carl had burned.

"Is the dome on fire?" she asked.

"Miribilium does not burn. There is no sign of fire or heat on these readouts. I will run a debugging script."

Jackie called a press conference in front of City Hall. With the elaborately mustached Yuri by her side, she announced that the city was safe.

"It was just a minor software problem, which is being repaired as we speak," she explained. "There is no cause for alarm." Yuri whispered in her ear. "Think of it," Jackie repeated, "as our own aurora borealis."

But the debugging seemed to make things worse. The next morning, three more auroras appeared in rapid succession. People stood outside their homes, looking alternately skyward and at each other. *Beautiful day*, they said to each other. *Isn't it?* They went to work and stared uncomprehendingly at merchandise or papers, drifting casually over to the window to check the sky. No one wanted to be the first to panic.

An hour of apparent normalcy went by. Then, just before noon, the entire dome erupted into color, as if blanketed by a huge, pulsating tie-dye T-shirt. Christmastown became a sort of lurid discotheque as the dome's faint hum, which had burrowed so deeply into residents' brains that they had come to register it as pure silence, grew louder, edged with a sharp, electric whine.

Jackie was already in Yuri's office, having arrived after aurora number two. "Yuri," she said as calmly as possible. The flesh of her arms reflected the mutating colors of the sky—turquoise, purple, green. She thought, for a moment, of Hunter. "Do you call this debugging?"

Yuri clattered away at his terminal. "It is as I suspected. The dome has been dealing with too much undifferentiated information. She is having a little nervous breakdown."

"Can you stop it?"

"I will need to reboot the system."

"What does that mean?"

"Like a gentle conk on the head. The dome forgets all her problems." Yuri knocked his own skull lightly with his knuckles and smiled. "But I can do nothing here." He reached into his desk and removed a pair of orange earplugs. "I must go down to the server farm."

Jackie called another press conference. This time she stood alone. Rather belatedly, she suspected that this did not inspire confidence. The crowd of reporters was smaller, and they kept glancing up at the dome as she spoke.

"Our engineers are rebooting the system," Jackie told them. "It will just take a little time."

"How long?" "What will happen during the reboot?" "How will you know that the dome is fixed?"

"Please be patient," Jackie said, because she didn't know the answers to any of these questions.

A woman came running up Commerce Street toward the podium.

"They're sucking the air out of the dome!" she screamed. "Can't you hear it? That hum? The air's thinner already. I can't breathe. We're all going to die!"

"That's ridiculous," Jackie shouted into her microphone. "Why would we even want to do that, anyway?"

The woman raced on. "Run!" she screamed, rounding the corner onto the multipurpose trail. "Get out before it's too late!"

It was Shelly Thayer, whom Jackie had finally allowed into Christmastown on a special mayoral dispensation. At the time, it had felt like the right thing to do, especially because Shelly had brought no family with her. She lived alone in a pale-blue house near a bend in the river. Jackie hadn't recognized her without makeup and genuinely frightened for her life.

"Ridiculous," said Jackie, turning back to the reporters. But all except one of them had fled, and the one who remained was loosening his collar and gasping.

Jackie jumped into her BMW and floored it back to her house. She burst into the home studio, where Mollie was bestowing a noontime benediction to CEDN's dwindling viewership. In light of Christmastown's financial woes, she now had to encourage Givers across the land to step up their game even further. *Double Your Giving, Double Your Loving* was the campaign Jackie had hastily concocted. Mollie's sorrowful expression suggested she felt the Givers were paying for someone else's mistakes. As was Mollie.

"Now's the best time ever to be a Giver," the poor girl murmured as the director made "bigger" motions with his arms.

Jackie snatched Mollie out of her chair and grabbed her mic. Mollie began whimpering.

"Citizens of Christmastown, do not panic. The dome can't burn. And there's plenty of air for one and all. Pay no attention to the rumors. This is a software problem only. Please remain calm."

The director screamed and ran out the door, right past the camera. Framed in a close-up, Jackie kissed and held her sobbing daughter.

By afternoon, steady streams of vehicles headed for the gates of Christmastown. Some residents, following Shelly's advice, fled on foot, carrying their children. Guest workers dropped their landscaping tools and piled into their trucks.

Jackie tried to personally halt the exodus from her own street. Cars shot past, regretful faces watching her through rolled-up windows. Barreling toward her came Pastor Mike's minivan. Jackie stepped into the street and waved him down.

"Pastor Mike, please. Don't go."

In the van, Mike's wife and five children huddled, pale and terrified. In the back sat Esther, holding hands with her two sisters. Esther had once saved Jackie, and Jackie had gratefully returned that act of love by showing her the path to Christmastown. Now Jackie needed her and Mike to help her again. If only she had gone to Mike's new church in Christmastown, at least once, expressing this need wouldn't have felt so awkward.

"Please don't go. This will all be over as soon as the reboot is finished," Jackie said to them. "As religious leaders of this community, please stay and reassure everyone."

"Jackie, it's the Rapture!" Esther shouted. "The time has come! Those aren't auroras! They're the Lord's eyes looking down on us!"

"His eyes, my hinder!" Pastor Mike said. "Those are his fingertips. He's reaching for us, but he can't get through the dome!"

"Come with us, Jackie!" Esther said. "We have to get outside so he can take us!"

"That's ridiculous," Jackie said, for the third time today. "How could he not get through the dome?"

She thought of Harry, who had disappeared while sailing through the sky. Had he been taken early, as a sign of things to come? He had not been the same sort of Christian as Pastor Mike and Esther and (maybe) Jackie. In fact he could not properly be called a Christian at all. But he was a good man. He had meant well, although, like everyone, he had made mistakes. He had dreamed. He had loved his son.

And the wind carried him away.

Pastor Mike reddened with anger. "The dome is the work of Satan. I should have known. Man has overreached again with his technology, just like with the space shuttle. This city is the idol, the false god! The wheat and chaff are separating. Get in the car, Jackie, while there's still a chance!"

Jackie glanced down the street. Some of her neighbors hadn't left yet. They stood on their front lawns, watching her for signs of what to do.

"Nothing is happening," Jackie said firmly.

"Suit yourself," said Pastor Mike. "May God bless you." He stomped on the accelerator. Esther, with both hands clamped over her mouth, watched Jackie wave a weak good-bye. As the van screeched around the curve, Esther closed her eyes in prayer.

Two turquoise auroras burst together overhead, and four new ones formed in their wake. They overlapped like irregular Venn diagrams, the intersections shimmering with interference patterns. This was something new. Was this the reboot? How long was that going to take, anyway?

Jackie ran back inside and found Kyle looking out the window of the game room, holding Mollie in his arms. Mollie fussed, but not excessively.

Kyle was really not that bad with her. She'd been meaning to tell him that. She'd also wanted to say that he smelled much better lately—not like beer and an old T-shirt, but like soap.

"Where's Caridad?" Jackie asked.

"She left. She said to tell you she was sorry, but she has her own children to think of."

Then Jackie observed the duffel bag on the floor beside Kyle. It was the one she'd bought him so he could go on tour, with the Thank You Coupon still stuck to the side. Next to it was one of Mollie's pink princess suitcases.

"I'm leaving, too," said Kyle. "And I'm taking Mollie. At least until this whole thing blows over."

"Nothing's happening," Jackie shouted. "The dome's not burning, no air is being sucked out of the city. All those lights and colors and that buzzing sound . . . they're not *real*. They're like the fireworks we have on holidays. Or our sun. The dome is a giant TV, Kyle. You, of all people, should understand that. The auroras are like a channel we can't tune in. Just scrambled signals."

"I mean, I'm leaving until this—whole—thing blows over." Kyle waved his free arm around the room, taking in Jackie, the ceiling, Mollie, whatever stood in its path. "CED. Giving. Winning. Domes and dolls and Quality of Life, the Green Space, and that giant fucking pyramid downtown. And you, Jackie. You need to blow over."

"You're just like the others. You won't believe me about the dome."

"Why should I believe you?"

From his expression, it was obvious Kyle hadn't meant to bring up Harry. But it was too late. So this was his true motive. Vengeance.

"I thought you said you forgave me." Jackie remembered how she'd laid her head on Kyle's chest, his heart pounding as that wild-haired woman on *The Weird Frontier* talked about . . . cannibalism.

"I do forgive you," Kyle said. "But I am also leaving you. At least for now. Mollie needs a break. This place is insane, Jackie. And Mollie's just a kid, for Christ's sake."

Where had Jackie heard that line before? From the Canadian doctor. And Harry. And, especially lately, her own conscience. Oh, Lord, what had she done to her own daughter?

Kyle was right. Mollie wasn't safe here. But not because of the dome.

Jackie had always thought Kyle didn't understand Mollie. She'd wanted to shield her from his doubts so she could carry out her special mission. That was why she'd hired Caridad to look after her—so she'd always be in the hands of a true believer. But as it turned out, Mollie needed Kyle's doubts most of all.

Kyle picked up his duffel bag and tucked Mollie's case under his arm. Mollie began to wail.

"We'll be at Enrique's," he said as he carried their baby out the door.

"I'm sorry," Jackie shouted after him. "I'm sorry about Harry. And Katie. And Mollie. Oh, Mollie, I'm so sorry!"

Mollie's shrieks pierced the walls of the van as it pulled out of the driveway.

"Get Carl out of the Facility!" Jackie yelled after them.

CHAPTER EIGHTEEN

After tucking Mollie into a smallish crib, which the Avilas had hastily borrowed from the neighbors, Kyle settled down on the couch and wrapped the sheet over the top of his head. He hadn't done that since he was a boy. Well, wasn't he a boy? What kind of man left his wife to burn to death in a fiery globe? Not a man, or a boy either, but a monster.

On the other hand, this was Jackie's chance for martyrdom. All her life she had wanted to be better than everyone else, a holy symbol of faith and sacrifice who made everybody else feel like shit. And what had that gotten her?

OK, so maybe Kyle did want a little revenge. Nothing extreme—just some sort of painless but memorable comeuppance. Not death in a fiery and/or airless globe. Of course Kyle didn't actually think anything like that would happen. Or did he?

What did Jackie mean when she said the auroras weren't real? TV wasn't real, but it had effects in the real world. People responded to stories and images. To myths, like Topper had said. But maybe the auroras really meant nothing; they were just scrambled signals, the harmless babblings of an overwrought system. The reboot might already have fixed it.

Untangling himself from the sheet, he got up and turned on the TV. With the sound off, he flipped through the channels. There was no breaking news about Christmastown—no fires, no meltdowns, no arrests of top officials. Jackie, evidently, was keeping it together.

Kyle turned to *The Weird Frontier* channel. But Topper was gone. His show was gone. The screen showed nothing but a log burning in a fireplace.

The next morning, to take his mind off Christmastown, Kyle offered to take Enrique and his father, older sister, and grandmother to the aquarium in Los Angeles. He called Katie at Stick's to see if they wanted to go, too, but got the machine again. He found it odd that the greeting still did not mention Katie's name. But that was too much to ask of Stick's grandfather, who was probably mystified by the device. Kyle left the Avilas' number with the true-enough explanation that he and Mollie were "visiting" Enrique while the dome was undergoing repairs.

In the carport of the apartment complex, the family gathered around the van. Hearing the commotion, neighbors came out to join them. They ran their fingers over the curves of the kelp fronds and called each other over to examine the details up close. Some took pictures of Enrique with the van. Kyle couldn't understand a word anyone said, but the women kept hugging and kissing Enrique, and the men repeatedly shook his hand and ruffled his overgrown crew cut.

Kyle allowed himself a rueful grin. In all these months, Enrique's family had never seen the van. It had never occurred to Kyle that they might want to, and Enrique had never asked.

The first thing Kyle did at the aquarium was buy a baseball cap for Mollie—navy blue and large with an ugly fanged fish embroidered on it. He pulled the cap down over her curls. Then he warily pushed her stroller into the lobby.

No one seemed to recognize her. Some people with similar-aged kids smiled at her and then at Kyle in parental solidarity. If they knew, Kyle thought, what a crummy parent I really am. But he was relieved. It wasn't just the hat that concealed Mollie's identity. Without her normal trappings—the celebrities, The Wall of Men, the CED and CarlsMart logos hovering in the background—she could pass for an ordinary kid.

Enrique's father, Roberto, who went by "Bob," was under the weather. Kyle lent him his cane to lean on as they peered into the aquarium's giant central tank. Enrique sketched furiously while his sister, Lupita, translated the wall text for their dad and his mother: leopard shark, starfish, rockfish, sheepshead. That last one made the old lady laugh out loud.

Kyle lifted Mollie up to the glass. She cocked her head and pushed her cap back from her face and smiled. She was examining her own reflection, not the fish. Naturally. She had spent her whole life being looked at. She didn't know how to be a spectator.

"Honey, look through the glass, not at it," Kyle told her.

Mollie leaned in.

"Those are fish," Kyle told her. "That one's a shark."

"*Tiburón*," Lupita said to her.

At the sea horse exhibit, they watched two creatures that looked like exotic plants, complete with multicolored, fan-like leaves, engaged in what could only be called a ballet.

"That's what I was talking about, Mr. M," said Enrique, tugging his sleeve. "They mate for life."

Kyle sighed. Animals, even bizarre-looking ones, were better than people. He bounced Mollie in his arms.

Did he want to leave Jackie for good? Did he want to get divorced and make a go of it somewhere else? In Morton? LA? Vegas? Did he want to fight her for custody of the girls, so that Mollie would once again become a football that people—this time, her own parents—practically killed each other to get hold of? And what would he do for a living? Impressions?

He wanted a drink. He wondered if the aquarium's restaurant served alcohol. He had been off the stuff, again, for two weeks. Two weeks, up against about twenty-five years of drinking history—Vegas history, Morton history, history.

Mollie pressed her hands against the glass and stared up at the sea horses.

"I want to live there," she said, pointing.

"They're pretty, huh?" said Enrique.

"Little girls can't live in fish tanks," Kyle said. He wanted to make that very clear to her.

"I can. I'm a mermaid."

"No, you are a human. Mollie, look at me. You are a human being."

Mollie gazed at him with the mixture of warmth and pity that had so captivated the masses these past two years. Did she mean it? Or was this just a trained reflex? The same could be asked of anything Mollie said or did.

Christmastown had done this, Kyle thought. It had turned his daughter into a freak. The town was a poisonous jellyfish slowly digesting the few remaining people trapped in its gut. He had never realized how much he hated it until this moment.

"What do mermaids eat, Mollie?" said Lupita.

"French fries."

"Now you're talking," said Lupita. "Maybe it's time for lunch," she said to Kyle.

"You all go," he said. "I'll catch up with you."

Lupita held Mollie's hand, and they walked off with Bob and his mother. Kyle had hardly ever seen Mollie walk. She was always being held, passed from one embrace to the next. On the rare occasion when she'd found her way to the floor and started crawling, or pulled herself up by the edge of a coffee table, someone, usually Jackie, immediately snatched her up to cart her off to her next obligation. Somehow she had learned to walk anyway.

Kyle put his face in his hands.

"Mr. M, what's wrong?"

They sat down on the bench.

"E," Kyle said, "you are one fortunate SOB. I know your family's life isn't easy . . ." Kyle thought of Enrique's mother, working her fourth shift in two days at the nursing home. "But you're all together. You love each other, and you support each other. Your parents work so hard and never complain. They are the real American dream; that's why they knew CED was bullshit from the beginning. They *believe*, you know what I mean? I gotta say, E, I really envy you."

Enrique listened with undisguised amazement.

"Mr. M."

"Kyle, please."

"No offense, Kyle, but you have no idea how much it sucks to be me. I've been getting my ass kicked at school every day since I was five. They call me Paco and Tubby Gonzalez. The football players steal my sketchbooks and tear the pages out and pinch my boobs, and in spite of all that, there's a better-than-even chance that I'm attracted to a certain quarterback. Meanwhile my dad has been coughing for two months. He used to work as a grape picker, and they sprayed the fields with crop dusters while the pickers were out there. But he can't go to the doctor because . . . because . . . they can't risk it."

Kyle understood. He sank against the wall. "You never told me any of that."

"You didn't ask."

"I'm sorry."

"It's OK. Working on your van kind of helped me forget things. In fact, I wish," Enrique started picking at his pinky, "that you would drive it around more. As an advertisement, like. I could make some cards, and if anyone asks who did your van, you could tell them."

"You got it," Kyle said.

That was something he could do, wasn't it? He could drive.

CHAPTER NINETEEN

About an hour after Kyle left Christmastown, the auroras stopped. Rather, they did not so much stop as fade, resembling at first a collection of bursting soap bubbles, then the faint skeletal outlines of some fossil coral. By about eight p.m., the dome had turned a solid midlevel gray—exactly like Melvin's glasses, or the sky on any foggy winter day in Morton.

Yuri called to tell Jackie all was well. "She is resting now," he said of the dome. "We will examine her for a few days, and then start her up again slowly. Of course we can't push her to her former limits, as I'm sure you understand. But soon we will have our beautiful days in Christmastown again."

Would anyone be there to see them?

In her backyard, Jackie stared up at the dull sky. Were those real clouds showing through the now-transparent dome? Or did the gray simply represent the dome's death, its—her—signal saying, *I am gone?*

The answer hardly mattered. Nor did the fact that Jackie had been right about the dome, and everyone who had fled had been wrong. For it would have been better to burn to death than to face this: the vast, barren plain of abandonment. Since childhood she'd grown accustomed to rejection in general. But the people she loved and trusted most on earth—Kyle, Katie, Mollie, Harry, Esther—all had now left her. And they had done so knowingly, even triumphantly. Saying, in so many words, *I'm not just leaving, Jackie. I'm leaving* you.

Had God left her, too? Where was that picture of Jesus she'd had on the bedroom wall back in Morton? She hadn't laid eyes on it after they'd moved. It was probably down in the Facility. Or even at the Salvation Army, where some other newly devout soul would find it and clasp it to her heart . . . at least for a time. *You don't need any pictures of the Lord,* Esther had said. *You'll know him when you see him.* Now Jackie knew that wasn't true. She would never see God because she did not know how to see him. She had confused her own selfish desires—for power, righteousness, glory, unmistakable and unconditional love—with his will. Her ignorance had destroyed not only her family, but a whole city.

She stepped out of her shoes and slipped into the deep end of the pool. She floated on her back. Her blouse and skirt billowed around her. Drowning, she had heard, was painless, even joyful. Wasn't there a saying, *rapture of the deep?* That made sense. Eternity would pull her down, not upward.

From the corner of her eye, she saw a figure hurrying toward her. She raised her head and then, amazed, paddled over to meet it.

"Esther?"

"Jackie, what in tarnation are you doing in there?"

Jackie hauled herself out of the pool and fell into Esther's arms, crying.

Jackie changed into her bathrobe and made tea. They drank it in Jackie's vast, empty living room.

"When we got a few miles outside the dome," Esther said, "Pastor Mike stopped the minivan. We said a prayer and waited for the Lord to take us up. But nothing happened. So then we got out of the car and stood there. The auroras were still going—we could see them in the distance. The dome looked like, I don't know, a disco ball stuck in the ground.

"So I said to Mike, 'Look. We're outside and the Lord's not taking us. Either it's not the Rapture, or . . .' And Mike says, 'We missed our chance! It's because of Jackie. She tricked us using witchcraft, in the form of luxury dwellings and consumer goods. We have been tainted. She's a minion of the Devil himself.'"

Esther paused and blushed. "I'm sure he didn't mean it," she said.

"Anyway we all started arguing. Mike and my sisters weren't ready to give up. They plunked themselves right down in the desert and prayed for forgiveness. Pretty soon evening came and the coyotes were starting to yip while heaven knows what was zipping around in the brush. But they kept on kneeling and praying. For all I know, they're still out there."

For the first time, Jackie noticed that Esther was covered in dried sweat and dust. She had walked all the way back to Christmastown.

"Why did you come back, Esther?"

"Because of you," Esther said. "I was thinking how you didn't run away with us. Even if you thought it was the Rapture, you decided to stay and help people. You put others before yourself."

"Actually," said Jackie, "I was only thinking of myself."

"Well, anyway, I like it here," Esther said. "And I want to help you. I want to help rebuild Christmastown."

"Mike may be right. Christmastown is the Devil's work."

Esther shook her head. "Not if you're involved, Jackie. It can't be."

Jackie wiped her eyes.

"Esther," she said. "I think I might have seen Jesus in the Inner Green Space."

"Now, that," Esther said, "would not surprise me one bit."

CHAPTER TWENTY

Scarecrow City
(Music by Stick Vortex [his stage name])
(Lyrics by Katie is Magic! [hers])

Did you ever notice
That all scarecrows are crucified?
I see them in the fields when I drive by,
And I say, Damn (Damn), Man (Man),
What kind of life is that
For a scarecrow?

Stuffed and mounted on the cross,
You know you are not the boss,
And the crows aren't scared of you anyway.
You see the others just like you,
Stuck in rows, mouths shut with glue.
You'll never eat the food you're here to save.

Scarecrow City,
That's where you and I gotta go.
That's where we pay for all the Man's mistakes.

So The Missing Link had a new house band, and tonight's crowd was standing room only. Word had spread about the punk-blues-metal protest band, with the lead singer with the husky voice and the skinny guitarist whose instrument sounded just like her. Together they broke your heart and blew your eardrums out.

Katie's dad sat right in front, with his pal Enrique beside him, and Mollie, of all people, on his shoulders. He looked kind of stunned. Something had gone down with Jackie, that much was obvious. Katie was only surprised it had taken this long to happen.

As usual, Stick had relayed the phone message to her at The Link, where she lived with Hunter. Kyle had called, out of the blue, saying he was in town for a few days and asking if she and Stick wanted to go to the aquarium. That was a big NO. Mainly because she really didn't like going out anymore. Outside the light was bright and harsh; the dry, toxic air abraded her skin. Humans staggered around, lobotomized by television and shopping. If a sliver of reality ever poked through their mental haze, they rushed out and bought more crap to wall off the awareness. Besides, she really didn't like to leave Hunter.

So she'd invited her dad to the show tonight instead. She figured if he was finally leaving Jackie, she could tell him the truth about her own life. They could talk about their decisions like adults.

Mollie watched her sister with great interest, smacking her dad's head in time with the music. Mollie was going to be a punk when she grew up, Katie thought with pride. She gave her a Black Power salute, which Mollie returned, then she brought the noise even harder. She wanted her dad to be sure to know that her life was working out exactly right.

After the set, Mollie sat on the bar, facing Kyle and Katie, with her feet dangling off the edge. Hunter brought Katie a beer, and Kyle raised an eyebrow at it.

"What'll you have?" Hunter asked him.

"Coffee," Kyle said.

"Good for you, man," Hunter said. "Giving up booze. You're a hero."

Kyle almost fell off his stool. "Don't say that. Don't even think it. That's so wrong."

Hunter clapped him on the shoulder. "And, uh, what for Mollie?"

"Got any juice boxes?"

"No. Got orange juice."

"Fine."

"He misses you," Katie told her dad, after Hunter had departed.

Strange, high-pitched singing came from the stage. The twins, in full Star Trek regalia, serenaded the crowd, accompanied by Stick on acoustic guitar. Enrique watched raptly from a nearby table.

"It's called filking," Katie said. "Science-fiction folk singing. They learned it at a *Star Trek* convention. When I'm not with them, the band is called The Coma Cluster. It's named after a bunch of galaxies."

Katie had long since quit struggling against the twins' aesthetic inclinations, and Stick's for that matter. In the process, she had discovered an important truth about punk. It was not about stripping everything away. It was about picking up what you found around you and making it into something new. Still, she hadn't understood why the twins stayed with the band, what with their other interests. The Missing Link was definitely not their kind of place. But, just now, she figured it out. They were looking after Stick, their little brother.

"I miss Hunter, too," said Kyle. "And I miss you."

"So what brings you back to Yokelville?"

"Didn't you hear what happened in Christmastown?"

"I don't, um, consume a lot of media these days."

"There was a glitch in the dome. A software problem. People overreacted, just like they always do, and ran off."

"You ran off, too."

"Sort of." Kyle hung his head. "I figured Mollie needed a break."

Hunter brought the coffee and the orange juice. Katie touched his hand, and their eyes stayed in contact for a long moment. Her father noticed, as she had meant him to. He leaned back on his stool and raised his eyebrows, but he said nothing. He had also not commented on her tattoo, which she had once hidden from him with a sweatband—a ring of capital Hs strung together like a fence around her wrist. Like a row of crosses. Scarecrow City.

"You know, if you and Mom want to break up, that's OK with me."

"It is, is it?" Kyle said. The shock of her directness made him laugh, though he did not look amused.

"I always thought she was too hard on you. She treated you like shit, actually. You didn't deserve it."

"I appreciate your support," said Kyle flatly.

"If I were you, I would go for it."

"But you're not me, and you don't know anything at all. Now, how about you tell me what that hideous thing is on your wrist. And how much beer you drink, and why you and Hunter look at each other in that yearning manner that I just observed."

So it was going to be the Dad act tonight after all. Katie decided not to push things by lighting a cigarette, although she really wanted one. She sipped her beer slowly.

"Hunter and I are together," she said. "It's been almost a year now. We're in love."

"That's a big mistake."

"You think Hunter's crazy, right? Well, he's not. He's just been through some intense stuff, as I'm sure you know."

She knew Kyle had no real idea. He had maybe an image of swamps and firefights, based on movies he had seen, but what really went down, Kyle could not possibly imagine. No one could, except for Hunter, and now Katie.

He told her the stories late at night, after she danced her private dance for him. Always Katie held her breath and took his words in without a sound. It was her way of assuring him she knew the stories were for her alone; she was to keep them safe inside her.

The stories were hard to hear. They tore down her throat into her stomach. But she needed them. She didn't know how she'd ever lived without knowing what humans were truly capable of—the worst, and also the best. Because Hunter had vowed never to hurt anyone again. That was why he never went outside, why he had her tie him up at night. Why he listened night after night to other people's sob stories, the same crap over and over, like a therapist who only charged the price of a few drinks. These burdens were Hunter's penance. Also his shield against the cruelty that he feared could well up again in him at any minute. He did not even eat meat, which was why he couldn't eat the mac and cheese with ham Katie's mom had once tried to bring him. That was kind of a funny story.

"He's my age, Katie, which is creepy and quite possibly illegal. And he isn't normal. Normal people go outside once in a while. If you stay with him, you'll be stuck here, and I mean right here"—Kyle pointed at the bar in front of them—"for the rest of your life."

"That's what I want," said Katie. "I feel more at home here than I've ever felt anywhere."

"That's an awful thing to say."

"I'm just saying, I feel like myself for the first time in my whole life. I know exactly what's right for me. Have you ever felt like that?"

Kyle shook his head.

"Well, it's awesome. And I'm not going to let anyone fuck that up for me. Even you."

Katie had him. She was prepared never to speak to him again if he resisted her, and he knew that. Anyway, what was he going to do? Challenge Hunter to a fight? Who would win that one?

"Daddy, I'm tired," Mollie whined.

"OK, sweetheart," Kyle said, obviously exhausted himself. "We'll talk about this later, Katie."

"Don't tell Mom," said Katie. "She won't understand."

"You'd be surprised. You guys have more in common than you realize." But her dad's sigh told Katie she'd won that one, too.

"By the way, I owe you ten bucks," she said, digging into her pocket.

"Why?"

"I saw Topper's last broadcast, the one where he broke down crying while talking to that crazy Bigfoot lady. He believed what he was saying all along, and it drove him nuts. So you win."

Sweating in their polyester uniforms, the twins handed out cassette tapes to the audience. On his way out, Kyle gave Katie's ten bucks to Oliver. They weren't supposed to accept any payment, but when Oliver looked over at her, she gave him a thumbs-up. He gave her dad both The Patients tape and The Coma Cluster one. Kyle gave the Coma tape to Enrique.

Stick slid onto the bar stool beside her and signaled to Hunter to bring him a beer. He liked ordering Hunter around like a trained animal.

He peeled the label off his beer bottle. With practice, he'd learned to do it in very thin, equal strips, which he then arranged on the bar. Tonight he decided to lay the strips down in a grid. Katie glanced at the pattern and then at her tattoo, picking up on the suggested connection: Hunter, trap. She smiled smugly, which made Stick want to kick her.

"Your tattoo," he said, "looks like somebody cut your hand off and then sewed it back on."

Katie studied her wrist. "Yeah," she said. "I'm thinking about doing the other one."

"Your dad's right," Stick said. "About Hunter. It's a big mistake."

"You were listening to our conversation?"

"Yes I was."

When he'd seen Kyle and Katie huddled together, and Kyle staring in shock at Hunter, Stick had cut the filking session short. Kyle, he'd thought, could be just the ally he needed. At the proper time, Stick had intended to jump in and corroborate her dad's concerns. Then Kyle, he'd assumed, would put his foot down.

But there had been no proper time, and Kyle had withered in the face of Katie's bravado. Like her father, Stick was too afraid of losing her—what was left to him of her.

"We have a great deal going here, Stick," Katie said, too unthreatened by him to pursue the matter of his eavesdropping. "All of us, The Patients, The Link. It works. Don't fuck with it."

"He weighs more than you and me combined. He could break your neck like that." Stick snapped his fingers.

"You're just like my dad. You think all Vietnam vets are crazy, but Hunter's the sanest person I've ever met. His goal in life is never to hurt anyone again. He walks the walk every single day. And night." Katie wiggled her eyebrows significantly.

Stick's sigh blew his label pattern to smithereens. The thought of Katie undressing and dancing—yes, she'd told him like it was no more than the plot of some TV show—in front of that tied-up, graffiti-covered hulk of bad hygiene . . . Stick gulped his beer.

He signaled Hunter again, twirling his index finger in the air: bring me one more, you dog. Hunter obeyed, and, Stick thought, sneered at him. He downed the refill.

It was way past time he got away from Katie once and for all. For more than two-thirds of his life, she had known of his feelings and refused to requite them and made him feel like shit just generally. It would mean breaking up

The Patients, but he would manage. He still had The Coma Cluster.

"I have something to tell you," he said a little blearily.

"Hang on. There's Francine."

"Hey, girl," Francine said. "Great show, as always." They embraced.

"You are so cool," Katie told her, tugging on her pink chiffon scarf. "This is so, like, French. Where did you get it?"

"CarlsMart, where else?"

They laughed. Francine leaned over the bar to pour herself a beer, and Walt slapped her ass.

Katie lighted a cigarette. "What were you saying, Stick?"

In addition to everything else, Katie was now the biggest poser this side of New York City. Hunter was her biggest pose of all. Look how I care about those who suffer. Really, what did Hunter have that Stick didn't? Stick, too, had known tragedy: two dead parents before he'd turned sixteen. True, he had not killed them himself, perhaps a shortcoming in Katie's eyes.

Say it, he berated himself. Say *Good-bye, Katie*.

"I love you, Katie," he said.

"Oh, God. That's terrible."

"I know."

"It's impossible is all. In fact, I didn't even tell my dad this, but Hunter and I are going to get married."

"Oh, fuck. When?"

"I don't know. Next year, maybe. I might have to turn eighteen first. Anyway, he asked me last week, and I said yes."

Stick slid off his bar stool, steadied himself, and grabbed her wrist.

"We have to get out of here, Katie. Come on. Let's go. You and me. We'll go to the desert. Or Christmastown. I understand there's lots of space available suddenly. I'll go anywhere you want, Russia, Guam, Alaska. But I can't let you marry that monster. He'll kill you."

"You're hurting me," said Katie.

"Maybe you'll listen to me then. You like guys who hurt you, don't you?"

"Are you fucking crazy? Let go of me. I'll call him over here. I'll scream."

"Do it."

Katie shrieked, long and loud. The room froze. She had learned from the master, of course—her baby sister.

Hunter arrived in a split second, placing his heavy arm around her shoulders like a yoke.

"What is it?" he wanted to know. "What's wrong?"

Katie smiled, victorious. Stick let her go.

"Nothing," she said. "Just practicing our new song."

"What's it called?" Hunter asked.

"My fucking life," said Stick. He went to help his brothers hand out tapes.

It was not that Katie didn't appreciate Stick's concern, or her father's. And she wasn't blind. Of course she was a little afraid of Hunter. Who wouldn't be?

In fact, Katie now believed—as her mother did, or used to—in demonic possession. It had happened to Hunter at My Lai. War spawned demons faster than any biblical hell. They jumped down people's throats at vulnerable moments and moved their bodies around like puppets. Hunter had watched and felt himself doing unbelievable things in that village, and he could not stop.

But that was what made him so good now. He knew evil as he knew his own body. He fought it every minute of his life, with every muscle, every cell. The demons came to him in dreams and he repelled them, thrashing in his bonds and crying out until Katie woke him with gentle kisses and held him.

His fight was her fight. His dreams were her song.

CHAPTER TWENTY-ONE

Under the gray dull firmament, the heat bore down on the two women as they walked. The temperature controls had gone off-line with the dome. But, hardy veterans of Morton, Jackie and Esther pressed ahead, conducting their census of the postexodus Christmastown. They split up, each taking one side of the street for greater efficiency. Once or twice on each block, in response to their knocks and shouted introductions, a door cracked open and anxious, yet eager eyes peered back. When that happened, Esther or Jackie shrieked with joy, jumping and waving her clipboard. The other raced over so they could greet the stalwart family together.

"Thank you for staying," Jackie and Esther said to them, over and over. "Thank you for believing in Christmastown." However, immersed as they were in the concrete symbolic system of CED, both Jackie and Esther felt odd expressing gratitude with words alone. So they began handing out Thank You Coupons along with their reassurances that the dome, and the city itself, would be up and running in no time. But the coupons failed. As their eyes fell on the proffered paper, or even the occasional Mollie doll—the replica now significantly younger looking than the original—the families appeared saddened. These people, Jackie and Esther realized, had been willing to risk their very lives for Christmastown. There was no way to thank them for such faith. Indeed, they did not want to be thanked.

"Esther," said Jackie one afternoon, as they rested in the BMW with the AC going full blast. "Giving isn't all it's cracked up to be."

In the evenings Kyle called, mostly so that Mollie could talk to her mother. Mollie enthusiastically recounted their adventures with the Avilas. The aquarium, the museum, the beach, the library. The library had amazed her most of all, for it represented the exact opposite of her former world.

"You can just take a book. It's free. All you have to do is bring it back," Mollie explained to Jackie, surmising, not without reason, that her mother could not conceive of such a thing.

"But you want to come home soon," Jackie said, taking care not to let her voice rise into a question. That way, when Mollie didn't answer, but instead described the book, *Harold and the Purple Crayon*, that she and Kyle were reading together, Jackie could tell herself she hadn't asked one.

When Kyle came back on the line, his tone was flat, his words monosyllabic. Jackie realized she'd always read her husband primarily through his physical features—facial expressions, body language. She had no idea how to understand what he *said*.

"I'm glad you're finally getting to spend some time with Mollie," Jackie said.

"Me too."

"But her home is here. I want her to come home."

"I know."

"I want her here. And you," Jackie said, becoming monosyllabic herself.

"We'll see."

We'll see? What did that mean? It meant, No sense in pushing things. She always managed to hang up just before she started crying.

Unlike Jackie's own family, Yuri had stayed in Christmastown, from a combined sense of professional duty and an almost unhealthy attachment to the dome. It made sense, Jackie thought. Though he never talked about it, Yuri clearly felt responsible for Carl's death. Inventing Miribilium had allowed him to make some form of reparations to Carl's father. Now that Harry was gone, too, that need had grown even more powerful.

Which was why Jackie had to find a new project for Yuri, and fast. Fortunately, with Esther's help, she had come up with a way to save the city.

Two weeks later, Jackie, her team, and Susan Ricker sat at the conference table in her office. Through the windows of the pyramid, the blue sky glittered, as if another perfect day had blossomed in Christmastown. However, at nine a.m., it was already ninety degrees outside. The dome remained off-line, and, if Jackie had her way, it would never come back on again.

From her seat at the head of the table, Jackie counted six people out and about downtown. The sight gratified her, given the temperature, although some of the shoppers were probably guest workers. Over the past two weeks they had kept Christmastown's basic services going, even as the vast majority of Winners had departed. Most of the stores had stayed open, with the workers mostly selling to each other.

Jackie let Susan go first.

"As you know," Susan began, "Christmastown One has been a debacle."

"There have been setbacks," Jackie agreed. "As with any new venture."

"The security expenditures alone," Susan said, "not only sucked up all the profits from CED's first year, they've also turned CarlsMart from a blue chip into a penny stock. On top of that, the aurora thing has been a PR nightmare. Mysterious glitches in the dome are not selling points, no matter how pretty they may be. Already Christmastown has been written up as a case study in the *Harvard Business Review*. It's called 'Paradise Tossed.'"

Susan was tall with pleasant features and a reasonable if somewhat rigid manner. She had come, Jackie knew, to offer her a "golden parachute." But Jackie was not into skydiving.

"Therefore, our decision is to sell Christmastown One to a real-estate developer back East," Susan said. "The amount is less than we'd like, but frankly it wasn't easy to find a buyer. This place is a sinkhole for resources. Money, water, energy. I've never seen anything like it. I mean no offense. It's a nice town in many ways."

"I enjoy the multipurpose trail," said Jackie.

"You and the other residents will have the option of purchasing your homes from the corporation," said Susan. "In your case, CarlsBad is prepared to subsidize the purchase, as well as provide a generous severance package. Or, if you choose, we will help you relocate anywhere in the contiguous United States. You will be welcome to avail yourself of our in-house job placement service, free of charge.

"In short, we're very grateful for your service to CarlsMart, Jackie, and we will do right by you as you transition into the next phase of your life. What do you say?"

"I say no."

Before Susan could properly express her surprise, Jackie pushed the button on her intercom. "Esther, Yuri, come in here, please." To Susan: "We have a counterproposal."

She flipped open her laptop and switched on the projector. Shades hummed down over the windows; a screen lowered itself down the wall. On it appeared the words *A Vision for New Christmastown.*

"If CED has proven anything, Susan, it's that information is the future. Gathering, securing, and productively deploying information. Information is the new gold. And we are sitting on a gold mine."

Jackie changed the slide. Up came a photo of Harry's old scale model, now in the Christmastown Museum.

"Christmastown as a Givers' paradise cannot, we agree, survive. It was a dream, an ideal. But our ideals are always reshaped by experience. That's life, as I'm sure you would agree."

Susan nodded sadly.

Jackie changed the slide again. The screen now showed a cutaway view of the Storage Facility. But instead of objects, its many levels were filled with ones and zeroes, glowing like fireflies.

"Christmastown is uniquely positioned to become a state-of-the-art corporate data center," Jackie said. "Instead of gifts, the Facility will be filled with impenetrable safes containing documents and disks, product prototypes, and other top-secret materials. We will expand the number of servers storing digital data, using sophisticated encryption software developed by our engineering team. We already have the necessary temperature and moisture controls, along with the ideally remote location. Once we make a few improvements, Christmastown will be the most secure possible site for sensitive information—not just CarlsBad's, but for paying customers around the world."

"What improvements?" Susan asked.

"First, the security of the Facility needs beefing up. As you know, we recently implemented cameras and doubled foot patrols both underground and on the surface. However, there are still a few black spots. We need total visibility and tracking underground—there can be literally no hidden movements. So I've asked Yuri here to develop a new form of Miribilium with tiny embedded chips that can be sprayed on all the surfaces in the Facility. This should be a relatively simple process. We already know Miribilium can be spun into fine fibers."

Jackie took a moment to picture her bedroom carpet, and the activities that had once taken place thereon. Those days, with Harry, had vanished. Yet the sun still came in through her window every day and transformed her floor into a pastel rainbow.

"I hasten to point out that the spray will be nontoxic," Yuri interjected. "Although Facility workers will be required to wear masks to avoid inhaling the chips."

Susan rested her chin on top of her clasped hands. "What about above ground?" she asked.

"Obviously most of the Facility's workers will live and shop and play there," Jackie said. "They will constitute the majority of New Christmastown's citizens. The location is a bit too remote for commuting."

Jackie brought up the next image, a silhouette of a large stooped man. He stood in the middle of Commerce Street like a lost traveler, a duffel bag slumped by his feet. Susan blinked.

"Who is that?" she asked.

"We can't know. That is the point," Jackie said. "I want one-third of the housing to be set aside for the outcasts of the world. The poor, the homeless, rehabilitated felons, haunted veterans. I want clinics, rehab facilities, food banks, job training centers. The town will be the kind of place where anyone who needs help can find it. No ID cards, no tracking. We take everybody in, no questions asked."

Jackie reached out and squeezed Esther's hand. Esther squeezed back.

"But that makes no sense," Susan said. "You have the world's most secure data facility below ground and a free-for-all on top. It's impossible."

"It's possible with Miribilium," said Yuri.

"Underground we'll have total surveillance and total security," Jackie said. "Up above, we're on our own. That's why the dome has to come down."

The next slide was an aerial view of a dome-free New Christmastown. The town looked rougher around the edges, a bit Wild West. Pinkish sand, rocks, and creosote replaced the once-green lawns. Tiny people wandered the multipurpose trail; kids played in their somewhat bleak front yards. Shapely clouds adorned the blue sky. The former Green Space remained a blank, a question yet to be answered.

"What about the heat, the cold, the rain, the flash floods for which the Mojave Desert is so famous?" said Susan.

"The weather will build character," Esther said. "Only the strongest souls will inhabit New Christmastown."

"Interesting," Susan said. "The charitable angle is compelling. And not having the dome would save a lot of money."

"The town itself could operate as a foundation," Jackie said. "Which would make CarlsBad look awfully good."

Jackie called up her last slide, a drawing of two hands, fingertips touching to form a sphere. Inside the sphere floated a red, white, and blue map of America.

"This is the future of American business," Jackie said, forming the same sphere with her fingers. "Harry was on to something, he just didn't work out the proper balance. Commerce and community can be two halves of the same whole. Both require us to focus on the needs of others and to see ourselves as part of something larger."

Of their own accord, Susan's hands had also formed a sphere. She looked down at what she'd made and nodded.

"I like it," she said.

Jackie gathered herself for her final pitch.

"I would like to lead the foundation," she said. "Christmastown is my home. I know its workings inside and out, and I love it more than anyone else ever could. I give you my solemn promise that my team and I will make New Christmastown work."

"You have certainly displayed impressive leadership qualities," Susan said. "All right. Let's give this New Christmastown thing a whirl."

The new partners stood as one and shook hands. The shades hummed back up into their ceiling homes, their work complete. It was probably a coincidence, but Jackie now spotted more than twenty people on the street below.

"Just imagine," Jackie said. "If we play our cards right, in a few years, no one will think of corporations as evil."

CHAPTER TWENTY-TWO

After a mere two weeks and two days of rebellion, Kyle returned to the belly of the beast.

Why did he do it?

First, he had overstayed his welcome at the Avilas'. No one had said anything to that effect, but he felt his and Mollie's imposition like a weight on his chest. The apartment, already cramped, had become stifling. Between her shifts at the nursing home, Enrique's mother had been cooking for eight people.

Then, perhaps to assuage his guilt, two days ago, Kyle had seriously embarrassed himself and the whole family. He had begged Enrique to tell his father that he would pay for him to go to the doctor.

Bob's "no, no" was clear enough without a translation. But Kyle insisted. "Tell him it would be my privilege to help."

Enrique translated, a bit reluctantly. Bob turned red and began to yell and gesture until his coughing knocked him back into his chair.

"He says no, thank you," Enrique said, picking at his pinky.

Second, he had gone to see Katie at The Link again. On the topic of Hunter, Katie had grown unresponsive and was working her way toward hostility. When Hunter had brought them their drinks, Kyle had clamped his hand on Hunter's massive wrist and said, "Don't hurt my little girl." Which was actually a terrible thing to say. Of course Hunter would never *intentionally* hurt her.

Hunter said, "I won't." He had looked ready to say something else, but Katie had patted his hand to stop him and glared at her father.

Kyle handed his ID to the guard in the booth. The guard nodded. "Welcome back, Mr. Majesky," he said. The name still had some pull around here. "That is one beautiful set of wheels," the guard added, leaning out to better ogle the van.

Kyle wrote down Enrique's name and number for him.

The guard peered into the backseat at Mollie. "So that's the old girl, eh?"

"Old? She's two and change."

"Yeah, but Jessie's the Christmas Spirit now, you know. She just did her first Gift of the Day announcement on the Giving Channel. God, she's gorgeous. Like a little angel."

Jackie had mentioned this Jessie to Kyle on the phone. She had seemed surprisingly receptive to the idea, if not to the child herself.

As he turned the van from Generosity Street onto Angel, Kyle passed a guy out walking a dog. Further down, a woman washed a car in her driveway. Life in Christmastown seemed almost back to normal. Or, rather, normal for the first time.

"We're home, we're home," Mollie sang, clapping her hands.

So that was the other reason Kyle had returned.

Put it this way: life was basically a matter of hopping from one rock to the next, across a huge, rushing river of pointlessness. Sometimes the rocks were close together and you could just mosey along on them, not even thinking about what you were doing. Other times the pointlessness rose up and threatened to knock you off your feet, so you stayed on whatever rock you happened to be on, even though you didn't want to be there. You wanted to be on that rock, over there. So you gathered your remaining strength, and off you went. And you fell in and had to scramble onto that new rock's slippery face, and when you finally got your footing, all you knew was that you really missed the rock you'd just been on. That rock had been pretty cool. Maybe, in fact, it was *your* rock, but now it was too late. Your only hope was to try to enjoy your rock in retrospect.

Christmastown, Kyle had begun to think, was his rock. It was definitely Mollie's. But both of them could still enjoy it in the present.

And Jackie? She was neither rock nor river. She was the riverbed, the foundation and the cradle of everything.

She saw the van in the driveway and ran out to meet them. She looked beautiful as always, in shorts and a tank top, her blonde-and-brown hair in a disheveled ponytail. Since it was too hot to run outside, she'd probably been on the treadmill in her home gym. Her dark eyes looked weary but also calm. They flashed to life when she saw her daughter.

Kyle set Mollie on the grass and let her run to her mother. Jackie knelt down and hugged her.

"Welcome back, sweetie. I missed you so much," she said.

"I missed you, too," said Mollie. "I'm a mermaid now."

"That's wonderful," said Jackie.

She stood. Kyle leaned against the van.

"How are you?" she said.

"Good."

"How's Katie?"

"Really good. I saw her band, The Patients. They play at The Missing Link these days. They're excellent," Kyle said. Katie's performance was one of those retrospective rocks, he realized. The Patients were great. He hadn't been able to appreciate that until now. "Stick's doing great, too," he added.

"Did you see Hunter?"

"Yeah. He's great. He asked about you, Jacks," Kyle lied.

He raised his head to examine the dome. The sky was perfectly blue, no auroras in sight.

"It's coming down next week," said Jackie, following his gaze.

Kyle's heart sank for a moment. The weather had certainly been one of the upsides of Christmastown. But then it occurred to him: without the dome, people would really need delivery services. For at least half the year, they would not want to go outside. Enrique would make a mint painting the vans.

Mollie danced on the lawn. "Scarecrow City, Scarecrow City, Scarecrow City!"

Jackie watched her. "I'm glad she's out of that whole CED pressure cooker," she said. "But you should see the new kid they picked, Jessie. She looks like a little baby alien."

"People seem to like her."

"Being the Spirit is no big deal anymore. Christmastown Two's been put on indefinite hold. Basically all Givers can hope for from now on is more and better Thank You Coupons. The stores will give them the coupons directly to save time."

"So people will be Giving to themselves."

"Same as it ever was."

They went inside.

"Look at this," Jackie said. "It's my new computer. It's called a laptop—I can take it anywhere."

Kyle touched the heavy, black, whirring thing. The screen said *New Christmastown: A Limitless Future.*

"It might not seem like it now, but it's actually going to be a lot better," Jackie said.

Nervously, she kissed him on the cheek. He hesitated. She folded her hands, as if in prayer, and touched her fingertips to her lips.

Kyle took her hands and kissed them. He kissed her lips, her cheeks, her neck, her lips again. They held each other, and Kyle sighed. After all these years, their bodies knew just where to settle.

Topper Moss went home, too. After thirty years, he had had enough of the weird frontier that was America.

The Myra episode had done it. The way she forgave the monster, who she thought had eaten her husband, had pierced Topper's exhausted soul. She embodied the exact notion of mythology that he had been trying to get across to his viewers: she had devised an epic tale that allowed her to live. However, she was also barking mad. In her, Topper had seen his future, the fate of everyone who traveled to the frontier's farthest edge.

So he went home to his old mum's house in the British Midlands. She was so happy to see him that she telephoned his four brothers and sisters, and they gathered around the table that evening to share what had once been Topper's favorite meal of kidney pie. It was revolting, but he could not have been more pleased to eat it.

That night his mum tucked him into bed in his old room. He'd been the last to leave home, and he had gone the farthest away. Perhaps that was why she had preserved his room like a shrine. His posters from boyhood still adorned the walls—cowboys, Indians in feathered headdresses, canyons, herds of mustangs kicking up red clouds of dust.

Topper sighed and turned out his light. Already America receded from his vision. From this distance he saw that it was not larger than life at all, but smaller. Its people and its myths grew opaque. They stiffened into action figures or pieces on a game board. One could reach down and move them about for one's own amusement.

CHAPTER TWENTY-THREE

One afternoon in January 1989 Kyle's van raced across the desert. He was headed to Vegas to pick up a disk containing specs for a new video poker machine. The disk would be stored in one of New Christmastown's underground vaults. As New Christmastown's director of transportation, and one of the fleet's regular drivers, Kyle traveled the country, meeting its citizens in all their random glory.

His van attracted attention wherever he went. People could not believe it was not an actual aquarium on wheels; enthralled with its beauty, they had no idea it carried billion-dollar secrets. Kyle gave the admirers Enrique's card. He had commissioned Enrique to paint Christmastown's entire fleet, a project that would be completed in approximately 1998. Enrique would eventually use the money for college, but right now he was helping out his family. His father, Bob, had died just before Christmas.

The people Kyle met thought he was a musician or a cowboy poet, an impression he encouraged by wearing a cowboy hat and a belt buckle with an eagle on it. He was also something of a raconteur. At bars along the interstate, at diners and gas stations and Native American souvenir shops, he talked. He picked up hitchhikers and talked. He talked about his childhood in Vegas, where he had walked a hit man's dog, whose name was Ruth. He talked about the night he met his wife. "She literally swept me off my feet," he said. "We swam in the casino pool with our clothes on.

That was the best night of my life." He mentioned how he had accidentally shot himself in the foot, and one or two people seemed to remember that, or a story similar to that.

"Weren't you on Letterman?" they asked, glancing stealthily at his cane.

At this point Kyle asked them about their lives, which had been his true purpose all along. He was greedy for other people's stories, and not only because they diluted the sometimes unsatisfying flavor of his own. His new thing was documentation.

When the workers had dismantled the dome last July, Kyle had suddenly felt overwhelmed by the fragility of the human species. If and when humanity's end came, most likely by nuclear war, the corporate secrets stored in the New Christmastown Facility would survive. The plastic toys and polyester clothes and cheap appliances churned out by CarlsMart's overseas manufacturers would live, in mutant forms, in oceans and landfills and drainage ditches the world over. But the stories wouldn't make it, unless he helped.

He recorded people telling their life stories with his camcorder. From time to time, he even thought about firing up the in-home studio and doing his own TV show. He would have to steer clear of the frontier mythology bit though. Look what it had done to poor Topper. No, better to be done with show business as such. Documentation was the name of the game now.

Kyle had convinced Jackie that the stories were every bit as precious as the gazillion bytes of secret data that formed the foundation of New Christmastown. He had his own section for storing tapes in the Facility. On his way to and from Vegas, he figured he'd make at least half a dozen more.

For example, here was this guy Kyle had just picked up by the on-ramp—a wild-looking old man with a backpack that reeked so badly Kyle had made him strap it to the roof. The guy looked extremely familiar. In his peripheral vision, Kyle caught him studying his face with an expression of mystified concern. The winter sun backlit the man's hair, twisted with twigs and leaves and dirt. His beard was long and similarly leafy. He looked like a woodland Santa.

"I'm headed to Vegas," Kyle said. "How far you going?"

"Dunno," the man said in a voice that sounded like tectonic plates grinding together. The rumbling died away, and he turned to look out the window.

"Vegas it is then," Kyle said. "That's where I'm from. I'm going to visit my parents."

This was, in theory, the truth. He didn't have to pick up the specs for the poker machine until tomorrow, yet he had made a point of going a day early so that he would be forced to do his filial duty. Kyle had not seen his parents in almost two years. His dad said he was losing his eyesight. His dad never admitted to any form of aging, so the problem had to be serious.

Kyle had been trying to picture how the reunion would go. In every scenario so far, he had ended up sprawled at his dad's feet, begging for forgiveness. And his father had kicked him. The half-blind old man had kicked him in the head.

"Where you from?" Kyle asked the hitchhiker.

"Where from," the man repeated. He picked at the glove compartment latch with his fingernail, black and ridged as a mussel shell.

So Kyle started in with his own tales. He told the man about his daughter, Katie—what a bright and energetic kid she had been, and still was, but in a different way now. They had been such buddies, Katie and Kyle. When she was, oh, six or seven, they used to play this game called "Freeze, Sucker!"

Kyle would spot Katie coming out of her room. Their eyes would meet and flare with shared conspiracy. Kyle formed his fingers into a gun and tucked it up against his left shoulder, and then he slipped around the corner.

Katie walked toward him, singing: "La, la, la. I just robbed a store 'cuz I'm a robber."

Kyle leapt out in front of her, his finger gun pointed at her head. "Freeze, Sucker!"

But suddenly Katie had her own finger gun (with a silencer): "Pshew! Pshew! Pshew!"

Kyle clutched his chest and staggered back into the living room. "You got me. Ah, kiddo, you got me."

He fell on the carpet and writhed, kicking his legs like a bug. Then he lay perfectly still until Katie came over and poked him in the shoulder with her toe.

"Dad? You dead?"

"RAAHR!" he shouted. He grabbed Katie around the knees and gobbled a mouthful of her checked bell-bottom slacks. Katie collapsed in giggles.

She still had that same spark, Kyle told the stranger. It was just that at some point, it had turned more volatile. She seemed to want to suffer. But the kind of suffering she'd chosen was pointless—she could never cure a man sickened by war. Kyle went to see her band perform at The Missing Link at least once a month, and she seemed happy, even at peace. But the songs she sang were sad and terrifying. Her tattoo, which she'd finally let him see, was a chain.

"It's weird," Kyle said to the stranger. "I always thought I owed Hunter a kind of debt. And now Katie's paying it."

Kyle had not planned to deliver this particular parcel of information. He always tried to keep his banter light with strangers. There was no need to burden them. Besides, what was this guy supposed to do about Kyle's problems, which had to be totally minor compared to his?

The man kept looking out the window. Kyle couldn't tell if he'd even been listening.

"You have kids?" Kyle asked.

The tectonic plates began to grind. "I think I have a wife," came the response.

Kyle stopped to let the hitchhiker out at the Welcome to Fabulous Las Vegas sign. As he collected his pack from the roof of the car, Kyle leaned out the window to ask if he would like to have his story videotaped and preserved for the ages. Old people in particular tended to say yes. They could record right there in front of the sign, Kyle said, which would be picturesque. But the guy had already turned away. In the rearview mirror, Kyle saw him heading back in the direction they had just come from.

So Kyle went and saw his folks in what was once their modern town house, in a formerly new development in Vegas. His mom covered his face with kisses, knocking his hat off.

"Mom," he said, burning with mortification. The problem was not just that he did not deserve her devotion. It was his the way his mother's ravaged face expressed it.

Kyle found his dad in his recliner, watching a World War I movie, the kind where men with dirty faces exchanged terse farewells before leaping one last time out of the trench. A glass of bourbon balanced on the recliner's arm. Kyle waited for Burt to tear his eyes from the screen.

"Look who's here," said Burt finally. He had on new glasses, rectangular with heavy black rims. His eyes swam like fat blue fish inside them.

"Don't get up," said Kyle. He tucked a thumb into his belt loop, which he'd never done before in his life, and leaned casually on his cane.

"What's with the cowboy look?" Burt said. "You a fag now?"

"I guess your eyesight's not so bad, since you're able to discuss my fashion choices."

"Not stone blind yet, sorry to disappoint you. Come back later for the white cane and pencil cup."

"I'm sorry."

"I'm on vacation now," Burt said, spreading his arms dramatically. "Pretty great, huh? The boss told me I had to use my days or lose them. I've been screwing up, see. Flipping cards, getting in fights with players. When my vacation's up he's going to inform me my services are no longer needed."

"He can't do that, Dad. Not after all the years you've given them."

"You think not? Every day I stood at that table, I was on the edge of a cliff. One false move and boom—no job, no food, no nice home for Kyle and Marian. I had to eat a mountain of shit every single day. And my only dream now is to go back and eat more."

"Burt, please," Marian said from the doorway, ice clattering in her glass. "Kyle's come all this way."

"I can't stay long," said Kyle.

"But we have dinner reservations."

"At Smuggler's Cove," said Burt. "They're comping us because they know I'm being canned. You don't want to miss out on my last fling, do you?"

Smuggler's Cove had undergone major renovations since Kyle had spent his youthful days there, wiping tables and dreaming of comedic glory. No more flimsy Jolly Roger flags drooped from the ceiling; no fake mermaids on fake ships' bows, distressed by fake salt spray, loomed over tables. The crossed plastic swords and pistols had vanished. Now authentic weapons gleamed in locked glass cases, with little plaques detailing their provenance. The place had become an actual museum, displaying sextants, spyglasses, worn gold coins dredged up from real shipwrecks. A gold button had, supposedly, once adorned Blackbeard's coat.

"It's classy, isn't it?" said Marian. "It always was classy, but this is a whole new level of class."

She grinned and raised her glass to Titus, an old family friend. He had been a pit boss at the Tahitian years ago. Now he managed the newly renovated nightclub, the Tiki Palace. He had joined the Majeskys for dinner, apparently by invitation.

"So Titus," Marian said, already loud from her second cocktail (or fourth, depending on whether the count began at home). "What's new at the Tiki Palace?"

"I'm glad you asked." Titus's thick fingers mauled a breadstick. "As you know, the Tahitian needs a new image. We can't afford to be the old lady from the fifties any longer, what with these state-of-the-art casinos popping up all over. Everything about the Tahitian has to be new—the décor, the food, the games, the vibe. For my part"—here Titus touched his lapel with an oily fingertip—"I have made it the Tiki Palace's mission to identify and groom new talent. So we now have an unknown as the opening act every Wednesday. The most popular acts will get regular gigs as warm-up acts for the big names. Eventually they could become headliners themselves."

"You don't say, Titus," Burt growled.

"But I do say."

Kyle snatched a breadstick from the basket. He stuffed a piece into his mouth but found himself unable to chew. He remembered his mother showing him a trick when he was little. If you were eating something you found you didn't want to swallow, you held your napkin up to your mouth like this, and gave a little cough: hm, hm! At precisely that moment, you spat your food into the napkin and gathered it all up, nice and neat. And then you . . . but this part had never been so clear.

"So Kyle." Titus turned to him, beaming in such a way that Kyle realized instantly that (1) Titus was genuinely pleased to be offering him, and Burt and Marian, this big favor, and (2) he had no doubt his offer would be accepted.

Titus had reserved the opening spot for Kyle this coming Wednesday.

"It's a perfect fit," said Titus. "If the Tahitian had a son, you would be him. We'll talk it up like a great big homecoming. Burt says your act is really good. You do a hell of a Reagan bit, he says."

With great effort, Kyle chewed his bread. The effort was too much. He spat his bread into his napkin and began to sniffle.

His mother grabbed his arm. "What is it, honey? Are you sick? Do you want to go home?"

Kyle shook his head.

"He's overcome by the great news. Aren't you, Kyle?" Burt yelled. Kyle felt himself sliding forward on his seat. In a moment he could be under the table.

"He'll take it," Burt said.

Kyle shook his head again.

"What?" Burt said. "Are you saying no to this gig?"

Kyle nodded.

"I can't believe this. Titus pulled some major strings here. You should be kissing his feet, not pissing on them."

"I'm sorry. I don't do impressions anymore. I thought you knew."

Kyle's prime rib arrived, throbbing on the plate like his heart.

"I have other things I want to do, Dad."

"Like what?"

"I can't say right now. But I have some ideas."

"You're going to drive around like a moron for the rest of your life doing errands for your wife? Is that it?"

Kyle threw his napkin, chewed bread and all, down on the table. Marian whimpered in between gulps of bourbon. Titus shrugged and snapped a claw off his lobster.

Bigfoot wanders through the desert. It's dusk, and he is looking for a place to sleep. He's overheated. His coat is thick. He is not a desert creature, that's for sure. Still, he likes it here. There is a clarity he has found nowhere else. Blue sky, red rocks. Finely detailed plants in green and yellow. Each pebble and grain of sand stands in relief, as if outlined by hand.

He's not sure how he got here. He has a sense of gliding, which may mean he has been in a car. A man was talking, maybe, and he seemed sad. But that's how all people seem to Bigfoot.

The sun slips behind the mountains. Bigfoot finishes off the liter of Pepsi the sad man must have given him. The liquid is warm and thick. He can feel it devouring what is left of his teeth. He has nowhere to put the bottle, so he digs a hole in the sand and buries it. As he tries to stand, exhaustion washes over him. He falls onto his knees and rolls onto his back as a jet fighter splits the sky.

For Bigfoot time is not an arrow, but a game of cat's cradle in the hands of an insane child. The line stretches and collapses and crosses over itself. Hours can be like days or seconds. Bigfoot leaps across a river and decades pass. A memory bursts in his brain, a young woman with braids smiles at him, and then an ocean roils with red foam. He sits on a rock and holds his head and tries to remember. He tries until his brain roars with fatigue, and in all that time the bird hopping across the leaf litter by his feet has only hopped once more.

A purple net drifts across the sky, catching the earth. Stars peer through the mesh. It seems to Bigfoot that these figures represent his ancestors. He's not alone in the universe, but the others are very far away. The sky turns deep blue and black. The stars leave trails as the world spins below him.

The Patients' song "My Fucking Life," music by Stick and lyrics by Katie, once again sent The Missing Link into raptures.

EPILOGUE

At last, Kyle was on his way home. He had locked the disk with the poker machine specs, plus hard copy, in the safe in the back. He had a full tank of gas and a freshly opened bag of Cheetos, along with an ice-cold Pepsi, at his side. He had an old Don Kirshner tape in the van's eight-track player. Kyle was rocking on.

You see, last night, he had landed a rock in the river that he knew, right then and there, was perfect. He was going to stay on that rock until he died.

He had been lying on the foldout couch in his parents' office/guest bedroom, replaying the god-awful Smuggler's Cove dinner in his mind. The whole scene had been so insane. Imagine: all his life, the one thing Kyle truly wanted was for his dad to approve of his dream. A word or two of encouragement would have sent him over the moon, but he would have settled for a simple absence of contempt. Neither of these things had ever come to pass. So Kyle had spent his entire life trying to put his rambunctious dream to bed. Night after night, he had lied to it so it would sleep. *We've got the Lions Club coming up, the drug talk at the high school— the kids will laugh and that's enough for us. No? OK, then, tomorrow, next year, we'll go for it. I promise. Go to sleep.* Two years ago he'd roused the monster accidentally, only to watch it flail about and break the furniture before setting itself on fire. He'd shoved it back under the covers and held it there until it stopped moving. It was finally dead.

Then, at the very moment Kyle had finished his mourning, Burt did an about-face. God only knew why. Maybe to make amends, since the old man was going blind or thought he was getting fired, both of which probably seemed like the end of the road to him. He wanted Kyle to have a chance like he himself never had. He resented the bejesus out of his son, but he'd hauled his old ass up and pulled those strings for him, which he'd sworn he'd never do again. He'd told Titus that Kyle's act was good. A *hell* of a Ronald Reagan bit. That was Titus's translation; his dad may have been more reticent, but still, the mere effort to say something not negative must have *killed* Burt. Showing his own flair for drama, he'd arranged a fancy dinner to announce the whole thing.

And then and there, what did Kyle do? He said no! He pulled the rug out! He had other plans! Burt could not believe his ears. Even at breakfast the next morning, he was still muttering and shaking his head.

But it was not this pathetic victory over his father that had made Kyle so happy. In fact, when he thought about it, the actual story made him miserable. Yet, when he had heard himself telling it in his mind, he realized he was practicing telling it to Jackie. He knew she'd think it was hilarious, in the way awful things—described in just the right way—always are. After everything they'd been through together, he *knew* Jackie would laugh. What a world, she'd say. Oh, what a world.

Kyle could not wait to get home.

On the other hand. Opening at the Tiki Palace was not nothing. Not by a long shot was it nothing. A budding comedian definitely could do worse. It was a good-size room, nice tables with candles stuck into the heads of little gods.

Jesus Christ, who was coming to the Tiki Palace next Wednesday? What did it say on the marquee over the entrance, which Kyle had noticed last night but had been too discombobulated to take in?

Rich Goddamn Fucking Little, that's what it said. Kyle had the chance to open for Rich Little. He slammed on the brakes and turned the steering wheel with all the force of a man seeing the flame of his final opportunity dwindle to embers.

The van fishtailed across two lanes, hit the median strip, and went airborne. It landed on two wheels on the other side, screeching away on an arc as an oncoming truck blasted its horn. Crashing through the wire barrier meant to keep desert tortoises off the highway, the van bumped over brush and rocks and took an arm off a Joshua tree before coming to rest atop a clump of creosote, like a giant tropical bird in a nest.

Kyle rested his forehead on the steering wheel as feeling trickled back into his face. He looked in the rearview mirror and saw no blood. His body appeared to be intact, if soaked with sweat. The windshield was scratched and dirty, but not cracked.

"You OK?" he said to no one but himself. He found his hat on the seat beside him, covered in Cheetos. With shaking hands he brushed off the orange dust and placed the hat back on his head. His Pepsi was a bottle of foam.

Carefully, he turned the engine off and went outside to ascertain that the van's doors were still locked and its precious contents intact. All was evidently well. The safe remained bolted to the floor. The van was going to need a good bath, and a few dings would need to be popped out. Enrique would have to do some touch-up work.

Kyle rested his back against the side panel, his legs wobbling.

"Kyle Majesky," he said aloud, "you are one dumb SOB."

In the bushes, some many-legged critter whirred and snapped. The desert lay all around him.

Somewhere between Kyle and the low rock formation in the distance, a shape strode, swift as the shadow of a cloud. He'd seen it on *The Weird Frontier* a million times. The striding monster had been one of its promo spots. There could be no doubt. No human being had ever moved that fast, and no ape had ever stood that upright. The creature's fur reflected purple undertones in the sunlight. His stride was longer than Kyle's van was wide.

Holy shit. Bigfoot was real. Not just myth real, but really, really real.

That meant anything could be real—or not. Kyle would have to start over from the beginning and review. Were his parents real? Rich Little? What about food? God had just rebooted his whole life. Kyle knew nothing at all.

But this was no time to stand there wondering in the sun. His future—fame, fortune, total comprehension of the universe in its true form—was getting away.

And so he ran. His right foot splayed out wildly as his cane lay useless back in the van.

His chest began to ache. His new boots bit into his feet. He stumbled over scrub and rocks. Kyle would never catch the creature, and even if he did, what the hell was he going to do? Shake his hand? He didn't even have his video camera. Not even Topper Moss, wherever he was now, would buy this story.

His ears rang like a jet engine powering up. Dust encrusted his eyes and lips. He could not even see the monster anymore. He had slid into the shadow of the mountains.

Nevertheless, Kyle ran.

These winter days in the desert were made for running. Inside her foundation director's office, which was also still the mayor's office, Jackie laced up her shoes. As always, she eschewed the elevator and ran down the stairs, out onto the multipurpose trail. The sun lit the glass pyramid's eastern face.

Jackie ran through the town, which looked into both the past and the future.

She ran through the neighborhoods. The houses appeared mostly the same as before, though water restrictions had long ago dried up the lawns. Xeriscaping with rocks and desert plants was the trend now. The cacti looked a trifle odd against the colonial-revival architecture of the houses. But New Christmastown was odd in many ways.

She loped through the Sidewinder neighborhood, where the foundation had helped her mother fund an artists' collective. Yes, Tessa had arrived at last. After the dome had come down, Tessa had drawn herself up to her full five feet and announced, "New Christmastown needs me." That was true. Jackie smiled as she ran past her mother's purple house with yellow and orange trim, where Mollie was, at this moment, receiving instruction in all manner of pointless crafts. Just like her older sister before her.

Mollie was thriving, loud, mostly happy, given to the occasional raging tantrum that nearly peeled the wallpaper off the walls. She sang along to Katie's tapes in the living room, spinning in circles with her arms splayed. She'd amassed a glorious collection of tropical fish in a bubbling tank, which she stared at for hours on end.

And what about Mollie's older sister? Jackie had gone with Kyle several times to see her perform at The Missing Link. The Patients were very good.

Katie's strange voice had found a home in their disturbing songs. But she'd seen the furtive glances her daughter had exchanged with Hunter and known immediately that they were in love. That worried her deeply. Would Katie be devoured by Hunter's pain, which Jackie herself had always wanted to assuage? Or would she sing her way out of The Link's stuffy confines and on to stardom? Would she be happy? Was she now? Jackie could not begin to say. All she could do was keep calling, keep coming to Katie's shows, and tell her she was good and that she loved her. Katie said she loved her, too, which was a new development.

Of course, Jackie had not told Katie that she knew about Hunter. She didn't know how to explain that she admired her fearlessness. She understood what she was trying to do, better than Katie could probably imagine. But Hunter was the sort of person, Jackie would have to tell her, who was best loved at a distance. And Katie would never in a million years accept that. So what to do? In any case, Jackie wasn't going to tell Kyle. He definitely wouldn't understand.

She ran along the river, now full from the winter rains. The rushing soothed her. She pounded across the wooden footbridge toward the former Green Space, now renamed the Harry Ricker Memorial Playa, where golfers were learning to enjoy the particular challenges of desert terrain. The animatronic sheep took the change in stride, grazing on sand and creosote contentedly.

Jackie passed Facility workers riding bikes or walking along the playa on their lunch break. They waved, and Jackie waved back.

"You're doing God's work," she called out. She was glad to see them getting sun. They smiled, their masks hanging loose around their necks.

She passed a group of homeless veterans, one of whom sat in a wheelchair pushed by Esther. Jackie waved at these men, too, though they did not exactly wave back. They were new here and still stunned. They didn't yet believe that they would really be taken care of. So many others, namely their country, had failed them in the past. Esther nodded as the man in the wheelchair turned to speak to her.

Jackie rounded the curve to where the forest had once stood. She had dispensed with her earlier plan for a water park. Instead, Tessa's Sidewinder group would build a sculpture garden. Jackie had no doubt it would be weird, especially because they planned to make it out of all the gifts abandoned in the Facility by New Christmastown's former residents. Her heart sank. Now that the debris from the logging was finally gone, the area looked even worse. Before, it had been a sad ruin. But now it was nothing. A vast patch of concrete had been poured in haste, after the remains of the trees had been uprooted and sinkholes had begun to form in their absence. The blasted spot hurt Jackie's soul, and yet she ran past it every day to remind herself of what she had once done instead of helping a lost old man. For that same reason, she had always kept the two gray river stones on her office desk.

What the hell, she thought, weird or not, let Tessa do what she wants with this place. Weird art was not the end of the world. In fact, New Christmastown itself was weird art. Anyway, she and Kyle could always laugh about it.

He would be back from Vegas soon. Tonight, they would go to dinner at Vichyssoise, a new restaurant downtown where you paid twenty bucks for a meal the size of a quarter. Jackie couldn't wait. She was dying to hear all about Kyle's adventures with his parents. If she knew her husband, he'd have at least one hilarious tale to tell.

She checked her watch. Barring unforeseen circumstances, it would be one hour and forty minutes until she saw him.

Her legs propelled her, powerful and fleet. Below, in the labyrinth of the Facility, masked workers moved through the bright darkness.

ACKNOWLEDGMENTS

This novel was born in 2004 in the form of a shambolic short story. Since then, it has changed radically and for the better, thanks to many attentive readers, constructive critics, and encouraging friends. Without them, *Bigfoot and the Baby* would not exist today, except, perhaps, as a collection of confusingly labeled files on an old laptop. A novel is a communal effort, and if you ever need to remind yourself of humanity's profound and instinctive generosity, I advise you to write a novel, tell everyone about it, and see what happens.

I'm deeply indebted to the following people for commenting on drafts, assisting with research, making connections, and providing inspiration at all points in the writing process: Shawn Allison, Tara Cottrell-Wright, Anita Feferman, Tom Gelder, Dana Heins-Gelder, Amy Hornstein, Linera Lucas, Kevin McLain, Vicky Mlyniec, Bob Rennicks, Sam Schieber, Kate Steilen, Tami Strang, and Sara Tung. I greatly appreciate Mary Cook's meticulous copyediting, which strengthened the story. For a writing education with a steep learning curve, I heartily thank my teachers and classmates from Stanford Continuing Studies and the 2005 Tin House Summer Writer's Workshop. For enthusiastically and creatively presenting my work to a wider audience, I thank Anthony Varallo and *Crazyhorse*, where the "Origin" section of this novel first appeared; I also thank Sally Shore and the cast of the New Short Fiction Series in Los Angeles. My eternal thanks and admiration go out to Bona Fide's brave and brilliant Kim Wyatt, whose faith in this book frequently surpassed my own, and whose editorial insights solved longstanding conundrums.

Bigfoot and the Baby both reflects and concocts mythologies of various stripes, and I consulted many, many sources over the years. Two of the most influential were Robert Michael Pyle's *Where Bigfoot Walks: Crossing the Dark Divide* and Fred Clark's Slacktivist blog, now at Patheos.com. However, any errors or misrepresentations are my own, and possibly deliberate.

Finally, I could not have forged through the writing wilderness without the love, confidence, and wisdom of my husband, Trevor Hébert. With love and gratitude, I dedicate this book to him.

This book is printed on 30 percent postconsumer recycled paper.

Thank you for supporting an independent press!

www.bonafidebooks.com